Chisto Healy

The Gateway in Apartment 8

Other titles by Chisto Healy

Sunnycrest Apartments Series
Accidental Murderer in Apartment 34

Other Books
Two of a Kind
The World Beneath
The Bucket List
Attack of the Killer Crabs
196 Days Later
The Guardian Book One

Originally published in Australia by Slashic Horror Press in 2023.

ISBN-13: 978-0-6457638-3-6
Cover design by Grim Poppy Designs
Interior design by David-Jack Fletcher and Lee Cross James
Edited by David-Jack Fletcher

ONE

The Good Doctor

November 17, 2021

1

Mark Stephenson had been happy to take on a new patient after what had happened with Roger. At least he was until he actually met her. There was nothing wrong with the young Asian woman seated before him (Chinese if he had to guess), at least not that he could figure in the first few minutes of their meeting. She was well put together and looked every bit like the average American college student. It was the words that came out of her mouth that rocked him to the core.

Mark had only just gotten back from visiting his last patient, Roger, at the Twin Spirits Mental Hospital that he now called home. Mark had thought that Roger was harmless, a lost soul that just needed to find his way and forgive himself for the sins of his past. He supposed he had been right—aside from the harmless part, as his story ended in terrible violence, a death that Mark may have been able to prevent. Guilt ate at him and twisted his stomach in knots.

He told himself he had done his part, that he wasn't at fault for Roger not taking his medication. Mark had prescribed it. That was his job. He even tried to call and follow up, checking to see that the man was taking them. It wasn't his fault. It wasn't. Was it? Even if it were, he couldn't let the guilt consume him. It was guilt that drove Roger to do the things he did.

It was a powerful poison, Mark thought.

He tried to smile for the girl sitting before him, the new patient. Alice, is it? No. Sarah. Her name was Sarah. Alice was the dead girl that had lived across from Roger. Maybe I should excuse myself, he wondered, apologize and tell her it's best if she seeks help elsewhere.

Sarah told Mark she lived at the Sunnycrest Apartments, the same place Roger resided before his new accommodations.

What about Maria? The voice in the back of his mind questioned. If you're not at fault for Roger, what about Maria? Mark shook his head and saw his new patient take notice. He had to focus and decide what to do. He had worked hard to put Maria out of his mind, to not think about what happened with her. It was awful.

Maria was a patient before Roger had even come to him. She had lived at Sunnycrest as well. She had also vacated her apartment to move into the Twin Spirits lodging, just like Roger, only she was in a more secure ward than he was. Roger, in his own way, was still a victim. He was a victim of his own mind. Maria's story was far more sinister. It caused Mark to seek therapy of his own. Maria was the reason for the pills in his own medicine cabinet, the liquor bottle stashed in the third drawer of his desk right now.

Now there was a third person from Sunnycrest wanting his help. Mark wanted to run from her, to run screaming through the streets. He wanted to demand that the building be evacuated and burned to the ground, but in truth, it was one of the oldest buildings in the city, a historic landmark that couldn't be taken down. It was a monolith that would forever be there, towering over him in his nightmares.

Mark had already told Sarah that he would help her. Even when she said the word ghosts—the word that attached itself like a spirit to that building and its residents—he told her it was okay. Mark told her he wanted to hear her story even though that was the farthest thing from the truth. Wasn't it?

Something in him called him a liar for that train of thought. Something in him knew for certain that curiosity would stick to him like glue, day in and day out, and drive both he and his wife, Claire, insane if he let Sarah walk out of his office without finding out what was bothering her. There were other Sunnycrest residents that came to him, people who lived there that hadn't gone mad or killed anyone. People like Tina, Ben, and Arnold.

Mark wanted so badly to believe that Roger and Maria both living at Sunnycrest was no more than a coincidence. Sarah could sway that one way or another. The implications of this were personal to him, to his own life, his own trauma. If ghosts were real…Mark saw a brown-haired boy in a red shirt behind his eyes. He had lived there for many years now, an image he couldn't escape, even in sleep.

"Is this a bad time?" she asked him.

Frowning, Mark shook his head, and leaned forward in his seat. He did his best to smile for her. "No, no. I'm sorry. I just got back from visiting someone at the hospital and I suppose I needed a minute to collect my thoughts. You're fine."

Sarah paled and put a hand to her mouth. "I'm so sorry. I was early. I just hate being late. It causes me anxiety. I didn't realize you wouldn't be here or would need time."

Mark put up a hand to stop her. "Punctuality is not a bad thing, though I would like to explore that anxiety at some point. I'm sure never being late makes you a good student. You go to Hunter, don't you?"

She grinned at the mention of school, and nodded. “Yes, sir. I’m in my second year, working on my Bachelor’s in Elementary Education in Chemistry. I want to be a science teacher.”

Giving a more genuine smile, Mark continued, “Hunter is a great school. My wife actually went there. She still speaks of it fondly.”

Sarah’s face lit up and she seemed to be much more at ease. “Let’s lose the sir stuff,” Mark said to her then. “Call me Mark. I’m a person, just like you. The only difference is I can prescribe meds.”

They shared a laugh. Then Mark saw clearly the right question to ask her. His fingers toyed with his bushy brown beard sprinkled with bits of gray. “Sarah, before you get started with your story, which I definitely want to hear, I would like to know how you heard of me. Was I referred by someone?”

Sarah’s eyes left him to rest on her lap. She nervously smoothed her dress. Mark tried to focus on her discomfort rather than her beauty. She was definitely alluring with her high cheekbones, unblemished skin and supple lips, but it was more important to discover why his question bothered her. “Sarah, did I say something wrong?”

The patient met his eyes, just for a moment, before looking away again. “No.” she said, her voice low, and conspiratorial.. “It’s just strange. I don’t take drugs. I don’t want you to think that I’m some kind of—”

Mark lifted a hand to stop her again. Leaned forward. "Sarah, you're making a lot of conclusions already. We just met. I have no preconceived notions. Let me tell you something about me. I'm pretty open-minded—open to a lot of things, really. My wife is big into astrology. My sister is a witch, and you're not the first person to walk in here with a ghost story. I think you needed someone a little less conventional and I believe you're in the right place. I was just curious, as I am with all my new people, what led you to me. Okay?"

"Okay," Sarah said with a small chuckle. She shrugged her shoulders and looked up at him. "Maybe you're right. Besides, if you can't handle the way I heard about you, then you definitely won't be ready for the rest of my story."

Mark was a little unnerved by that, but he did his best not to let it show. How did she come to find me? "Alright," he said with a gentle clap of his hands. "You've definitely tugged at my curiosity. Let's hear it."

2

Sarah trotted down the stairs to the first floor. It was only one floor and she didn't like elevators. It felt better and more practical to jog down an open stairwell than to trap yourself in a box, especially that box. Every time someone took it she felt like they were going to die. She listened to it creak and rumble as it went up and down.

No thank you, she thought.

She supposed she might feel different if her apartment had been on one of the upper floors as opposed to the second, but it wasn't, so she didn't. She learned a long time ago that no good came from thinking about What ifs.

When she came out of the stairwell, Sarah waved to Tom, the maintenance man and janitor of the building, who was on his way out. She wasn't sure why she always waved to him. He rarely waved back and he was a generally unfriendly person. Sarah supposed it was just in her nature to be friendly. Maybe it was due to the fact that she knew his demeanor was likely connected to the fact that his job was often a thankless one.

Sarah looked at the mailboxes across from the stairs in the lobby, and couldn't help but notice Roger's name was missing from its usual spot on the seventh floor. She wasn't home the day he was taken away, and she didn't know the details of what happened. That was curious in itself. Most apartment places she knew were full of gossip and talking neighbors. Sunnycrest was a different animal. The residents never talked about each other's secrets or situations. There was a strange code of respect among them. The most anyone said to her regarding Roger was that it was terrible what happened, or so sad. That poor child that had always walked with him must have left the building when he did because Sarah never saw her anymore. She hoped nothing bad had happened to the girl. She was always so sweet, the way she jogged around and played with her ball.

When Sarah first met Roger, he tried to warn her about Sunnycrest—he told her it was haunted and wasn't safe.

She thought for sure he was crazy. Over time, she'd run into him coming and going, getting mail and the like, and she came to realize he was just incredibly sad. He had anxiety and depression and something was eating him alive from the inside, but he seemed nice enough. He even apologized for his outburst, blaming it on stress with an awkward smile.

Sarah wanted to tell him he shouldn't apologize, that he had been right in what he said. She had wanted to tell him she believed Sunnycrest was, in fact, haunted, and that she was the one who should apologize for not listening or believing him. She didn't say any of that though, because she didn't know what she believed at that point. She couldn't wrap her brain around what was happening in that building.

Now she would never have the chance to say anything to him. She didn't even know where he went. He was just gone and everyone said it was terrible. There was something in the paper about a tragic accident, but it didn't contain any useful details. It was a small column at the bottom of a page. That was all.

What happened to you, Roger?

It was a strange thing for someone to be there and then just be gone. It made her think of when she was young and her grandmother passed. Her parents didn't want to explain death to her so they said that Maa Maa had just gone away. It was harder for her to adjust and understand, and when she got older she vowed to never do that to her own children. If someone died she would sit them down and talk to them about it.

Did Roger die? Is that what happened?

She ran her finger over the still-sticky place where his name used to be above the mailbox for Apartment 34. With a sigh, she moved her attention to her own mailbox. She opened the door with her key and started to pull out everything crammed inside.

"You alright?" someone said to her.

Sarah looked over to see a woman coming out of the elevator. She was surprised she didn't hear that death box arrive with its signature rumble. She must have really been in her own mind. The woman was around her age, maybe younger even. Sarah didn't know her, but she was pretty sure the woman lived on floor seven. Roger's floor. Was it worth asking her if she knew anything?

She probably won't even tell you. Just let it go. "I'm fine. Just thinking," Sarah said. "Hey, don't you live in Apartment 31?"

The young woman laughed and shook her head. "You must have been talking to the crazy guy," she said. "He seemed to think we were all in Apartment 31 when he wasn't screaming or rolling on the floor. No dear, my name's Tina. I live in Apartment 32. 31 is actually vacant."

Sarah chewed on her lip. "Now that I'm thinking about it, I think he did tell me that the nice old black lady lived in Apartment 31, too."

Tina gave another laugh. "Mrs. Jackson. She's in 35. My point exactly. I think we're better off with that one gone. I hope they background check the next one they rent to more thoroughly. That guy was way off his meds. I just feel bad for Tom that he had to clean up that mess. So much blood. Anyway, I'll see you around."

Sarah watched Tina saunter out of the building and close the heavy front door behind her. She frowned at the shutting door. She never asked the woman what had actually happened. Tina had mentioned blood though, so Sarah thought, maybe she didn't actually want to know. She thought about the paper and the article she'd read.

Tragic accident.

Sighing, Sarah closed the mailbox and locked it. She fumbled with the mail in her hands and it spilled from her grip, cascading to the floor. She bent down to retrieve it when the front door blew open with a bang. Sarah couldn't help but wonder what kind of breeze could blow open a door that heavy. Were they in the middle of a hurricane she somehow failed to hear about?

Whatever caused the breeze, it made its way in through the open door. Sarah shivered and hugged herself against the sudden rush of cold air, trying hard not to drop the mail she was still in the process of picking up. Most of it is probably junk mail anyway, she thought.

Something small—a piece of paper maybe—blew in

on the swirling breeze. It drifted around, fluttering like a leaf that had fallen from an autumn tree before landing at her feet with the rest of her dropped mail. Then the air was gone, though the chill remained in her bones. Sarah jumped as the door fell suddenly shut with a loud Bang!

Curiosity tugged at her and she reached past the envelopes and circulars at her feet, picking up whatever the wind had brought in. Lifting it before her eyes, Sarah saw it was a psychiatrist's business card. "Dr. Mark Stephenson," she said as she read the words.

Maybe it's a sign, she thought, tucking the card in with the mail in her arms.

With everything that had been going on lately, she could use a professional to talk to, someone to tell her whether or not she had gone mad. Sarah thought about Tina talking to someone else at the mailbox and saying, "Oh you must have been talking to the crazy lady in Apartment 8."

Sarah got to her feet. As she moved toward the stairwell door, mail in her arms, she made the decision to give Dr. Mark Stephenson's office a call.

3

Mark shivered as if the phantom breeze she spoke of was actually in the room with them. Across from him, Sarah hugged herself, her body language saying she felt the chill as well. Mark laughed and it sounded awkward in the silence of the room. He cleared his throat. "Alright. Well, it seems the universe had it in the cards for us to meet, literally. Who can argue with fate? Not me." He laughed again. "Funny part is, I haven't had business cards in a long time. Years, actually."

"Weird," Sarah said quietly.

"Weird indeed. So now that we've cut the weird ribbon, why don't you go ahead and tell me why you feel your home is haunted?"

Sarah started looking around the room, her eyes flittering about like a buzzing housefly. Mark felt anxious—her behavior and body language reminded him of Roger during their last session. Right before everything went bad.

Is this the behavior of someone who's haunted? He wondered. Mark was beginning to feel like he was haunted himself, haunted by the trauma of all of this. Behind his eyes, he saw Maria's face, her mouth contorted into a violent scream of agony and rage. He closed his eyes for a moment to blink it away.

"I don't know where to start," Sarah said. Her hands were in her lap, thin fingers kneading at the fabric of her dress.

"The beginning is a good place," Mark chuckled. "You're the only appointment I made today because I knew I was going to the hospital and I don't like to bring people in too late. You've got plenty of time. I'm not going to tack on any fees if you go over. I'm a psychiatrist not a cell phone provider."

Sarah gave a genuine laugh this time.

Mark watched as her hands unclasped from her dress, her body releasing tension.

"Thanks," she told him, "for making this easier."

Mark smiled and nodded, not speaking because he didn't want to take the moment back. He wanted to make sure it remained hers, and motioned for Sarah to continue when at her own pace.

She took a breath. "I don't know how long you've been here or how well you know the city, but have you heard of the

Sunnycrest Apartment building?"

"I know it well actually," Mark said, trying to sound reassuring. In his head, he added, Unfortunately. "It's been around a long time," he told her. "Longer than you or me, that's for sure." Mark had actually thought about paying Sunnycrest a visit, of walking those halls himself and seeing if anything spoke to him, stood out and said, This is why we chose you. He always decided against it.

Something about that place felt dangerous to him. Rational or not, Mark couldn't shake it, no matter how hard he tried. Claire had told him she didn't want to hear the word Sunnycrest again. She said it was driving them both mad and it wasn't healthy. He didn't need his years of schooling or the degree framed on the wall behind him to know his wife was right. He knew just as well that he couldn't so easily put Sunnycrest out of his mind. Instead, he forced himself to stop bringing his work home with him. Now, this girl comes in and tells him that the building sent her to him.

To hell with Sunnycrest.

Sarah took a deep breath. "Right. Well, when I first got there, I was just looking for something cheap to get me through while I went to school. I'm sure you know that cheap isn't easy to find in the city, but the commute every day would've been terrible. My parents said they would help me with an apartment if need be. Sunnycrest seemed like a dream come true. It was old and tucked away and a fraction of the cost of everything else in the area. I didn't care how pretty it was or wasn't, you know? Beggars can't be choosers and whatever. Back then, I didn't believe in ghosts." She paused and licked at her lips. "Before I even signed the lease, a guy—Roger—from one of the upper floors came running down. He tried to warn me that the building was haunted, to convince me to leave and not sign. I was more scared of him than anything he was telling me."

Mark almost choked at the mention of Roger's name. He could picture the man running frantically at Sarah, trying to save her, even though the poor guy really needed to be saved from himself. Mark felt his eyes cloud and he removed his glasses, rubbing at them. When he replaced his glasses, he said, "And yet you still signed. Haunted or not, that would have been a red flag for me."

"I did," Sarah said with a shrug. "There are crazy people all over the city. You can't escape them. You have to learn how to live with them. Anyway, there was no way I could pass up the one place near school that I could actually afford to avoid one crazy guy who lived on a different floor. I had to take it."

"I understand that. I probably would have made the same call if I had been in your position. Has that crazy... Roger...has he caused you problems during your time there?"

Sarah shook her head. "No. Actually, I talked to him some. He seemed to be troubled but I don't think he was actually dangerous."

If only you knew, Mark thought. Out loud, he asked, "So at some point, you decided Roger was right. What brought you to that conclusion?"

Sarah took a deep breath, and returned to the nervous habit of kneading, and then smoothing, her dress. "There were things that made me wonder, even before my own story, things that just didn't make sense, unsettling things."

4

Sarah knew enough to stay away from the guy on the seventh floor—who'd practically assaulted her when Gary was showing her around—but she didn't know about the others. With thirteen floors to the building and most apartments occupied, there were a lot of people at Sunnycrest. She felt she should at least know the workers, the people she would see all the time. Her father had raised her to not wait for people to introduce themselves to her, to make the first move and live with power. It was important for people to know you were self-assured. Her father was a pretty successful businessman so she tended to listen to his advice.

She was coming home between classes and saw the groundskeeper, Willie, planting flowers around the big tree out front. With a smile, Sarah marched his way. "Hi," she called. "I'm Sarah. I moved into Apartment 8 on the second floor."

The man looked over his shoulder at her, then said, "Okay," and went back to what he was doing. Sarah chewed on her fingernail. She didn't want to just walk away and leave this bridge burning as it was.

"What's your name?" she asked him.

"Willie."

"Nice to meet you, Willie. You been working here a long time?"

"Mm."

"Those flowers are pretty."

"They're anemones."

Sarah beamed. She'd finally gotten through his wall. "The flowers symbolize protection and sacrifice. Which one are you going for?"

Willie stopped. He turned to face her, a spade in his dirty gloved hands. "Both."

Sarah paused. Her smile fell away and she shifted from her left foot to her right Considered slowly backing away. She tried again. "Sunnycrest seems nice. There's a lot of children here, huh?"

Willie gave a snort and got to his feet. He looked her dead in the eyes then and said, “In a sense.” Then he turned his back to her, knelt in the dirt, and got back to his plants.

Taking a deep breath, Sarah said, “Right,” more to herself.

She turned and went into the building, wondering what Willie had meant. Could he have been messing with her, trying to get in her head? Maybe he just wasn’t a people person and he tried to give people a reason not to speak to him again. There was a boy in her high school like that. Cameron. Sarah managed to befriend him, but she had to literally push her way into his life to do it. When they graduated, he thanked her for doing just that and said he wouldn’t have made it without her. Sometimes things worked out. Maybe she would try again with Willie, but there was something about their conversation—if you could call it that—that made her want to give it time.

When she got inside, she went to the stairwell and started to climb the two flights to her floor. She was halfway up, on the landing between floors, when she heard the laughter of children. Sarah turned and saw several young kids charging up the steps right toward her. She yelped and pressed herself against the wall to let them run past. Then she straightened herself and turned back to the stairs ahead, the door to her floor at the top.

She meant to yell at the children running toward it, to

reprimand them. To demand they slow down.

She meant to tell them it was dangerous to run like that on stairs. Dangerous for them and for the other people around—people like her.

She meant to say lots of things.

But she didn't say anything. Not even when she saw them pound their way through the closed door without slowing down.

In her mind, she heard Willie mutter snorting, "In a sense."

5

Mark blinked and rubbed at his face. "Wow," he said. "Assuming you're telling the truth, that seems pretty clear, and as you said, definitely unsettling."

"Assuming? You think I'm making it up? Why would I—"

"No, no." Mark held up a hand. "It's just…that's a lot. I believe you. What are you looking for from me exactly?"

Settling into her rhythm of kneading and smoothing, Sarah frowned. "I guess I was hoping you would tell me it could have been a trick of my eyes since I was at the bottom of the stairs…or it could have been my imagination, right? Acting up after the strange conversation. Or maybe, I don't know, maybe I'm schizophrenic or something and need meds. I don't know."

Mark smiled and nodded. "I could tell you those things. They're certainly all feasible, but I can't say any of them for certain because I wasn't there. After we talk for a while I can determine the last thing, but I'm not in the habit of diagnosing people a few minutes into their first session. I don't think I would be any good at my job if I did that."

"I guess you're right. I suppose I just don't know that I believe in ghosts or that I even want to, but I do know that something strange is going on in that building."

That part I definitely agree with, Mark thought. "Well, it's obvious you want to avoid leaving since it's convenient and affordable and those things are rare. So what are you feeling?"

Sarah was tight-lipped for a moment. "I don't know. The story gets a lot more complicated."

It always does, Mark thought. His fingers toyed with the handle of the drawer in his desk that hid his whiskey bottle. He would never open it with a patient present but knowing it was there brought with it a sense of comfort. "You've seen other things…things like the children that run through doors? Have you seen another child in that stairwell, a blond girl?"

As Mark was trying not to see the image that plagued

his nightmares, given to him by one of Roger's stories, Sarah said, "The jumper. No. She only comes at certain times of the year and Tom does a good job of locking things up. That's the only time I use that rickety old elevator."

Mark paled. His lips felt sickeningly dry. "So she's real," he said, his voice little more than a whisper.

Sarah frowned and shrugged simultaneously. "As far as I know. Like I said, I've never seen her myself, but if she's not real, there's a strange conspiracy going on with the staff and residents."

Mark's stomach churned, he could feel acid rising, like he was going to vomit. His fingers on the handle of the desk drawer began to tremble, his resolve cracking and his hand wanting the whiskey tucked within. He had hoped with every fiber of his being the child was part of Roger's addled mind. If she was, then it was possible that Sarah was right and there were people there helping to drive people crazy. Behind his eyes, he saw the terrified blond child climb the railing and go over it. He squeezed his eyes against the vision his mind conjured, blocking it out, but his mind was still filled with the wet smack of her impact. He put a hand to his mouth. Reel it in, Mark. You're not looking very professional right now.

Mark contemplated excusing himself to go to the bathroom but instead, he took a deep breath to regain composure and said plainly, "It sure sounds like you believe in ghosts, but you're trying to deny your own reality. Why do you think that is?"

Exhaling, Sarah's shoulders slumped, like the air she released had been previously holding her upright. "I don't know. It's not, like, anything about my parents, or my childhood, or anything like that, if that's what you're thinking. I guess if I accept that ghosts are real and all this stuff is real, then I have to accept that what's happening in my apartment is real, and I don't know if I can do that and hold onto sanity."

Mark's eyes popped open wide. His fingers left the desk drawer and his hands gripped the desk. He leaned forward and looked at her intensely. "Wait. What's happening in your apartment?"

With a deep sigh, Sarah said, "Yeah. I guess it's time I get to that."

6

Sarah had had a long day at school. Her feet ached and her lower back was sore. She was glad to be home. As much as she loved school and the idea of the career she was working toward, sometimes all of it was overwhelming, especially being an hour away from her parents and friends. Maybe she should have found a place with a roommate so the house wouldn't be so quiet when she got home every day.

At least a pet, she thought. Something.

She plopped on her couch and kicked off her shoes. With a groan, she rubbed at her arches, wishing she had a girlfriend to do it for her. She was in the big city, but school didn't really leave her the time or energy to go out and meet people. At least, that was her excuse, and she was sticking with it. She didn't know how so many people went to college and partied like they did. Even if she had been in a party school, she wouldn't have been able to bring herself to spend her study time drinking. She had always been goal-oriented. She had an end game and liver failure wasn't it.

Letting her sore foot drop from her hand to the rug below, she let her head fall back against the big plush couch cushions. It felt like drifting into clouds and she loved it. Her eyes slid closed and she considered sleeping right there tonight.

Then there was a loud thump.

Jolting awake, she jumped out of her skin, shivering. Now she was definitely wishing she had gotten herself a dog.

Sarah groaned with the effort, a hand to her lower back as she pushed herself up from the couch to see what had caused the sound. Her closet door was ajar. Something must have fallen off the shelf and hit the door. At least, that's what she told herself to calm her nerves. She covered her mouth against the yawn that broke from her lips and then cautiously crept toward the closet.

Sarah pulled the closet door open. When she did, a snow globe rolled out and landed at her feet. She stared down at it for a moment, perplexed. It wasn't hers. It never had been.

It had the statue of liberty in the center and seemed like a souvenir you would get at the airport or something. She never wanted to seem or feel like a tourist, as she grew up on Long Island and considered herself a New Yorker. She never would have purchased something like that.

Running through the files in her mind, she tried to see if she could locate any memory of where someone had given her the tacky ornament. As far as she could recall, no one ever had. She shook her head slowly and bent down to pick the object up. She looked at her closet and saw everything else as it had been when she left. There was no room for anyone to hide in all the clothes and things she had packed in there. It seemed like a bizarre crime for someone to break into someone's apartment and leave a snow globe in their closet. Take that! Okay. I will! She laughed to herself.

Sarah turned her eyes to the object she held. She turned it over in her hands and her mouth fell open. A date on the bottom read: Jan. 11th, 1987.

She hadn't even been alive then. Sarah was pretty sure her parents hadn't even met yet. She hadn't seen the nineties, never mind the eighties. "Where did you come from?" she said out loud.

Stepping away from the closet, Sarah placed the snow globe on the end table. She went back to the closet, but looked over her shoulder. A nagging sense told her the snow globe would disappear if she took her eyes off it.

It sat right where she left it. She almost sighed with relief and wasn't sure why. Sarah moved the coats in the closet and lifted her photo albums, flipping through them. She didn't know what she was looking for, or expecting to find. Whatever it was, she didn't find it.

The nagging feeling remained as she bent down, rummaging through the things stacked on the closet floor. There was a broom and dustpan, a vacuum, and a bowling ball bag, without a bowling ball in it. She was meaning to get a new one, mainly just because she loved the bag so much with its aged leather and rainbow design. Then her hand stopped and her eyes grew wide.

She was touching a pair of shoes that didn't belong to her. They were a man's work boots—filthy and caked with fresh mud. Sarah trembled. She stood and slammed the closet door shut, as if locking the shoes away would negate the threat of a random man's boots sitting in her closet. She put her back against the door and stared at the table where she had left the old snow globe that was clean and looked new. It was right where she left it.

Sarah's eyes darted around the room and landed on the front door. It had been locked when she came in. She was fairly certain it had. She had used her key, but what if it hadn't been locked at all and she just didn't check and used her key out of habit to unlock an already open door? It was possible, wasn't it? If the door wasn't actually ajar, she would just follow her routine, none the wiser. No, she told herself, that's anxiety speaking. It's irrational. But was it? It nagged at her, nonetheless.

Sarah's heart pounded in her chest. She looked at the windows. One of them was open and the curtains were blowing in the breeze outside. But I left it open, didn't I? I'm on the second floor. There's no fire escape. How would someone even get to it? A ladder? In broad daylight? What the hell sense does that make?

Sarah wondered if the intruder could be there somewhere, watching her. Waiting.

She went into the kitchen and grabbed the biggest knife she could find. She checked the cabinets—even though it felt insane to do so—and then she headed for her bedroom, tightly-gripped knife held out before her, quivering in her nervous hand. She opened the bedroom closet and found nothing out of the ordinary.

Icy fingers grazed the back of her neck, and she spun on a sore heel to find herself alone. Dropping to the ground, she peered under her bed, which was way too big—what was she thinking? Wow, she really needed to get out. Is that a stain? She needed to wash her bedding. Hey, what if there was a gorgeous lesbian hiding under the bed that wanted to know if she liked the snow globe. Oh my God, she would see that grisly stain. Sarah laughed at herself, breathed the last of her fear away, and got to her feet.

There was no one in this apartment, no one but her. At least, not at this moment. She could see the bathroom from where she was. The shower curtain was wide open. There was no one in there either. Whoever was there, leaving bizarre gifts in her closet, they were gone now.

Sighing, Sarah made her way back to the living room. She paused at the closet door, clenching the knife and steadying her hand. Ripping the door open—like there was going to be someone standing behind it that she could give a piece of her mind to.

Empty.

She grabbed the boots and pulled them out. Then she sat on the floor and looked at them more closely. There were initials written in black permanent marker on the cloth loop at the top back of each boot. KT.

Sarah was sure she had seen those initials before. She tried her best to remember where. Then it clicked. She ran to the window and Sarah stared out at the big tree in the front yard. The tree Willie had planted flowers around when she first moved in.

Those initials had been carved into the tree, surrounded by a heart. KT & RJ. How long ago? She wondered. Something in her gut told her it was January 1987.

Sarah shivered and told herself it was due to the breeze blowing through the open window. She hurriedly closed it and latched the lock in place, but the chill had settled into her.

And something drew her back to the old snow globe that was now swirling a festive New York winter scene. Sarah grabbed the souvenir and threw it in a box, shoving it under her bed, unsure why she didn't throw it right out the window.

7

Mark blew out a puff of air and then pulled his glasses off to rub at his eyes. "Well that's definitely strange, to say the least, but it doesn't necessarily scream ghosts. That's not to say I have a better explanation, because I certainly don't. Was that the end of it or was there more? Have you asked the other tenants about RJ and KT? Maybe one of your neighbors has been there long enough to remember them."

Sarah watched him with a twinkle in her eyes , which he found strange. Was this all some kind of joke? Did someone send her to him, put her up to this? That would be a cruel prank if that were the case. His fears fell away when she said, "That would be good advice if that was the last thing that happened, but that was only the beginning, Doc. I'm sorry, Mark. This story is just getting started."

Mark nodded. I should have known that, he thought. Nothing was ever simple when it came to Sunnycrest. "Yes. I'm sorry. I jumped the gun on that one."

Sarah gave a small, humorless laugh. "There's definitely more—a lot more—and I believe plenty more to come that I don't even know yet."

Mark took a deep breath and leaned back in his chair, which creaked under his weight. "Well, I am glad you came to me Sarah, and I definitely want to hear all of your story. But I'm afraid I'm not going to be able to do that today. Why don't you try to give me a little bit more and then we'll call it a day and resume again next week? Same time?"

Sarah nodded. She stood from her chair and walked to the window. She looked out at the busy city street, life passing by at high speed while they suffered through this slow conversation within these walls. A place like this was a respite of sorts, she supposed.

"Alright," she said. "Yeah. I'll come back next week, but first I need you to at least give me some kind of advice on what to do."

Mark nodded. "Okay. What to do about what, exactly?"

Sarah gave another laugh that Mark feared bordered on madness. She seemed like a bright, together girl though. Maybe she was just stressed and needed his help. He would help her if he could. He would do anything to not let another person end up like Maria or Roger. Was there anything he could really do though? Mark was beginning to believe that Sunnycrest couldn't be stopped once it got its claws into someone. He couldn't remember ever being so afraid of anything. Then he thought maybe it was time to make an appointment with his own psychiatrist—or the bottle in his drawer.

Sarah turned to face him. "I need to know what to do with the doorway in my closet." Mark peered at her closely. He realized she didn't say the doorway to my closet. She must have seen or felt his confusion because she elaborated then by saying, "The doorway to 1987, to the people that lived in my apartment 34 years ago."

Mark eyed the drawer in his desk that contained the whiskey.

"I've gone through it," she said. "I've seen them, and I don't want to be crazy, Mark. Please, help me to believe that I'm not crazy."

8

Sarah stood facing her open closet. The items didn't come every day, or in any specific pattern of time, but they always showed up there. Behind that door, in the living room closet. There had to be some way they were getting through, some kind of gateway or something. She knew Sunnycrest was a strange place and that each person tucked within its walls had their own story.

This must be mine, she thought.

She didn't know if it was ghosts or something else, but she knew it was real. There was a shoebox under her bed filled with things she received from…wherever…the past, she supposed. Was it here? Were they living here in Apartment 8 simultaneously? Were they finding her things as well? If they were then she needed to pay closer attention. She hadn't noticed anything going missing, but that didn't mean that nothing had.

Sarah ran to her school supplies and grabbed a notebook and a pen. She went through the closet, writing down everything she saw, making an inventory. Then if anything came or went, she would know. She could update the book every day, and keep a log of it.

As she was doing so, she reached to the back and felt the wall. It was solid enough. She didn't feel any loose paneling or holes in the wall. She bit her lip and then came to a spontaneous decision. Reaching in with both hands, she pulled everything out onto the floor. Then Sarah crawled into the closet, pulling her knees to her chest below the line of coats. She reached up, grabbed the handle, and tugged the door shut.

She sat there for a moment, holding her breath. She didn't know what she expected to happen. Nothing seemed to happen at all. She sighed, frustrated with herself for giving in like that. Then she reached up and opened the door to let herself out. When she emerged, she said, "Shit."

She was in her apartment, but it wasn't her apartment. It was completely different, down to every last detail. She contemplated seeing if she could take The Cure poster back with her as her eyes scanned the room. I shouldn't, she decided.

So, was this KT's place, or RJ's, or both? She edged toward the bedroom and stopped short when she heard voices. They were laughing about something but panic still rose in her gut at the sound. She raced back to the closet, opened the door, and found it full of their belongings.

Shaking now, she looked over her shoulder and feared she would see angry people behind her wanting to know what she was doing in their home. She reached into the closet and ripped out some all-too-familiar work shoes and then squeezed herself in, the other belongings raining down in an avalanche of someone's life. She closed the door harder than she meant to and cringed at the bang!

Sarah knew she had to open the door again, but she feared it hadn't worked. That she hadn't gone back and she was stuck there. She feared opening that door would just alert the homeowners to her hiding place, that they would be standing there, staring down at her. She told herself she was being irrational again but was any of this really rational?

Sarah stared through the dark at the closed door before her. Part of her was waiting for the knob to turn, for a foreign hand to open it from the other side. They would see their shoes on the ground and wonder how they got there. They would want to put them back.

She couldn't breathe. She felt like the sound of her

heart was a drum echoing through the apartment, that it would give her away. She knew she had no choice, but she was so frightened. Her hand shook and she reached up.

Twisting the knob with frightened, trembling fingers, she pushed the door open, falling out into her own living room. She scurried away from the closet in a hurry, terrified that someone would follow her back. When she got to her feet on shaking legs, she quickly closed the door and then stepped back, staring at it. She stayed like that for several minutes, just waiting, and waiting. She vowed to herself that tomorrow she would get a new doorknob and a lock, maybe a chain too, and a deadbolt.

In the meantime, she would go the rest of this night without sleep and somehow hope she could make it through classes in the morning. Sarah thought, at that moment, that she could do with taking up drinking after all.

TWO

Going Home

9

Mark Stephenson sat silently, blinking at Sarah. He was trying to collect his thoughts, to word them accordingly. He'd found in his time in mental health that it was important not to dismiss people, even when their stories were far-fetched. They needed trust in order to remain open, and the moment you shot down their wild tale, that bridge was on fire and almost impossible to extinguish.

After a moment, he said, "I thought we were talking about ghosts. This sounds more like time travel. The people you encountered were alive and talking, correct?"

Sarah nodded and sucked her teeth. “Yeah, but I feel like they’re trying to tell me something. Something about someone that died.”

“Why do you feel that way?” He looked over at the clock on the wall and thought about how Claire would be waiting on him if he didn’t get out of here soon. “Have you gone back after that?”

Sarah sighed. She got to her feet, smoothed her dress, and grabbed her purse from the floor by her chair. “I haven’t, no. I was afraid, but I opened it and things continue to appear. The last thing was chilling, to say the least. It was a newspaper from 1987.”

Mark watched as she reached into her purse and his eyes widened when she pulled out a folded paper. His mouth fell open when she walked over and placed it down on the desk before him.

“Take a look when you get the chance. It doesn’t say anything that specifically pertains to RJ and KT or my apartment but it says something. See what you can make out of it. I’ll see you next week, Mark. Thanks for listening. I’m glad that old business card found me. It seems things from the past like to end up in my hands.”

Mark forced himself not to look at the paper yet. He kept his eyes focused on the woman at his door. As she pulled it open, he said, “Remember to live, Sarah. Don’t let this consume you. Get out and have some fun, and meet some people that live in 2021. I'll see you next week."

Sarah laughed and gave him a wave before she walked out and let the door fall closed behind her. Mark let out a long, slow exhale and immediately opened the drawer in his desk, pulling the whiskey bottle free and setting it before him. He took out a small crystal glass as well. He liked his whiskey but he wasn't a heathen. Mark poured two fingers into the glass and then returned the bottle to the drawer. He realized his hands were shaking and he frowned. Mark let his eyes fall shut and sipped the amber liquid. He left his eyes closed and just breathed slow steady breaths. Then he opened his eyes and picked up the paper in front of him.

From the way she had it folded, the first thing he saw was the date. She was right. It was either from January 17th, 1987, or it was a beautiful forgery. The paper was far too crisp and white to have been sitting around for 34 years. It would have yellowed, the ink fading.

Unless it was new, he thought. Jesus. Do I believe this? It's Sunnycrest. It makes anything seem possible and all of it seem terrible. Maybe when I get home I'll talk to Claire and see if she wants to move away from this city. We can start over somewhere else.

Below the date, Mark read the cover headline. **The Manhattan Mangler Murder Mayhem Continues!**

Mark unfolded the paper and gazed at the picture. It was an apartment building. It wasn't Sunnycrest, but another just like it. His fingers ran through the bristles of his beard as he sipped the whiskey and read the article. The writer was discussing the fourth attack and shared his belief that the killer had no idea of stopping. Women were being butchered in the safety of their own homes, all of which were busy, crowded apartment buildings. The killer wanted to make sure everyone knew that they weren't safe anywhere, and apparently so did this journalist.

Mark leaned backward in his seat and tried to think back. Unlike Sarah, he had been alive in 1987. He was a child in the eighties, but old enough for people to have been talking. Kids in school never let things like that go. He lived in Jersey then, but he thought he might remember something. He was drawing a blank. Mark took a deep breath and looked at the bottom of his empty glass. Not remembering a killer—from when he was eleven—didn't mean they didn't exist. He wanted to take out his laptop, to search the Manhattan Mangler and see what came up, but his eyes went to the clock and he cussed. He left the glass on his desk, stuffed the paper into his coat pocket, grabbed his shoulder bag, and headed out of the office.

Jessica smiled at him from her chair out front. She had everything packed up and her giant pocketbook resting on her lap. As usual, she was ready to go and waiting on him. "You look pretty shaken," she said. "You alright?"

"I'm good," he told her. "Go ahead and schedule Sarah for the same time next week."

Jessica spun on her chair until she was facing her computer. She typed quickly and then said, "Done."

She switched the computer off and the monitor went black. Then she got to her feet and led the way to the front door. "I'll see you tomorrow, Mark."

"I'm right behind you," he said, following her out the door. Before he closed it, he looked back into the office like he expected something. Maybe someone or something that shouldn't be there. He didn't know what he expected, but he knew it frightened him. Sarah's session probably just left him unsettled. It was evidence that the past had a way of coming back to haunt you. In his mind he saw a brown-haired boy in a red shirt, and hoped he could keep his own past at bay.

10

Sarah thought the doctor's parting comment was interesting. He somehow read from her that she needed to get out and meet people. They hadn't even touched on that. Either he was really good at his job or she was very obviously a lonely shut-in. She hoped it was the former.

She didn't bother with the subway or hail a taxi when she left. Even if something was a hundred blocks away it somehow felt like it was within walking distance in the grid that was the city. Besides, walking was good exercise and a chance to catalog your thoughts and clear your head. As she walked today, Sarah wondered if she had been right to give the paper to the doctor. Part of her didn't want it around because it gave her the creeps and it threatened her sanity. She wanted, no, she needed to share it with someone. Not just the paper, but all of it, her truth. That's why she went to him, wasn't it?

At the same time, if he didn't bother with it and just threw it away, she'd lose her proof. Proof of what? she asked herself. She wasn't even sure herself. She wished she had more time to explain things to the doctor, to talk through it with someone, but she understood she had already gone over the allotted hour and couldn't stay in the man's office all night. He probably had a family to get home to.

Mark seemed nice enough, though a little on edge. He had said he'd come from the hospital. She probably caught him at a bad time and then dropped a bombshell in his lap. He still handled it better than most people would have. Sarah looked at all the people walking by her in both directions, the constant ebb and flow of city life, and she imagined what the street may have looked like in the late 80s. She pictured the same passing people in 80s attire, and wondered if the world through her closet was happening simultaneously—if those people were walking this very street in place of these people, right now. She imagined them overlapping like layered animation cells. There was something equally frightening and alluring about the concept.

Sarah thought about the fact that Mark had known

about the jumper in the stairwell. He obviously wasn't new to Sunnycrest. Maybe he wasn't new to its ghosts and monsters either. Perhaps she should have asked him some questions when she had the chance. There could have been a good reason he was frightened. Although, if he'd gotten the information from patients he wouldn't have been able to disclose it to her anyway. Nothing was ever simple and easy.

Her mind went back to what Mark had told her when she was leaving—to live her life and not let this consume her. *What life do I have?* It was school and her apartment. That wasn't much. She knew she was the only one capable of changing that and she knew just as well that she hadn't the slightest idea how to go about doing it. There was a girl who shared several classes with her and they talked from time to time. Melissa. Sarah was pretty sure Melissa was straight, but a friend was a good place to start. She should ask the girl to hang out sometime, go dancing or something. Sarah loved to dance and she hadn't done it since she moved to the city. It wasn't fun to dance alone, though the release was cathartic.

Sarah didn't feel like cooking. Cooking was worse than dancing in that regard. When you're the only person there, it is hard to motivate yourself to make a meal every day. It would be different if she had someone else to cook for. She didn't though, and decided on a burger and fries. She would have preferred something better, at least better for her, but it was something she wouldn't have to wait long for. Sarah was already tired and she had class early in the morning. She just wanted to get home.

As she walked, Sarah ate her fries, cringing with pangs of guilt every time she passed by the sad, desperate faces of the homeless while stuffing food in her face. Eventually, the guilt won over and she handed the bag with the burger inside to a man who looked like he hadn't had food in days. He thanked her profusely and as she started to walk away, she saw him feed it to his dog. Apparently, love was more powerful than hunger, and maybe even survival. To her surprise, there were tears in her eyes. She wiped them away and kept going.

The current train of thought brought Sarah's mind right back to RJ and KT. They had been in love enough to carve their initials into the tree out front. What did that mean for them? Where did it lead them? The answers to those questions could be right through a door in her living room. But what else could be through that door? The Manhattan Mangler?

She had no idea. That was the part that frightened her the most. She didn't know what to expect, what to think, what she would find. That unknown left her feeling helpless and she hated to feel that way. She was out here on her own, going to school and trying to pave the path to her career, to show how not helpless she was. Now, this. But I did something about it, right? I called Dr. Stephenson and even went to go see him. I'm controlling what's in my power. That's all we can do.

Sarah made it to Sunnycrest but she stopped before going to the heavy front door. She felt drawn to the tree or—more to the point—to the carving in its bark. There it was, a symbol of love from the 80s. She traced it with her fingers. Sarah imagined two people sitting there on a picnic blanket, both of them laughing, one of them scratching their love into the tree that hung over them like an umbrella. She realized then that she had no idea what they actually looked like. As she stood there, fingers tracing the carving of their initials, Sarah found herself wanting to know.

Control what's in your power, she told herself. I have to go back through.

11

Mark double-tapped the button on his keyless entry and waited to hear the answering beep that let him know his car was locked. There were too many break-ins on this road for him to be overconfident. His car had an alarm, but so did half the others he watched from the safety of his living room window.

He climbed the brick porch to the front door. He was glad to find it locked even though Claire was already home. He spent most of the car ride trying to decide if he should tell her about Sarah's time-traveling closet or not. Mark knew he wasn't supposed to talk to her about patients, but he also knew no one would ever find out. Claire would never breathe a word of it to anyone. She was great, far better than he, or anyone, deserved.

Mark moved into the house and shut the door, immediately turning to lock it. As he did, he called, "Sorry I'm late. I hope you're not starving."

Claire swaggered to the foyer to meet him with a sly smile pulling at her thin lips. "I know you by now, husband. I ate a sandwich a while ago to hold me over. Now you can get started cooking the good stuff."

"Yes ma'am," Mark said with a wide smile. Somehow Claire always made him forget about the stress. He loved cooking and he loved her so it was a winning combination. He hung up his coat and hurried to the kitchen where he washed his hands. Over the running water, he asked, "Do you believe in time travel?"

Claire sat at the table behind him. "You know everything I believe in by this point, don't you?"

"Humor me," he said, cutting off the water and drying his hands.

Claire shrugged her shoulders. "Anything is possible, but I've never seen any evidence of it. Why is that the first thing out of your mouth when you get home?"

Mark tossed some butter and minced garlic into a frying pan to brown as he began slicing an onion on the nearby cutting board. "I just had a new patient with a peculiar story today."

Claire poured herself a glass of wine from a bottle already sitting on the table. "And you're buying into it? Is this another Sunnycrest person?"

"They have a way of finding me," Mark sighed. "Go get the paper out of my bag. See for yourself."

As he worked to sauté the onions and garlic, Claire did as he said. "Smells good already," she told him. She didn't say anything else and Mark left the sizzling frying pan to turn and face her. He saw her staring at the paper.

"Looks real, doesn't it?"

"It does," she admitted. "And new. I need to know the story on this one, Mark."

She brought the paper back to the table. "There's an ad for Harry and the Hendersons in here. Apparently, it comes out in June," Claire laughed. "This is wild."

Mark continued with dinner, the scents of stir fry filling the house. As he cooked, he did his best to fill her in. When he was retelling it he realized how many details he was likely missing and wished he could have let the session go over longer, stayed around to hear the rest. "You should go," Claire told him when he was done. "Ask her if you can see it for yourself."

"You want me to show up at my patient's house and request to climb into her closet?"

"Why not?" Claire said with a shrug and a sip of wine. "She's obviously dealt with crazier than that already."

"Maybe," Mark admitted, setting a plate of food down in front of her.

"Of course, if this were a movie," Claire added with a laugh, "it would turn out that you actually were the Mangler and the reason you were never caught was that you were from the future."

"You know I could never do anything like that," he said, shaking his head and smiling.

"I know, but maybe somebody else could. Who lived there between the 80s couple and Sarah?" She spooned a mouthful of stir fry. "Oh my God, this is delicious. I love your nights."

Mark wasn't eating though. He was just staring at his wife and processing what she had just asked him. Maybe the killer had been caught. He didn't know what transpired after the paper came out. He let his fork fall onto his plate and threw his chair back with a screech. Then he ran to his bag and got his laptop. It was time to see what the internet knew about the Manhattan Mangler.

12

Sarah got inside and stared at the closet door. "Did you leave anything for me?" she asked. She felt anxious and afraid but also intrigued and energized.

She wanted to teach kids because she wanted to make a difference in someone's life. Maybe she could do that now, with this. Maybe there was a reason the past and the present were connected. She had seen a million movies like that. She had a soft spot in her heart for Frequency, the movie with the short wave radio that connected the past to the present. It was beautiful. Perhaps Sarah's story would be beautiful too.

Maybe there was some wrong she could help right, something she could align in the universe, or maybe she just wanted there to be.

Maybe Sarah was just desperate for a higher purpose, for some meaning.

Maybe that was the same thing she was seeking through wanting to be a teacher.

Sarah sighed at the thought.

If her mother knew anything about this, she would yell at Sarah, and tell her to leave dark things alone, and insist she move to a new apartment, or even a new city. Her father was all business. He cared for her mother but not her superstitions. He would never dare try to change her though. Her father worshipped the ground her mother walked on. Sarah had always dreamed of finding a love like that. It was refreshing to see how different they were and how little it mattered.

America was so full of division these days. There was so little acceptance. Differences were deal breakers with her generation. It made social anxiety that much more powerful. You had so much more to fear in being open and honest with new people. One wrong opinion could end everything forever. Boom: canceled. That kept Sarah in her books, her dreams, her own head. She was safe there.

She wondered what her father would say, if he were here now. He'd probably ask what her end game was and want to help her develop her strategy toward reaching that goal.

He'd probably even whip up a PowerPoint some spreadsheets. The man adored spreadsheets.

He was successful and she often told herself she should listen more to what he had to say. His accolades were proof that his advice was sound, but it honestly all felt overwhelming to her, especially the spreadsheets. Sarah had ADHD and that was a lot to focus on and keep track of. It gave people like her father peace of mind and people like her anxiety attacks.

Sarah took a deep breath to steel her nerves, then ripped her closet door open before she could get too caught up in her thoughts and change her mind. Some things fell from the way she haphazardly stacked them after last time, and it was enough to make her jump.

In all, it looked no different than any other ordinary closet. Would anyone believe otherwise, if she were in danger or went missing? Would the paper be enough for Mark to bring help? Would he? She didn't know him well, but he seemed trustworthy enough. The universe steered you to him, she reminded herself Believe in that. But is that me or my mother? I don't know what I believe. Dad would say, "Believe in results." Ugh.

Maybe it wasn't the universe at all. Maybe it was this place. Sunnycrest. With all the things that went on here regularly, wasn't it possible that the building's reach extended beyond its walls? Mark could be connected somehow, or maybe it wanted him to be—was trying to draw him in for some reason. Perhaps the building knew more than all of them.

Now you sound like a mad woman, Sarah thought, laughing quietly at herself.

Sometimes she wished she actually had a little of her mother's faith and superstition. It would probably do her well. She admired her parents equally for different reasons and often wondered what they really thought about her. Of course, they showered her with love and praise, but that was their job. What did they say to each other when she wasn't around? She knew they'd given up on the prospect of grandchildren.

Just go, she told herself. You're stalling. Go. See. Go on.

Sarah swallowed a lump in her throat and licked her lips. Then she moved slowly toward her closet like it was a dog that might bite her if she wasn't careful. With a deep breath she climbed in, more things falling out from under her, but those things didn't matter. What mattered was the truth, the story. Maybe I should change my major and go into journalism. There's something really exciting about the pursuit of the truth. "And dangerous," she knew her mother would say. "Stick to teaching."

Sarah reached up, grabbed the knob, and tried to pull the door closed. It wouldn't come and hit something, stopping its movement. Sarah grumbled in frustration and looked down to see the left shoe from a pair of combat boots that she totally would wear but definitely didn't own. She reached down and grabbed it, lifting it before her to see if it had initials on it. Before she could see any details, the door slammed shut. She yelped, cast into darkness.

Sarah immediately grabbed for the doorknob, for an open door and light, her heart racing. When she found what she desired and the ability to breathe came with it, she was facing a bed that wasn't hers in a room that was. Sarah got to her feet and stepped cautiously out of the closet on trembling legs, her eyes darting around the room, searching for threats. She kept her ears peeled, listening for the voices—the ones she heard last time, or new ones. The apartment was eerily quiet. She heard her own breaths, her own heart, and nothing more.

Why did she come out into the bedroom this time? She had thought the closet led only to itself in a different time, but it seemed the Sunnycrest time travel system was a bit more complicated than that. She was immediately drawn to a picture on the nightstand. It was of a beautiful young white woman, all black hair and blue eyes, and an equally attractive ebony man on her arm. They were smiling at each other, that twinkle of love in their eyes. "RJ and TK," Sarah said quietly. "Are you okay? What happened to you? Where are you now?"

Sarah looked around the room and found that things were more feminine than last time. Was she in a different place or was it just that the female got to be the decorator of the bedroom? There was a boom box with a tape deck. Sarah wanted so badly to press "Play" but she didn't want to draw that kind of attention to herself. She hit "Eject" instead. When the drawer loudly popped open, she pulled the cassette out of the deck and looked at it. It was a Bauhaus album. There was definitely a Gothic theme with these two. Sarah liked it. Ever since she was a child she had been drawn to alternative things, things outside the mainstream, things her classmates' Baptist church didn't approve of.

She considered pocketing the tape and wondered what would happen if she did. Would it somehow mess with the time-space continuum? She didn't think so, but she did think it was probably rude and invasive to the person who owned it. It felt wrong being here in that sense, like she was a burglar or a peeping Tom or something. It was a clear invasion of their privacy. Sarah had to admit to herself, although shamefully, that was part of what made the whole thing so invigorating. I'll bring that up with Mark at the next session, she thought, giving herself a pass.

Sarah wished she could inspect the closet but she was afraid she would be sent back if she did. She didn't want to mess with the closets until it was time to go, though she was intrigued. People tended to keep secrets in their closets and not just metaphorically. Instead of allowing herself to be drawn to the magnetic pull of the closet, Sarah went to the dresser and opened the drawers. There were some fairly elegant undergarments—Sarah was impressed but felt wrong touching, especially the wide assortment of fishnets—but nothing to explain why she was connected to this place. She did her best to put everything back how she found it and silently apologized to the goth girl for touching her underwear. She wondered in part if this was just how Sunnycrest worked. Maybe there wasn't a mystery at all and the past was just connected to the present there. Maybe the building was a loop of some kind where the timelines coexisted.

And maybe I watch far too many movies. I really do need to get out and meet people. Mark is right.

Sarah left the bedroom then and headed into the living room and the sight of it changed her mind. This was definitely not the same living room she had been in last time, though the décor was very much the same—a Siouxsie and the Banshees poster graced the wall behind the overly bulky tube television. There was a piece of paper on the coffee table with legs of winding black roses. Sarah leaned over for a closer look and her mouth fell open. Scrawled on the paper were the words, "I knew you would come. Please help me."

Is that for me? It couldn't be…could it?

Sarah backed up and looked around suddenly feeling like she was being watched from somewhere. Was this note from RJ or KT? Was it meant for one of them or could it be as it seemed? Something in her gut told her the answer. Even if she were wrong, and it wasn't to her, it felt like it was. That was enough to get under her skin. *How? How did you know I would come? How do you know me? Could they be coming* to my time too? Watching me in my sleep? Showering? Eating? What do they want from me? You're paranoid, Sarah. Get a grip.

Sarah had one thing nagging at her, something that wouldn't let go. She crossed to the front door and opened it. Then she peered out into the hall to make sure no one was watching. The hall looked pretty much the same as it did in the present day, except in far better condition. She didn't expect any different. What she wanted to see was what hallway she was actually looking at. She stepped out and turned to face the door of the apartment she was just in.

53.

That meant she was all the way up on the eleventh floor. Either RJ or KT—whoever was the female—had lived on the eleventh floor, it seemed. It frustrated her that she still didn't know which pair of initials belonged to which person. Either way, that meant the other's apartment could have been on any floor as well. She had assumed it was her apartment and that the couple lived together. She was now beginning to suspect Sunnycrest had no rules. The building did what it wanted to do when it wanted to do it, but what did it all mean?

A door started to open nearby and Sarah hurried away. She didn't have time to think and ran down the hall to the elevator. It was dumb. She scolded herself. She should have gone back inside, gone back home—back to 2021—but she hadn't, and now someone was in the hall, and even though her suede overcoat and knee-high boots weren't that outlandish they may have seemed so to the 1980s crowd. Plus, the farther she got from the closet in the apartment, the farther she got from her way home, and her reality, her sanity. The idea of being trapped here, fourteen years before she was even born, was absolutely terrifying to Sarah.

"Are you looking for someone?" a voice said from behind her. Sarah's eyes went wide. She hit the "Down" button and tapped her foot nervously. She could hear steps on the tiled floor—not yet chipped and broken—coming behind her. Come on. Come on. Come on.

It wasn't until she was in the elevator, facing the thin bald man in too-large plastic glasses taped in the middle that it occurred to her, she never takes the elevator. He eyed her with a peculiar expression through the deteriorating space between the closing doors, and it unnerved her. Fortunately, this was thirty-four years in the past and the car moved smoothly and soundlessly as it took her down. Out of instinct, she hit the button for the second floor when she got in.

She could have added the lobby to that, but then what? Sarah licked at her suddenly dry lips. She felt like her heart sounded impossibly loud in the acoustics of the metal box but she knew that was only her imagination. You're trying to be a science teacher, she reminded herself. Get it together. A little more Scully, a little less Moulder.

When the doors slid open, the hallway was clear and Sarah breathed a sigh of relief. Sarah watched a lot of movies, especially now that she was single and didn't have much time where she was awake and not in school, studying, or writing papers. Movies made a nice companion while she worked and let other voices into her apartment. They made her less lonely. She'd seen enough time travel movies to know that doing things in the past could screw things up in the present. Of course, she already touched things and ejected that tape. Dammit. What if I go back and have a sixth toes or my mom and dad split up or this building was torn down ten years ago and I have nowhere to live? Okay. I just need to do better. She didn't want to talk to anyone while she was here. She had no idea what the ramifications would be. Maybe even being seen just now would set something in motion. It was so much to think about and Sarah felt like her brain was going to break. The stabbing pains in her temples evidence enough of her imminent breakdown.

Sarah told herself to use the stairs and make her way back to floor eleven, wait for the bald man to be out of sight, and then head back into Apartment 53. Still, even as she told herself that, she found herself walking toward the door to Apartment 8.

What are you doing? she asked herself. I have to know, she answered. Curiosity killed the cat, she reminded herself. Good thing I'm not a cat. But what happened to worrying about the effects on the present? I have to know. For God's sake, I'm arguing with myself and losing.

Against her better judgment, Sarah knocked on the door. She held her breath and waited.

"You looking for Kevin, because I saw him leave a while ago."

Sarah stiffened. She looked over her shoulder and saw a long-haired man in a denim jacket snorting coke off his sleeve. Sarah blinked. It's the 80s, she reminded herself. "Okay," she said, not knowing what else to do. "Thanks."

She moved to walk down the hall, and the man said, "You want a bump? Mama taught me to share."

"No," Sarah said, clearing her throat. "Um, no thank you. I'm good."

She looked in the direction of the stairwell, but she didn't want to go up with this guy following her. He smiled. "Your coat is pretty fresh, like something out of Lost Boys. That movie is mint."

Sarah hadn't thought much about how the language would be different. She did, however, know the movie he mentioned. It was a classic in her opinion and one of her personal favorites. She had the Blu-ray collector's edition tin on her entertainment center. She'd watched the special features before. It led her to say what she said next. "Lost Boys doesn't come out 'til the summer."

The man laughed. "I understand why you didn't need

the blow lady. It came out last weekend. How fucking wasted are you, Betty? You've been smoking those chongers. Got any doobies left to share?"

"My name isn't Betty," Sarah said in confusion.

The man laughed. "Most Bettys probably aren't named Betty, but I guess I shouldn't pass judgment like that. You're probably rad as hell with that Lost Boys jacket and kicker boots. Well, Not-Betty, my parents call me Bill but my crew calls me Baggins. Pleasure to meet you."

"You too," Sarah said coyly, brushing hair behind her ear. She didn't know the slang and she felt like saying too much would complicate things further. "I gotta go."

Before she could take the first step toward the stairwell, Baggins said, "How do you know Kevin Thompson? I didn't think he knew girls other than Regina even existed."

"Oh," Sarah said with an all too obvious start. She frowned at herself which she felt probably didn't help the situation. Then she remembered this guy already thought she was high. "School," she said.

"Like high school? Because Kevin's not one of those dweebs going to college. He's got a job."

"I meant work."

Baggins laughed, a deep hearty laugh that bounced off the walls of the otherwise empty hall. "You're a trip, Not-Betty. Don't worry. None of this is real."

Sarah jumped. Her fingers kneaded at the fabric of her

dress. "I'm sorry. What?"

Baggins gave her a big enough smile that she could see he needed better dental hygiene. "She needs closure. Sometimes the dead communicate in bizarre ways. Sunnycrest helps with that. See you 'round, Not-Betty."

Sarah stood there dumbfounded as the man went back into his apartment and closed the door, and she was left simply facing a number seven. She told herself to go, to get back to her own sensible world. A question nagged at her though. Why did it jump from January to July? What did Regina want her to know? To see? Regina and Kevin. RJ and KT. Sarah's headache was getting worse.

Just to see, she tried the door to Apartment 8. It was locked. Sarah took a big deep breath and exhaled it slowly. Then she headed for the stairwell. Her legs burned as she made her way all the way to floor eleven. Sarah was glad she didn't see the jumper on this long trip. Maybe this was years before the girl took her jump and became tied to this stairwell. Maybe it just wasn't part of Regina's story. Either way, she was glad. Just hearing about it from her neighbors, Sarah never wanted to witness that with her own eyes. As it was, in her imagination she could hear the girl screaming and falling past her to land with a thud.

When she got to the eleventh floor, Sarah eased the door open. She peered into the hallway. No bald man anywhere. She slipped through the door and closed it quietly. She had already talked to Baggins. She didn't know why she was still fearful of this guy. Maybe it wasn't all about the past. There was something in the way he looked at her that unnerved her. Whether this was the actual past or the past a ghost created for her, Sarah didn't know what the rules and dangers were. She didn't know if these people could touch her or hurt her and she really didn't want to find out the hard way.

The question was answered when a hand grabbed her shoulder. Sarah gasped and jumped away from the contact, spinning on her heel to come face-to-face with the man she had been working to avoid. He peered at her with hungry eyes through his giant wood-grain plastic frames. "I'm glad she brought you here. You're pretty," he said, reaching up to caress her face with a stubby finger.

Sarah recoiled and the man laughed at her. "I'm in 55," he said. "Don't run away next time."

That's exactly what I'm going to do. Sarah turned and ran for Apartment 53. She looked over her shoulder to see if he was following, but he remained where he was, giving a smirk and a wave when he caught her looking back. Sarah shivered and opened the door, practically falling into the apartment. She didn't bother closing it behind her, just ran for the open closet and climbed inside. Shaking, with panicked breaths, Sarah tugged the door closed.

She planned to rip it back open and escape into her own reality when she realized that she wasn't alone in the darkness of the closet. Sarah turned her head and saw eyes peering at her in the pitch black. A finger lifted to full lips, to keep Sarah quiet. Her trembling grew worse, knowing someone was in there with her.

"This is where I hid," the girl said in a whisper. "It created a doorway. Listen."

Sarah heard footsteps, someone walking outside the bedroom closet. Was it the man she'd just run from? Had he found them? Could he have hurt Regina? Is that who she was sharing space with in the dark? Something inside Sarah said yes. It had to be her.

"You're going to want to open the door now," Maybe-Regina said from the darkness beside her, "before they do."

They who? The bald man? Sarah didn't need to be told twice. She lunged forward, twisted the knob, and exploded from the closet into her own living room. She was shivering furiously now. She kicked at the closet door with her trembling leg and it slammed shut. Then she lay on the rug, panting and shaking. What the hell is going on?

13

Sarah couldn't sleep. How could she? There was a whole world created just for her, a threatening dangerous world, only a door away. Sarah had received items from that world but nothing ever left the closet unless she took it out.

That didn't stop the thought from nagging at her. What if?

What if the people on the other side of that door started coming through into our world? What if they came through into her apartment, and stood over her while she was lost in dreams? She imagined herself sound asleep when a hand came over her mouth. She thrashed as more hands grabbed her arms and legs, and held her firmly to her mattress, while she screamed muffled cries and tasted the sweat of their palms.

No. Sleep wasn't happening. Part of her knew she should call it quits, move away, and keep her focus on school. Even if that were actually feasible and she could somehow find a way to afford it, Sarah knew she couldn't walk away now. She would only spend the rest of her life thinking about all this, wondering what it meant. There was no way she could walk away before she had answers.

Sarah's gut twisted in knots over the fact that this was happening for a reason. The girl in that closet, hiding in the darkness beside her, needed her help with something. May-be-Regina was trying to reach her for something, something important. Sarah didn't yet know what her role was, but she knew Regina, or whoever's spirit, was in some kind of trouble. Something terrible had happened to that girl over the summer.

The summer of 1987.

Sarah just knew it, with a strange certainty, like someone had told her. Like an instinctive knowledge in her DNA. Somehow she knew it was true. She wished she didn't have to wait six days to see Mark again. Sarah needed to not be in this alone. She needed to tell someone what had happened when she went back in. Anyone other than Mark would either laugh or have her committed. Mark may do that too before it was all said and done, but at least he was actually qualified to make that assessment.

When she got herself together, Sarah went to class, but her mind didn't. She couldn't focus on anything that was being said or shown to her. All she could think about was Regina, the bald man, and Kevin. She knew there was a piece missing, details she hadn't seen yet, and Sarah believed that if she thought about everything in an endless cycle, the answer would just appear.

She told herself it was a ridiculous notion, but she couldn't let it go. The world through her closet was becoming an obsession. It just kept going in her mind, spinning end over end like an astronaut lost in space, spinning through the endless void.

It made Sarah think of the man from the seventh floor, the man who tried to warn her about moving into this place. Roger. That was his name, Roger. What was he dealing with before he disappeared? Before whatever tragedy befell him? Is that the way it was going to end for her? Would no one even talk about it outside of Tina saying "Good riddance" to someone by the mailboxes? She hoped her life would mean more than that, but Roger probably hoped for the same thing. Am I to be the next Roger?

When classes ended and Sarah had ingested enough coffee to kill a bear just to get through them, she still sleep-walked her way home. She was exhausted, confused, and frightened, and it felt like she was trudging through fog-laden streets when she knew the fog was only hers, just like the world behind the door. *Why me though? Is it truly just a coincidence because I took that apartment, Kevin's apartment?*

When Sarah found herself back at Sunnycrest, having somehow navigated the fog without being mowed down by an angry city driver, she stood on the walk and stared up at the second-story window that led to her place. It wasn't really hers though was it? It was Kevin's. It had been Kevin's for thirty-four years and it was still Kevin's.

Sarah couldn't help but wonder what happened to him. Did he get hurt too? Did he find the love of his life lying dead somewhere? She pictured the beautiful girl tucked into the closet, broken like a child's doll, a leg over her head, and her boyfriend standing before her, his hand over his horrified mouth, a scream caught in his throat like a fish bone. *Or maybe he's the one who did it.* The vision revised itself to show him staring down at the broken girl with a twisted smile, a bloody knife gleaming in his hand.

Sarah shuddered and looked away from the window. She decided then that she wasn't ready to go up. She wasn't ready to find out more, even though she desperately wanted to. She needed a break, a moment to breathe, to be Sarah and not just the person in Apartment 8, another piece of the puzzle tucked away up there.

She stumbled to the big tree and ran her fingers over the carving. A chill ran through her. It felt like electricity and it actually elicited a moan from her, which left her looking around for nearby neighbors, her cheeks burning with embarrassment. Sarah sat below the thick scrawling branches. She took a notebook and a pen from her school things and she worked to write down everything she knew up to this point. It wasn't much.

Kevin lived in Apartment 8 on floor two. His girlfriend, Regina lived in Apartment 53 on floor eleven. The gifts came from January. Maybe that was when their romance started? Something happened to at least one of them in the summer, July or August, when Lost Boys was still new. Baggins lived there at the time. He could have been involved. There was an unnamed bald man on the floor who was definitely creepy. Was it him? Lastly, the world wasn't real so none of this may be correct, or at least that's what Baggins told her, but could he really be trusted? That was frustrating enough to make her pull her hair out.

Sarah closed the notebook with an exasperated sigh. She dropped it in the grass at her feet and leaned back against the tree. Exhaustion took hold then and Sarah quickly fell into dreams. She was walking the dark, cold halls of Sunnycrest, voices whispering to her from everywhere and nowhere. Someone was following her, someone with ill intent. She couldn't see them but she could feel them. She was trembling and her heart was pounding like a prisoner screaming for freedom from his cage. She knew she was going to die there, knew it in her soul and tears streamed down her cheeks as she nervously walked, footsteps tapping rhythmically behind her. Gasping, she spun around and—

Then, Sarah's phone rang in the waking world and awoke her with a start. She jumped and looked around the front yard for anyone that may have seen. When she saw no one, she tucked her embarrassment away and answered the phone.

"I'm sorry to bother you." It was Mark. "But would it be possible to meet up for coffee somewhere? There's something I think you need to see."

"That's a bit unorthodox, isn't it?" she replied, her eyes still combing the area for onlookers, unable to shake the feeling of being watched from her dream.

"Yes. I'm sorry. It pertains to your situation. I did some research and I want to share my findings with you. That is, if it's alright of course."

"How much will it cost me? Not your usual rates I hope."

Mark laughed. "Just the price of a cup of coffee."

"Alright. It's a date."

"No, it's not. My wife would kill us both," he laughed. "There's a diner not far from you. It's called Diner on the Corner. Do you know it?"

"I do. Sometimes I get breakfast there before class. They have really good home fries. Does this mean you believe me, Mark?"

"I believe you. I have an appointment at four. I'll see you there at around five thirty."

"Five thirty."

Sarah hung up and took a deep breath. She could still feel the skin-crawling unease of hidden eyes roaming over her. Her mind showed her the hands covering her mouth and pinning her arms in her sleep again. She shivered and decided that she would just go to the diner early and have some coffee until it was time to meet Mark. What did he want to show her? She would find out soon enough. It was good to feel like she wasn't alone in this anymore.

As she stood, she could have sworn the initials carved into the tree glowed orange like they were burning hot, like they'd been branded rather than carved, and someone had only just done it. Sarah gathered her things and hurried away from Sunnycrest, from her home, from that tree, and from the molesting gaze that still followed her from somewhere unseen.

14

Coffee or not, Sarah was falling asleep in her seat at a corner booth in the diner while she waited on Mark. She tried to turn her mind onto things from school, but she couldn't concentrate enough and she was beginning to get a headache from trying.

The server, Leremy, looked at her book with a grin. "Here's some science for you," he said jovially. "People need sleep to function. It's actually been proven. More coffee?"

"Sure," she said. "Do you believe in ghosts?"

The young pink-haired man shrugged his shoulders.

"I think everyone has ghosts. I just don't think their ghosts are always spirits. In this city, we're all haunted by something."

Sarah nodded. "You're probably right. So what haunts you?"

"My ex-fiancé," he told her as he poured dark black sludgy coffee into her mug. "The fact that I had no closure, that I have no idea why he left. The ghost of that relationship and the fact that I may never know what killed it follow me through every day of my life. He got an apartment down the road to be closer to me. When my lease was up, we were gonna move in together before we tied the knot. Then he was just gone, no note, no cussing or yelling, nothing. Sometimes I walk over to that Sunnycrest Apartment building and just see if I can see him, just hoping to run into him, but I never do."

Sarah's eyes widened at the mention of Sunnycrest but she didn't want to tell Leremy she also lived there. "That sounds hard. I never thought of it as haunting but it definitely is like that. Maybe that's why they call it ghosting someone." She sipped her coffee and gave a supportive smile. "I hope it gets easier."

Leremy shrugged again. "I don't know. So what about you? What's your story?"

I have a gateway in my closet that leads to a fictional 1987 created by a dead girl that may be tied to a serial killer. "I don't know," Sarah said with a shrug of her own. "I guess something pretty similar."

The server sighed and looked at her with sympathy. "Well on behalf of the 'haunted by our exes' club, I'm going to bring you a slice of cheesecake, on the house."

Sarah chuckled and thanked him. She watched him strut away, and when she turned back forward Mark was standing before her. He waved shyly. "Thanks for meeting with me," he said as he sat down. "I don't usually meet with people outside of the office."

"I understand. It's okay," she said to him. Sarah considered making a joke but she could tell he was uncomfortable and thought cracking on him about meeting up with college girls would only make it worse. He was the only ally she had right now. She couldn't afford to burn that bridge. "You said you found something."

Mark nodded. "You look like you haven't been sleeping. Are you alright?"

Sarah looked around the restaurant for patrons that might be prying. She hesitated then said at last, "I went back in."

Mark's eyes widened. Before he could say anything, Leremy returned and placed a plate of cheesecake down before her. Mark ordered a cappuccino. Before Leremy left he stood behind Mark and pointed at him, mouthing to Sarah, Is this him?

Sarah shook her head and Mark turned to look behind him. The server just smiled and headed away, walking swiftly.

Mark turned back to Sarah with one eyebrow raised high.

"What did you find?" she asked him.

Mark nodded. "I did a search for the Manhattan Mangler just to see. He was definitely real and this was his last killing before he disappeared." He reached into his bag and pulled out a printout, placing it on the table before her.

Sarah looked at the piece of paper. It was an article about Regina Johnson's brutal murder at the hands of the Mangler, killed in her own apartment just like the rest. Sarah picked it up and read it further, absorbing the details. No one at Sunnycrest seemed to see anything strange or anyone coming or going that didn't belong. Sarah gave a humorless laugh at that, knowing well that everything at Sunnycrest was strange so the killer probably just didn't stand out. Regina's boyfriend—who also lived at the building—was inconsolable and wound up being committed to the Twin Spirits mental facility. Didn't someone say that was where they took Roger? People say a lot of things. Who knows if it's true?

Sarah put the paper down. "I wonder where he is now," she said.

Mark seemed to know who she meant. He said, "He's not still there. I checked. I can do that. He left years ago."

Mark reached over and retrieved the paper. "She was the last one. The Mangler was never caught. It just…stopped."

Leremy returned with Mark's cappuccino and asked if they needed anything else. They both declined. When he walked away, Sarah said, "When I went back, there was a bald man on her floor. Something about him was off. He gave me the creeps." Sarah was trying to decide whether or not to include the part about Baggins and what he told her. "She hid in the closet. I think that's what opened that door, what turned the closets into the gateways they are now. I saw her, Mark. She was in there with me when I was trying to come back. He was there too. I could hear him walking around on the other side of the door, looking for her, scared the shit out of me."

Mark looked at her with alarm. "Be careful. We don't know if he can hurt you or not. I don't think you should go back in until we know more."

Sarah wanted to argue, but she nodded. As she dug into her cheesecake, Mark said to her, "I didn't print them for you, but there were photos of the scene. I found images of the others too. It was brutal, Sarah, a level of violence beyond what I could imagine. I was sick after seeing the images of it. Whoever he was, you don't want to be anywhere near him."

"Noted," Sarah said with a nod. "But what if that's the point? Ghosts are known to be looking for closure to unresolved issues right? Maybe Regina knows something and wants to share it. Maybe she wants that son of a bitch to get caught."

"Maybe," Mark quietly agreed. "But it would be safer to figure that out in 2021 where there's not a serial killer hanging around your apartment."

"That we know of," Sarah responded with a forced smile brought on by nerves that made for an awkward moment. "But you're right. I do need sleep or I'm going to flunk out of school. I just can't sleep there."

"I don't blame you," Mark told her as he sipped his drink. "Is there anywhere else you can go, even if it's just for a day or two?"

Sarah placed the fork on her now-empty plate. She wiped her mouth with the back of her hand, then met Mark's eyes and shook her head. "I've been a bit too much of a loner since I got here and my parents and friends are too far away for me to commute to school."

Mark frowned. "Can you miss a day or two?"

Sarah gave a sarcastic laugh. "Are things going to be different in a day or two?"

Mark sighed. His fingers toyed with his beard. "Maybe," he said, his voice giving away how far his mind was from the present. "...if we can figure this thing out."

Sarah was taken aback. Mark was really in. He was committed to this. She was thankful but couldn't help feeling guilty all the same for dragging him into her crazy. Of course, she definitely understood how impossible it was to let something like this go once it got its teeth into you. "Where do we even start in figuring this out, Mark? You wanna come by and go in the closet, experience it for yourself?"

Sarah jumped when Mark immediately stood. "Sorry," he told her. "I gotta… I just… Be careful. Get a motel or something. I'll see you at the office." He reached into his bag and took out the paper she had given him, dropping it in front of her. Then he went to the counter and paid for the meal. Sarah watched with wide eyes, still trying to figure out what caused that reaction. He didn't think I was coming onto him, did he? Maybe he's right to run.

She watched Mark give her a nervous wave and hurry out of the diner. Sarah blew out a frustrated breath. She was realizing just how alone she was. She was away from home and had literally no one—except her psychiatrist, whom she'd only just met, and he just ran away from her like she herself was a ghost. I'm not, right? This isn't like The Sixth Sense or something, right? That would really suck.

Sarah felt someone beside her and turned her head to see a smirking Leremy. "I charged him for the cheesecake," he said. "That's what he gets for running out on you. Take that!"

Sarah laughed and shook her head. "My hero. I'm sure he learned his lesson." As she was looking at the server and matching his smile, Sarah realized this was the chance she'd been looking for. "You wanna hang out when you get done with your shift?"

Leremy looked serious as if he'd just sobered. "You know… I'm not—"

Sarah chuckled. "I'm not either."

Leremy looked equally shocked and impressed. He

nodded. "Okay then. Everyone needs a wingman. Where do you live? I'll come get you once I've freshened up."

Sarah felt a surge of panic. If she was going to be friends with him she was going to have to tell him where she lived but she wasn't ready to yet, not after what he told her. "It's complicated," she said then. "Can I just meet you back here?"

"You want me to go out in my work clothes, smelling like french fries? What kind of heathen do you think I am?" he huffed. "Well, I can't have you come to me because my roommate is awful and you'd end up running away like the guy that was just at your table. Fine. Be here at ten and bring something to help me smell better, preferably cucumber melon."

Sarah belly laughed. "I'll do what I can. See you then."

She was headed for the front door when an image crashed into her head. It was Regina's face, terrified and screaming. Her fingers pulling at her cheeks and dragging her eyeliner into black streaks like claw marks, staring at Sarah from behind her own troubled eyes. Sarah put her hand to her head and hurried out of the diner.

15

Sarah found herself standing by the big tree, staring up at the eleventh floor of Sunnycrest. She didn't know what that image was, but she knew what it wasn't. She hadn't thought it up because it came out of nowhere, caught her off guard, and left her with a headache. It wasn't a memory because the only time she'd seen Regina had been in the darkness of the closet with her, and in the photo in her room.

It was something else.

Maybe it was Regina's way of begging her to stay, of asking her not to give up and walk away. Maybe even in death that poor beautiful soul was afraid of something. Sarah remembered what Baggins had said. The dead have strange ways of communicating.

"You know, staring at it from the outside doesn't change what's in it?" a voice said from behind her. Sarah turned to see Tina standing there. "You know they say the eyes are the windows to the soul, but in this case, the windows are the windows to the soul. We're all a mess, huh? I know a good psychiatrist if you need one."

Sarah laughed. "I've actually got that base covered. Thank you. So something strange has happened to you here too? You've seen things?"

Tina smiled. "Honey, there's no one at Sunnycrest without a story. Hey, this may be overstepping because I'm known for it, but there's a girl on your floor, Felicia. She swings your way. Sometimes having someone to hook up with makes this shit easier. You might wanna knock on her door when you have a chance."

Sarah was startled. As Tina sauntered away, Sarah called to her. "Wait, how did you—"

"Call it woman's intuition," Tina said with a chuckle as she went up the steps and opened the door. "Plus we're friends, Felicia and I. You're too buried in books to notice her and she's too shy to make herself known. That's why this world needs busy bodies like me."

Before Sarah could respond, Tina disappeared, feeding herself to the mouth of the building and letting the heavy door fall shut behind her. Sarah just shook her head. This was one wild day. She looked back up at the window to what was once Regina's apartment. It looked like every other window. Sarah couldn't help but wonder who was living there now. Was their closet a doorway too? Maybe they could be an ally, and they could solve this thing together. She promised herself she would find out, just not right now. She wasn't ready yet. Tonight she wanted to take care of herself, have some fun and make a friend. She needed at least a sliver of sanity in this mad, mad world.

Sighing, Sarah pulled her eyes from the window and made the decision to go somewhere else until it was time to meet up with Leremy. She yawned and covered her mouth with her hand. She was exhausted. I hope I can even make it to hang out. I might just fall asleep and miss the whole thing.

Sarah glanced over at the big tree and gasped. The letters had changed. Scrawled in the crudely carved heart shape, the letters RJ & KT had been replaced with Help!

Sarah turned and hurried away from Sunnycrest as fast as her legs would carry her. At least she didn't feel tired anymore. In truth, she wondered if she would ever sleep again.

16

Sarah considered going to the park, somewhere full of nature and people where she could relax and feel safe, but she was too tired for the crowds the city parks tended to draw. She wasn't in the mood to deal with joggers and lovebirds, actors working on their lines, and people playing frisbee with their German shepherds. She opted instead to go to the cemetery. The dead there were much quieter than those at Sunnycrest. So were the living. There was one in particular of the former that interested her.

Sarah walked until she found the tombstone. She

hadn't been there in a long time. When her parents finally told her the truth, she and her father would come to visit. She was sure her father still did, but she and he lived in different worlds now. Still, she had loved her Maa Maa when she was alive, and her resting place felt like a safe place when she needed one.

Sarah sat by the grave. Maa Maa had been wise in life. Sarah wished she could seek the woman's advice now. She talked to her even though Maa Maa couldn't respond. Maybe she would show up at Sunnycrest. Sarah didn't know if there were rules about that kind of thing. Her paternal grandmother made for a great sounding board though. There was no one else and people weren't shocked by superstition in a place like this. Sarah could talk about ghosts all she wanted to, out here. And she did. It turned out to be just what she needed.

Sarah patted the stone. "Thank you for listening, Maa Maa," she said with love. Then she balled up her overcoat and used it as a pillow. She lay down in the quiet of the cemetery, surrounded by her grandmother's love, and fell into a deep, dreamless sleep.

When she woke, she felt someone staring at her. Sarah lifted her head with a yawn. She stretched and turned. There was a thin older man with scraggly, long, dirty-blond hair, and a swollen bulbous pink nose squatting beside her. Sarah yelped and jumped.

She hit the tombstone and fell back to the dirt, scrambling like a crab onto the grass to put distance between her and the odd stranger. How long had he been there? Was he looking to rob her? Sexual assaults happened daily in this city. She should have been more careful. She was just so tired.

Before she could ask who he was or what he was doing, the stranger volunteered the information she sought. "I'm Harry. I live out here. It's quiet, usually, but tonight this old woman showed up when I was having my drink. She told me to wake you or you'd be late to meet your friend."

Sarah looked at the time and realized he was right. She cussed under her breath and got to her feet. "Oh, and Sarah," Harry said then, drawing a surprised look from her. "I don't know what it means, but she said to stay out of the closet. You queer or something? You shouldn't feel bad if you are. I gots a cousin who's queer, great guy. I think ya'll are alright."

Sarah laughed despite how creepy this entire encounter was. "Thank you," she said. She dug into her purse and came out with a twenty-dollar bill, then handed it to him. "Buy yourself another drink."

Sarah hurried away then, not wanting to be late to meet Leremy. She was still shaking off the remnants of sleep as she traversed the paths of graves in the cemetery. "Thank you, Maa Maa," she said as she walked briskly. "I wish I could stay out of the closet, but you know I can't. Is Regina there with you? If she is, tell her I'm listening. I think she needs to know that. I love you, Maa Maa."

Then Sarah left the cemetery and hurried down the street toward the diner, an old woman with sad eyes and a tight frown watching her go.

THREE

New Friends, Old Haunts

17

Sarah got to the Diner on the Corner and found a scowling Leremy waiting outside with crossed arms. "I was beginning to think you weren't going to show," he said. "Cucumber melon?"

Sarah cringed. "I'm sorry, no. I fell asleep in the cemetery. Is there somewhere we can buy some now?"

Leremy's scowl increased. "Well, that's dark. Sure. Let's run to the late-night body spray shop. No."

Sarah frowned. "I'm really sorry. I'm having a crazy week to say the least. I think french fry is a nice scent, myself.

They should bottle that stuff." That elicited a laugh from the man, and his posture softened. "So what should we do tonight then?"

Leremy cracked his knuckles and stretched. "Well, not sleep in a cemetery for starters. Do you dance?"

Sarah smiled. "I'm a little rusty, but I've got some moves. Full disclosure: you're my first friend since I moved out here."

Leremy's eyes widened. He wrapped an arm around her shoulders. "Oh my. Well, darling, that's terribly sad, but I'm honored to pop your friend cherry. Let's go celebrate. It's 80s night at one of my favorite clubs."

Sarah stiffened for a moment at the mention of the 80s but then she relaxed and let him lead the way. "If you could go back to the 80s, would you?" she asked him.

He huffed as he pulled her along. "That's tough because the music and the movies were fucking incredible but the status of the LGBTQ community was rough. I wouldn't mind visiting, but I don't think I'd want to live there. Why? Do you have the armoire that leads to 80s Narnia?"

"Something like that," she admitted. "If you could see one band from that era live, in their prime, who would it be?"

Leremy stopped. He turned in a circle, tapping on his lips with his index finger which was practically covered in rings. "Just one?"

"Just one."

"Shit. Okay. Echo and the Bunnymen."

Sarah laughed and her cheeks burned red. "I have no idea who that is."

Leremy sighed. "This is why you need friends. I'll get the DJ to spin something for you."

"Awesome." Sarah locked elbows with her new friend and they walked along, talking and laughing, and she realized that Mark had been right. She needed this. She needed to live, to enjoy the moments between the chaos. It made everything feel easier. When they got to the club, they danced their hearts out for hours. Leremy introduced Sarah to his friends and she even allowed herself to have a drink and loosen up some. She discovered so much great music that she had never heard before. When they left the club, still laughing at a joke she couldn't even remember, Sarah thanked her new friend and kissed him on the cheek.

"So, what did you think of Mickey?" Leremy asked her.

She shrugged. "She seems nice but she's a bit rough around the edges for me."

"Well, there's a lot of fish in the sea. We'll find you a good one. Where are you headed? I'm over in Hell's Kitchen."

Sarah's smile fell away. "I didn't want to tell you, because I didn't think you would hang out with me if I did, but I live at Sunnycrest."

Leremy stood there for a moment, staring at her with

his mouth open. "You've gotta be shitting me."

"No shitting."

"Shit."

"I said no shitting."

Leremy laughed then and shook his head. "Have you seen a guy named Collin?"

Sarah's face tightened. She shook her head. Then she stammered, "There are thirteen floors though, five apartments each, sixty-five in all, so maybe I just don't know him. I don't know a lot of the people there."

Leremy looked down and kicked a stone. "I don't think he's there. I think he dipped without telling me. He was on the fourth floor. Then he wasn't. I asked his neighbors. No one saw him leave, but his door was left open and so many of his things were gone. I wish he had at least left a note, something to let me know why."

Sarah took a deep breath and let it out slowly. "Maybe he wasn't running from you," she said. "Maybe he was running from Sunnycrest."

"Is it that bad?"

"It's…" Sarah stopped, unsure of how to finish that sentence. She didn't need to. Leremy jumped back in as if she had said something complete.

"Why wouldn't he come to me if that was the case? I could have helped him or we could have left together. He didn't even try."

Sarah smoothed her dress, her fingers tugging at the fabric and then smoothing it back out. "There was a guy on the seventh floor. He warned me not to sign the lease, and said the place was haunted. I spoke to him a few times after that and he just seemed like a lost soul. Then one day he was gone and no one would tell me anything. I never saw him again."

"No wonder it's so damn cheap," Leremy said, laughing snidely. "Well come on. I'll walk you over to that enormous brick monster." When they started walking he asked, "Is that why you asked me if I believed in ghosts earlier?"

"Yeah. Some of my neighbors definitely do and I've seen and heard some weird stuff, but I don't know what I believe."

"I had a cat that used to see things I couldn't see. I thought he was crazy though or maybe that he had a drug habit he was hiding from me."

Sarah laughed. "I'm glad I met you," she told him. They continued to talk and have fun as they walked along, but the laughter stopped when they reached their destination. They both got quiet and serious when they saw Sunnycrest looming before them like a tower of the damned, kudzu spreading like scrawling veins up its red brick sides. A breeze picked up then, pulling leaves from the big tree and swirling them around the two of them.

"Alright," Leremy said nervously, his voice cracking. "Text me." Then he hurried off and for a moment, Sarah considered going with him, but she didn't move.

When he was gone, she took a deep breath. The door opened ever so slowly on its own, inviting her in. Sarah swallowed the lump in her throat and accepted the invitation.

18

When she got inside, Sarah jumped when she was accosted by an old man. She rolled her eyes. He said the same thing he always said, the only words she ever heard from him. "Have you seen my wife? I think something has happened to my Kathy."

Sarah shook her head and moved past him. No one's answer ever changed but the man never stopped very aggressively asking the question. This time Sarah wondered what had become of Kathy. The old man seemed less crazy than he had before.

An elderly woman came out of Apartment 1. She bent over and looked at the empty space before her. "There you are," she said to whatever it was that only she could see. "I've been looking all over for you. Come on." Sarah watched as the woman gestured for whoever or whatever was there to enter her apartment. After a moment she seemed satisfied and went in with a smile, closing the door.

Sarah just shrugged and ascended the stairs. If this building wasn't full of ghosts then it was definitely full of madness. Maybe the truth was that it was full of both. There could definitely be a link between the two, in her opinion. She came out on her own floor and stopped in her tracks when she saw Felicia going into the apartment next to her own.

That was the girl Tina advised her to talk to. Should she shoot her shot? Felicia was certainly beautiful, hair red as fire and skin like snow, with a perfectly placed spray of freckles over the bridge of her nose that could be seen between the thick black 60s chic cat-inspired frames of the glasses she wore. She saw Sarah stop and turned to look at her curiously. Sarah felt like an idiot. She hated how inept she was at social interaction. She gave a shy wave and mumbled, "Hi."

"What?" Felicia seemed to not hear her and wandered over.

Sarah trembled with nerves. She had never been good at this. Dating was not her forte. She cleared her throat and then cringed at how loud it was. "I said hi. Hello. Hi." She punctuated it with an awkward laugh. Did I just snort? Oh God, tell me I didn't just snort.

"Hi," Felicia said back, adjusting her thick black glasses. "What's up?"

Sarah scrunched her face up thoughtfully but came up with nothing. "I don't know. You know. Stuff and whatever. How about you?"

Felicia laughed, and Sarah noticed that the girl had a freckle right on her dimple. "I'm actually writing a paper on the history of Sunnycrest. Maybe you can see what I have so far and add something."

Sarah excitedly said, "Do you know about RJ and KT?"

Felicia grinned. "Of course. That was a high-profile case that garnered national media attention. It was one of the things that tied Sunnycrest to actual history in this city. Crazy to think a serial killer had been in this very hall, huh?"

"Yeah," Sarah said, breaking eye contact. "And my apartment."

"Not that the evidence shows. Regina was killed in her own place up on floor eleven. What makes you think that he was in your apartment? Kevin lived there but he wasn't home when things went bad. He found her later and completely lost it, did some time in Twin Spirits and then left the city for good when he got out."

Sarah was processing everything she said and then realized that the other woman had asked her a question. "Oh, yeah I guess you're right. I just had my facts wrong. Thanks for clearing that up. Hey, do you want to hang out sometime?"

Felicia laughed. "Yeah sure. When are you free?"

"I don't know. When are you free?"

After another chuckle, Felicia said, "How about tomorrow night? We can grab dinner."

"Yes. Good. Great. Tomorrow's good. Tomorrow. Cool. Yeah." Before she could say anything else to ruin things, Sarah opened her door, went inside, and closed it behind her. Then she leaned against it and panted. Was it a date? They hadn't specified. It probably wasn't a date. Maybe it would lead to a date though. Calm down, she told herself. Take it slow. One step at a time.

Sarah hit her bed and somehow fell fast asleep despite everything, credit to exhaustion. She awoke several times during the night, feeling like someone was there, in the room with her, but each time she saw nothing but darkness. Still, she couldn't shake the feeling that she wasn't alone, and just the same she couldn't keep herself from falling back to sleep.

19

Sarah woke up and looked at the clock on the nightstand by her bed. She had already missed her first class and cussed under her breath, jumping out of bed. Her feet got tangled in her sheets and she spilled out onto the floor. Crap, crap, crap.

Fighting the clawing hands of her bed linens, Sarah finally got to her feet, frustrated and panicked. She opened her closet to select clothes for the day and stopped moving, despite the need to rush and not miss more than she already had. There in her closet, hanging among her clothes, was a shirt that didn't belong to her. She'd never seen it before. It was a black t-shirt with Soft Cell on it, and it smelled like a boy.

Sarah didn't want to freak out, but she understood the implication that came with this shirt. The closet was a two-way street. She had been right when she woke in the night. Someone had been there. She reminded herself that the things she'd discovered were more like gifts than threats. They were messages. This may have been in Kevin's closet and just showed up in hers all the same, as it was the same closet. It didn't mean Regina came into her room and put a shirt in her closet. On the other hand, it was the living room closet she had traveled through and this was in her bedroom. She hadn't checked the closets in their bedroom because she was afraid they would also be doorways. Was this confirmation of that? Or was it confirmation that someone had to have come through the living room and physically put the shirt in her bedroom closet on purpose? Is this what the road to insanity was like?

"Everything's okay," Sarah said to herself. "Just get ready and get to class."

With a slow deep breath, Sarah took the t-shirt from the closet. "Alright. I'll wear it. Is that what you wanted? You want me to wear it? Vintage is cool now, I think, and who doesn't love Tainted Love."

Sarah carried the shirt with her to the bathroom. She turned her shower on and waited for the steam to rise. Then she hung the t-shirt on the towel rack and started to undress. She heard a squeak as she was stepping out of her panties and looked up to see what caused it.

An unseen finger was writing in the steam on her shower door, each stroke squeaking as it dragged along the glass. Suddenly feeling vulnerable, Sarah quickly covered herself.

Whoever was in her shower spelled out, Come Back.

Keeping her eyes on the shower door, Sarah bent down and dragged her underwear back on. Then she stared at the words. She decided at that moment she couldn't get in the shower. She had no way to know if whoever wrote the message for her was still present, taking up what looked to her like empty space.

Nope. I'm willing to listen and help you, not shower with you. Sorry. Sarah shrugged on the t-shirt and thought about asking Felicia if she could use her shower. Would that be awkward? Not as awkward as showering with a ghost.

Just to know for sure, Sarah slid the shower door open. She nodded when she saw no one inside. Shivering, she reached in cautiously to turn the knobs and cut off the water. She hoped she was reaching around the finger painter and not through them. "Sorry, sorry, sorry," she said with a grimace, just in case.

Sarah headed back to the bedroom to find pants when something grabbed her ankle and tugged her off her feet. She hit the ground with a thump and screamed. Then she was being dragged backward through the apartment. Her fingers grabbed at the carpet, trying to dig in and restrain her movement, but to no avail. She looked back, panic gripping her heart, but she could see no one pulling her. Whoever had a hold of her was just as invisible as the writer in the shower. Sarah screamed.

As she was dragged along against her will, she stared back at the nothing that was forcing her and saw the living room closet door open on its own as she traveled toward it. She screamed louder, but it made no difference. In a moment, Sarah was pulled past her empty bowling ball bag into the darkness of the closet and the door slammed shut, cutting her off from the world she needed desperately to hold onto.

20

Sarah's scream cut off abruptly when the closet door re-opened, shedding light upon the darkness that held her. She stayed where she was, on a pile of someone else's belongings, staring out into the light of their living room. It was quiet—so quiet that she felt like a single spoken word would resonate as another scream. Sarah just blinked and watched, waiting, expecting something to happen.

After a minute, she reached forward and pushed the open door further. No one rushed at her, grabbed her, or even stood before her. Sarah held her breath and climbed free of the closet. She saw no sign of Regina or Kevin. She just stood in the center of the room and listened. Regina wouldn't have literally dragged her back here for nothing. Why am I here?

Nothing was happening. Could the world be waiting

for her? Was there something she was supposed to do? The aggressiveness of it sapped her willingness to help, which had been thriving before today. She just wanted to go home.

Sarah released her pent-up breath and went to the bedroom. She eyed the dresser when she stepped into the empty room. Then the front door opened and she stiffened. Sarah moved out of the line of sight of the doorway, pressing her back against the wall. She heard movement from the other room, then voices.

"That was the best pizza ever," Regina said happily.

There were sounds of kissing. "It tastes even better on your lips," said Kevin, eliciting a giggle from his girlfriend.

"You're a loser," she told him.

"I just went on a date with the most beautiful girl in this city. Pretty sure that makes me a winner."

Regina laughed. "I want to do this forever," she said. "I want to be this happy, this in love, always."

"Of course," Kevin told her. "As long as we have each other, nothing can hurt us."

Regina laughed. "That sounds like a line from Stand By Me or something."

Kevin chuckled. "Stay here. I have something for you. It's a surprise."

Sarah heard footsteps coming her way. They were the ones that brought her here. What would happen if they found her? Somehow, she still didn't want to know. She was in her panties and one of Kevin's t-shirts. Somehow, she felt like that could ruin their date night. The whole thing started to feel like a setup. Was that the point? Was this Regina's way of telling her that Kevin was a cheater? She was grasping at straws, reading into things, but what else could she do?

Sarah scurried across the room and slid under the bed just in time as she watched Kevin's feet enter the room. He went to the dresser she had looked at when she entered the room, and opened the top drawer to rummage through. When he had what he wanted, he turned and left without even closing the drawer.

"What is this?" she heard Regina ask a moment later.

"It's a promise ring. Forever is real," Kevin answered.

When the sounds of kissing resumed, Sarah slid out from under the bed. She bit her lip and looked around. I wonder if the bedroom closet will work here too. Maybe some of my clothes are hanging up in there.

It was worth a try. She opened the door slowly, doing her best to be quiet, and slipped inside. Then she eased the door back shut. A few seconds ticked by. The only way to know for sure if it worked was to open it again, but what if she caught the young lovers in a tryst in doing so, or more importantly, what if they caught her? What choice did she have? Sarah sucked in a deep breath and then pushed the door open. She stepped out into another bedroom, and an angry-looking Indian man standing before her.

"What are you doing in my closet?" he demanded to know, and suddenly Sarah became all too aware that she was in her underwear.

21

Sarah swallowed hard and stared at the stranger. How did she begin to explain how she got there? It's Sunnycrest. Just tell him the truth.

"I asked you a question. What are you doing here? Are you in trouble? Where are your pants?"

Sarah frowned. "I'm really sorry. I'm not sure what happened. I went into a closet on the second floor and when I came out I was here."

The man returned her frown and turned his back to her. "There are pants in the dresser," he told her. "Put them on and go before someone sees you. My wife would never understand or forgive me."

"Yes sir. Thank you," Sarah said shyly but with real appreciation.

The man nodded without turning around to face her. "And quit messing with these closets before you end up like the girl that used to live here," he said. He walked out of the room before she could offer any response.

22

Sarah was still flushed when she left Apartment 53 on the eleventh floor in the present day. She kept her head down in hopes that no one would spy her heading out of the married man's apartment. That wasn't even close to who she was, but she felt like it would be hard to explain, even at Sunnycrest.

There was no way she was going to take the stairs all the way back down. She wanted to get out of these pants and this shirt and into clothes of her own. So much for not missing any more classes, she thought as she hit the button for the elevator.

When its rickety doors opened for her, Sarah hurried in and pressed the button for floor two. It felt like a shameful eternity that she had to wait for the doors to close once more. When they finally did she found herself sighing with relief, glad that no one else was around to see her like that. She was dressed now but she still felt naked in a stranger's clothes. Her anxiety told her that people would know and they would think the worst.

The journey down felt more like a roller coaster than an elevator, the barely functioning rusty box tossing her back and forth as it cranked along with a rumble. Sarah felt nauseous by the time it stopped. When the doors rattled their way open, she couldn't get out fast enough. She hurried to her apartment and found the door open.

Why? No, no, no. Nothing else, not now, please. I just want to wear my own clothes and not a married man's pants. What if someone knows him and recognizes the pants? They're just jeans, Sarah. You're being paranoid. Shit. I just got dragged back to 1987 by a ghost. How the hell am I supposed to not be paranoid?

Sarah stood on the threshold of her apartment, cringing at the open door, unsure of what to do. She had only woken up, late as it was, and was working to get ready when she had been dragged into the closet. She hadn't gone anywhere yet today, and knew for certain she hadn't left the door open last night. She saw herself in her mind coming in after talking to Felicia. She closed the door and leaned against it.

Someone had opened her door while she was gone. Of that, she was certain. Were they still there, inside her home? Were they rummaging through her things? Sarah wanted to call the police, but what if the intruders weren't alive or they weren't from this time period?

Maybe I should try to go through a closet and call the police in 1987. They wouldn't believe me any more than the police in 2021 would. Sarah reached into her pocket for her phone and realized that these weren't her pants. She cussed under her breath. Her phone was in the apartment with the intruder. Well, that's just fricking great. What am I supposed to do now? Go. You're supposed to go, Sarah. Just go.

Even though the voice inside her mind told her to run, to get far away from all of this, Sarah stepped forward. Slowly, she stepped through her open front door.

23

Felicia jumped when Sarah walked in behind her. "What are you—" they both started to say and simultaneously stopped before finishing.

"I heard screaming," Felicia said, starting again. "I called to you, and you didn't answer. I thought you were in trouble. After the conversation we had last night, I got scared. I called Gary and he came and opened the door."

Gary was the building manager. Sarah rarely saw him. Usually, it was just to show an apartment or renew a lease, but he lived on the first floor and it did make sense that he would have copies of the keys.

As she thought about this, Gary stepped out of her bedroom. "And obviously everything is fine and everyone is okay," he said. "I didn't touch anything. I promise. I was just looking for you or any sign of trouble."

"No trouble here," Sarah said, forcing a smile, "but thank you for checking on me."

Gary gave a simple nod and walked past her out of the apartment. When he was gone, Felicia looked at her with a mixture of shame and confusion. "I called Gary to bring the key. I never left the hall, never took my eyes off the door. I heard you screaming, or at least I thought it was you."

Sarah sighed. She had two choices: lie to someone that she was hoping to forge a relationship with, or try to explain all this and hope Felicia didn't run in the opposite direction. "How much time do you have?" she asked.

"How much time do I need?" was Felicia's retort.

"A lot."

It was Felicia's turn to sigh then. "Okay. Hold on. I have a bottle of rum at my place. I'm going to get it."

"Isn't it a little early for that?" Sarah asked as the other woman headed for the hall.

"Not today, it isn't."

24

While Felicia was retrieving her alcohol, Sarah seized the opportunity to change her clothes. She took off the pants, wondering if there was a right way to go about returning them. She tugged the shirt off too and just pulled on a dress. It was a floral print hip-hugger, something that wouldn't ride up and show anyone else her panties. One stranger was enough for today. It did show off her form however, and might impress Felicia—or, at least, she hoped it would.

When she got out of the bedroom she found Felicia on her couch. The bottle she mentioned was on the coffee table before her with a glass next to it. There was another glass, already full, in the woman's hand. "I brought a second glass in case you wanted some."

Ordinarily, Sarah would have declined but her neighbor was right, today was different. She took the liquid courage and used it to help her get through her wild story, starting at the beginning. She expected a lot of questions, but Felicia seemed content to wait, to sit in silence, and let her finish before saying anything.

"So I took the elevator back down here and found my front door open, and you know the rest," Sarah said, her fingers tugging at the fabric of her dress.

"That's completely insane," Felicia said. When Sarah closed her eyes and hung her head, she added, "Oh I don't mean that to say I don't believe you. I completely believe you. That doesn't make it any less insane though."

Sarah opened her eyes, lifted her head, and peered at the redhead seated across from her. "You believe me?"

Felicia took her glasses off and rubbed at her eyes. "It's a lot to process, but yes. I believe you. If we lived anywhere else, I may not have, but we don't, do we? And that's why I end up drinking liquor before noon."

Sarah nodded. "Have you seen and heard things here?"

Felicia raised her glass. "Of course. We all have. Nothing quite as personal as what you have this far, but everyone within these walls knows what kind of place this is."

"What do you think I should do?" Sarah asked her.

Felicia laughed. "Move?"

"I can't," Sarah said with a sad smile. "I'm going to call this our first date. I can't walk away now before we even have our second."

Felicia raised her eyebrows. "That's presumptuous."

"Sorry," Sarah said quietly, finding anything but Felicia to rest her eyes on. "Truth is I can't walk away without figuring this out. I feel like all of it is happening because Regina needs me to understand something. She's looking for help. It's been so many years already. I can't just turn my back on her."

Felicia refilled her glass and took a sip. "So does that mean there's not going to be a second date? I was hoping for a proper one. You can definitely wear that dress again though."

Sarah flushed. "You like it?"

Felicia laughed. "I'm not a huge fan of floral print but I definitely enjoy the way it fits you." When Sarah's embarrassment visibly increased, Felicia giggled. "Hey, do you want to crash at my place for a little bit until we know it's safe here? I'm right across from you so it will be easy to get everything you need every day."

Sarah looked at her with shock gleaming in her eyes. "You called me presumptuous and you're asking me to move in before we've even had our second date."

They laughed together. "My couch is actually more comfortable than my bed," Felicia said. "It's made of clouds,

I'm pretty sure."

"Sold," Sarah said. "Thank you."

Felicia nodded. "I'll dig up everything I have on our lovebirds. We can go over it together. Maybe we can figure something out."

"I'd like that," Sarah told her.

Felicia stood and grabbed her bottle. "Just come by and knock tonight, whatever time you need to." She headed for the still-open door and looked back when she reached it. "And try not to bring any ghosts with you."

Sarah tried to force a laugh and it sounded awkward. She grimaced at herself. Once Felicia was gone, she walked to the closet, opening the door. She stood before it and said into the mish-mash pile of things, "If you want me to help you, you can't do what you did today. You can't drag me against my will, force me to go there. If you do anything like that again, I will leave. Do you hear me? Understand?"

There was an answering crash behind her. Sarah jumped and turned around, adrenaline coursing through her. A picture had fallen off her wall. It was a framed family photo her parents had given her when she moved to the city. The glass of the frame had completely shattered. It was all over the carpet. What does that response mean? she wondered. Was that just Regina's way of saying yes or was she angry? Upset?

Sarah closed the closet and walked to the broken picture, trying to avoid stepping on glass with her bare feet. She failed and growled under her breath. Carefully, she bent and picked up the photo. Everyone in it looked so happy, so full of love. Was that what Regina was trying to tell her? That she and Kevin had been happy? It was definitely a happy moment she'd dragged Sarah back to.

"I know you were happy," she said, giving it a try. "I'm sorry for what happened to you. It was horrible. It's not fair. It's not."

Sarah waited a moment. The apartment was quiet. There was no further response. She sighed and hopped her way to the couch to see how deep the glass was in her foot. She couldn't even see it. It must have been like a splinter. Great, she thought.

Feeling someone's presence, Sarah looked up and saw a man standing in her open doorway. He was tall, well-built, and blond. His piercing blue eyes were locked onto her. Before she could say anything—ask who he was or what he wanted—he turned and walked away. She would have chased after him and demanded answers had it not been for the glass in her foot.

Sarah had no idea who that man was, but now she felt even more glad for Felicia's invitation.

FOUR

Looking at the Past and Hoping for the Future

25

As Sarah made her way across the city to meet Leremy for dinner, she felt proud of herself. She was definitely the product of her parents. She had enough of her mother's upbringing to not be closed off to the supernatural, to embrace the strange things that were happening, and to regard them as truth. Just the same, she was her father's daughter, learning from his business mind; goal-oriented and focused enough to see the end game and not be rattled by the ghosts that roamed the halls.

Sarah's parents were very different people but there

 124

was a reason they worked so well together—she was proof of that. They were opposites that complimented each other and covered all the bases. Now Sarah just had to figure out how to get through this without screwing up school, and the future she dreamed of. As an educator, Sarah felt she could pass on the strengths her parents had bestowed upon her. She would have to toe carefully around the superstition and spiritual side of things these days, but that part of her would still be useful in the classroom setting. A teacher that could see the magic in the world could more easily validate a child and understand their fantastical perspective.

Sarah understood that there was a dark and a light to everything. It was balanced and balance was necessary. She was going to have to face the darkness in order to help Regina find peace and restore some light to the world. Her mother would tell her the darkness would leave a stain on her and to avoid it at all costs. With nothing to compare it to, she just had to hope that wasn't true. Was that what Maa Maa believed too? According to the cemetery's permanent resident, she'd tried to warn Sarah away. Now Sarah started to doubt herself. What if she was wrong? Maybe Leremy would have some insight.

"Then again, I've now had two alcoholic drinks in two days. Maybe I have been letting the darkness in," Sarah joked to Leremy once they met up. She failed to mention anything about ghosts though. She didn't think their friendship was ready for that just yet.

"A little bit of darkness is good for you," he said with a chuckle. "I don't suppose you've seen the ghost of my heart roaming the halls."

Sarah frowned and shook her head. "Sorry." She thought about the strange man that had been staring at her. That couldn't have been Collin, could it? She hoped not because that guy was creepy as hell. Sarah decided not to tell Leremy, at least not until she saw him again, because if Collin matched that guy's description, she didn't want to get his hopes up. "So I met a girl, I mean…I already knew her. I've known her for a while actually, like, she's my neighbor, literally, but I mean, like, I met her in a different capacity. Is that a thing?"

"So I want to hear all about hot hallway girl over dinner," he said, leading her into the restaurant. Sarah looked at the place and frowned. It looked fancy—really fancy. When they got to the hostess, Leremy said, "Montgomery, party of two. I want a corner booth in the back, dear. Thank you."

"This way," the woman said, leading them.

"Hey! There's a wait! What the hell?" some guy barked behind them.

Once they were seated, Sarah didn't even look at her menu. She glanced around at all the people seated at the tables around them and realized with embarrassment just how underdressed she was. Leremy wasn't dressed up either, but he was always stylish it seemed, even when he was serving tables in a far less fancy restaurant.

"What's going on?" she asked her friend, who answered with a devious grin. "I cannot afford this place."

"Oh I can't either," he told her with a wave of his hand. "Not by a long shot."

"So what are we doing here?" Sarah's skin felt hot. She felt like she was going to spontaneously combust in that chair. It felt like everyone was staring at her, mocking her. This was horrible. If this was what having friends was like, she felt like she had been better off alone. She wanted to actually get up and flee the scene, running through the front door and not stopping until she got all the way home. At least at her apartment, she couldn't see the people staring at her.

"Breathe darling. You can order anything you want. This place belongs to my father."

Sarah's eyes bulged. "Your father? If your father owns a place like this then why do you work where you work? Tips have to be bigger here, don't they? Why don't you work for your dad?"

Leremy scoffed. "Because this lovely establishment is owned by my father and my father is a monster, but he doesn't want anyone to know that so publicly he will still pretend that he loves me. I come here to make his skin crawl and force him to pay for my meal when he won't even speak to me outside of the public eye. It's my little way to get something back from the creep."

Sarah covered her mouth to stifle the laugh that followed. It snuck by anyway, and drew the attention of the people seated around her. She cleared her throat which probably only made things worse. "I think I might love you," Sarah said to the young man grinning at her. "I mean, not like that of course, but you know."

Leremy shushed her. "I love you too, dear. Now pick up that menu and tell me all about this new girl." Once Sarah filled him in, he declared far too loudly for the atmosphere, "You're moving in with her? Are you insane or brilliant? I can't decide."

Sarah laughed. "I'm sleeping on the couch and it's just for a few days."

"Well, I hope those days are full of wild sex," he said, his eyebrows bouncing up and down with each syllable.

"Me too," she admitted.

Soon they were eating and drinking and the food was as outrageously tasty as it was pricey. They shared more laughs that clearly made people uncomfortable. Sarah realized she no longer felt that way, and took note of the fact that wealth and prosperity were not the only power. "I feel like I could learn a lot from you," she told Leremy as he ordered a triple chocolate truffle mousse with praline pudding for dessert.

"Oh honey, you will. You also just had alcoholic drinks for the second time today. Bring on the darkness, girl. Bring on the darkness."

Sarah laughed. "You know, all jokes aside, things have been dark lately. Troubling. You were the first light in a while, honestly."

"Well, let's have it," he said, waving her on. "Share your deep dark secrets with Leremy."

Sarah laughed again. "Well if you talk about yourself in the third person, you're probably already crazy so, I might as well." He waved her on in dramatic fashion like she was making an awards speech and needed to speed it up. "Okay, okay," she said. She took a deep breath and then began to fill him in on everything that had been going on at Sunnycrest.

When she was finished, Leremy wiped cheesecake off his mouth and said, "Well that would explain what happened to Collin. He was obsessed with the 80s. If his closet was a doorway, he definitely took it. Here's to hoping the Mangler mangled him for leaving me for Boy George."

Sarah choked on her final bite of cake and quickly sipped her water. Then Leremy took her hand and led her back to the front. "Put it on my tab or whatever Daddy does," he said to the hostess, who looked unsure of what to do or say. Sarah noticed a man by the door to the kitchen. He was dressed in a fine suit and staring at them with hard eyes. She didn't need anyone to tell her who he was.

"I can't believe we just did that," she said when they got outside.

Leremy hugged her. "And don't you just feel so alive?"

"I do," she agreed.

"A fine contrast to the people you live with," he laughed. "Have fun with Felicia." The way he sang the woman's name made Sarah roll her eyes.

"I'll try," she told him.

As she walked back toward home and all the madness that waited for her there, Sarah found herself feeling light of foot, and unafraid of what was to come. She was still smiling when she made her way into the usually ominous building and her smile actually widened as she climbed the steps to the second floor, prepared to knock on Felicia's door. It didn't even fall from her face as the parade of children ran by her through the closed door up ahead.

26

Felicia looked tired when she opened the door, but she smiled. "Come in." She closed the door behind Sarah and engaged several locks. "It's not to keep you in. It's to keep them out," she said. "I made up the couch with a pillow and some blankets. I didn't know if you planned to bring your own or not, but seeing as you're not carrying any, I feel like I made the right choice."

"Yes, thank you," Sarah said shyly. "It's wonderful. I really appreciate you doing this." Felicia smiled again and nodded, and then headed for the kitchen. Sarah took a seat on the couch that was to be her bed. Felicia hadn't been exaggerating about how comfortable it was. "Something smells good," she said, the scent tickleing her nose.

Felicia returned with a bowl of popcorn and set it on the coffee table. She climbed onto the couch next to Sarah. "I use real butter. Let's munch and talk," she said.

Sarah grabbed a handful of popcorn and munched it, moaning with delight and giving Felicia the thumbs up. Then she told Felicia what happened with the photo on the wall after she left. "Sounds like she was saying her happiness had been shattered," Felicia responded between bites of popcorn. "It really is just horrible luck to find true love and happiness just to be the random victim of a serial killer."

"What if it wasn't random? Maybe there was some way the Mangler targeted people. Some reason he had for choosing them?"

Felicia looked thoughtful. "It was the 80s. Maybe he was racist and didn't like her being with Kevin?" Then she shook her head. "That doesn't add up with the rest of his victims though."

"Maybe they were all happy," Sarah said, her eyes cast down at her lap. "What if that was what he was actually killing? Happiness and love."

Felicia reached over and took her hand. "That's actually a good theory. And it's something that's easy to miss."

Sarah looked down at their intertwined hands then,

and asked, "What if you come with me? To 1987? Maybe you can see something I didn't."

Felicia had eyes full of empathy but a frown on her lips. "Will it work? For me, I mean. From what I've heard, Sunnycrest has a tendency to haunt people, not places. I may just find myself sitting in the closet waiting for you. I feel like I've already spent months doing that."

Sarah giggled. She leaned over and kissed Felicia, who kissed her back with surprising passion. When their lips finally parted and they were looking into each other's eyes, Sarah said, "I like the idea of having someone waiting for me. I haven't had that for a long time. I don't know if it will work, but I know if it does, I'll feel a lot better having you with me, and if it doesn't, it'll help to have someone to come back to."

Felicia kissed her again. "Okay," she said afterward. "Tomorrow. I have other things I want to do tonight."

Sarah's cheeks flushed and she felt hot again but it was for entirely different reasons this time. She looked at Felicia and bit her lip, feeling a hunger she could tell was mutual. Felicia kissed her again and Sarah leaned into it. They collapsed onto the cloud-like cushions of the couch. Sarah felt like there was someone else in the room, someone watching. Behind her eyes, she pictured the locks on Felicia's door and couldn't help but wonder if they really kept out the dead. I'm not gonna let you ruin this, she thought as Felicia's fingers tugged at her clothes. Go away.

She leaned her head back, moaning in delight. Her eyes flicked open, and she saw Regina's terrified face staring at her. Sarah snapped her eyes shut again and squeezed them tight. Her fear intensified at the moment and made her heart race and pound even harder. She sat up and took control, tugging at Felicia's clothes, kissing her wildly. She could still feel the eyes on them, and she waved her arm in the air as she kissed her way down Felicia's belly.

Sarah tried to focus on the incredibly sexy woman beneath her. She made her way back up on a trail of kisses and stared into Felicia's eyes. She saw a frightened, white-painted face adorned with black lipstick and eyeliner in the reflection of her glasses. Sarah's breath caught in her chest. She reached over and removed the glasses, folding them and placing them gently on the nearby coffee table.

"I can't see without those," Felicia told her.

Sarah put a finger to her lips. "You don't need to see," she said gently. "You need to feel."

A few moments later when Felicia was biting back screams, Sarah felt satisfied that she was doing just that. It filled her with pride. She had needed this for a long time—intimacy, passion, connection. Knowing that Regina was there for it made her feel dirty though. It felt wrong and right simultaneously.

Balance, she told herself. This is all just part of the balance.

27

Sarah excused herself and went to the bathroom. She turned the lock in the doorknob and then looked around the room.

"Are you here?" she whispered. "What is the point of hanging around during that? I'm trying, Regina. You have to give me time…and a little privacy. Okay?"

A blur of movement went past the glass of the bathroom mirror. Instinctively, Sarah looked behind herself, but she shook her head. She knew better. The faucet turned on. Sarah reached over and turned it off.

"What are you trying to tell me? It's not easy to interpret this stuff. I want to understand. Is there a way you can be clearer?"

Regina appeared in the mirror then, but she wasn't the beautiful girl Sarah had seen before. She was torn to pieces, the flesh stripped from her skull in peeled ribbons. What was left was swollen and discolored, a mess of shattered teeth in a lipless mouth, one empty cavernous eye socket and one eyeball still hanging there, dangling over a shattered cheekbone.

Sarah fell to her knees and vomited in the toilet. She puked far more than she had eaten and her throat burned from the acid. Her gut contracted and spasmed. There was a knock at the door. "You okay in there?" Felicia said from the other side.

Sarah stood. She did a quick clean of her face and rinsed her mouth with sink water. Then she opened the door. Felicia was standing there looking at her with real concern. "What's going on?"

Sarah frowned. She looked over her shoulder and saw that the mirror had returned to normal. When she turned back, she said, "I forgot my toothbrush. I should go get it."

Felicia's eyes on her as she walked past, heading for the door. "You're gonna bail on me aren't you?"

Looking at the floor, Sarah stopped, and bowed her head in shame. Then she started toward the door again.

"You live directly across from me. You can't bang and

run. We see each other all the time, Sarah. What's going on? Talk to me."

Sarah stopped at the door and turned to face Felicia. The sight of the woman made her heart break in her chest. She wanted nothing more than to make this work, to have someone like her. She sighed deeply. "You were right," she said at last. "It's not my apartment or my closet that's haunted. It's me. I brought here with me."

Felicia huffed and slouched. "Okay. It's weird, but it's not like she's trying to kill you. It's not like you've put me in danger. You don't have to run away."

Sarah grabbed the knob and turned it, but didn't open the door. "But someone killed her and what if they follow her to me, to you? I can't. Also, I really did forget my toothbrush, and I need it now. If I don't use it, you'll never kiss me again."

Felicia frowned when she opened the door. "Go get your toothbrush, and then come back. If there is danger, then all the more reason you shouldn't be alone. I'm not like go die on your own! If you don't come back, I'm going to come looking for you. Please don't leave me in the hall all night. I don't like these halls at night. Remember our ghosts aren't the only ones here."

Sarah wanted to protest, to argue, but she didn't. She just nodded and crossed the hall to her own apartment. She didn't have to look back. She could feel Felicia's sympathetic gaze up until the moment she closed the door.

28

Sarah went to her closet. She opened it and jumped backward, not sure what she was expecting but still ready for it. For this moment at least, it was just a closet. She sighed and grabbed the empty bowling bag. There was finally an excuse to use it for something.

She went to the bathroom and brushed her teeth, then put her toothbrush in the bag. Sarah felt a little better now that it was the taste of spearmint instead of the taste of vomit that lingered in her mouth. She took the bag back to the bedroom and opened the closet, holding her breath when she did.

Nothing jumped out at her. She was just standing before her clothes. Sarah exhaled the breath she was holding.

Grabbing a few dresses, she threw them in the bag. Then she turned and moved to her dresser. She opened a drawer and grabbed some leggings and jeans and tossed them in too. Then she moved to her vanity so she could grab some of her makeup. There was something written on the mirror in lipstick. It said, He's still out there.

Sarah stared at it for a full minute. If she asked a question, would the lipstick rise into the air and write an answer? Was that more than she could handle? She bit her lip and then took a deep breath and said, "Do you mean Kevin or the Mangler?"

Sarah stood there for several breaths. Her heart rate was increasing by the moment, beating harder and faster. The lipstick remained on the counter. The mirror never changed. Sarah let out her frustration and then stepped forward to scoop some of her most used products into the bag.

There was a thump behind her and Sarah jumped, a chill dragging itself over her bones like fingernails. She turned to see what had made the noise and found that something had fallen out of the closet. Sarah walked over for a closer look. She bent down and picked up a hairbrush that wasn't hers. It was full of matted hair. Was this Regina's answer? She didn't understand the significance if it was. What is she trying to tell me? I don't get it.

Sarah threw the brush in her bag and walked out of the room. She almost collided with Felicia, and she screamed. "Really?" Felicia said with a laugh. "I told you I was going to come looking if you didn't come right back."

"I'm ready," Sarah said, showing her the bag. "If we're to do this properly, I had to make sure to bring you all my baggage."

Felicia smirked, shook her head, and led the way back. "This is by far my most interesting first date ever," she said as she opened the door to Apartment 7.

"Is this date one: part two? I thought this was technically date two. Maybe we can keep doing parts and just first-date forever," Sarah said back.

Behind her, words came like whistled notes on the wind. "Come back."

29

Felicia decided Sarah shouldn't sleep alone and invited her to bed. Despite everything that had happened, Sarah had the best sleep she'd had in a very long time, curled up in Felicia's arms, blanketed by her warmth. When she woke up, she was alone in the bed, and it felt huge. It had to be a King. Her own was just a full. It was plenty for her, but this made her feel like actual royalty. She yawned and stretched, then slipped out of the bed. Rubbing her eyes, Sarah headed for the kitchen and found Felicia already there, in a green apron, frying eggs. "There's coffee if you want some. It's over there," she said, pointing with her spatula. "Sugar is above and cream is in the fridge."

"I drink it black," Sarah said, shuffling over to it. "You shouldn't spoil me like this. I could get used to it."

Felicia cracked up laughing. "This isn't for you. This is what I do every day."

"Is it too soon to say I love you?"

"Yes."

They sat down and ate the eggs together, and Sarah filled Felicia in on everything that had happened. "Can I see the brush?" Felicia asked when she was finished. Sarah nodded and went to get it. She came back and placed it on the table before her. Felicia picked it up and studied it for a moment and then put it back down. "This is definitely not Regina's brush or hair. It has to be Kevin's. It probably was her answer."

"Shit. Okay, that makes sense. So do you think telling me that Kevin is still alive means he knows something she wants us to find out, or that she wants us to tell him something?"

"I don't know, but I liked how it sounded when you said us."

Sarah chuckled. She took the dishes to the sink and began to wash them. "When Regina showed herself to me in your mirror, it was the aftermath of what the Mangler had done. After our conversation about him killing happiness, I thought maybe she was warning me. It freaked me out."

Felicia came up behind her and wrapped her arms around Sarah's waist. "So you thought she was saying if we were happy together the Mangler would come get us? That must have been a lot."

"It was."

"That's why you wanted to run."

Sarah nodded. "And I puked in your toilet and needed to brush my teeth."

Felicia laughed. "You know I really do adore you. I have for a while."

"That's what Tina told me. That's why I forced myself to talk to you."

Felicia backed away. "That makes sense. Tina is an acquired taste. She's abrasive and outspoken, but her heart is usually in the right place. Also, her produce is really good."

"I don't really know her," Sarah admitted. "I just talk to her when I see her around, but she may become my best friend after last night."

"I thought I would become your best friend after last night, but I do agree that we owe her. Threesome?"

"Seriously?" Sarah paled.

"No." When Sarah sighed with relief, Felicia laughed. "Tina is very straight."

Sarah thought for a moment and said, "Would you if she wasn't?"

Felicia shrugged. "Only if you wanted to."

Sarah watched her walk away and just blinked. She felt like she was as bad at understanding the cues of the living as she was the dead. When she was diagnosed with ADHD she thought it was just about focus, about paying attention in school. She didn't realize it messed with her social cues and left her feeling constantly like she was saying and doing the wrong thing. It gave her a constant feeling of rejection, even when it wasn't there. She ended up afraid of initiating anything because she feared rejection that hadn't happened yet. It was called RSD, rejection-sensitive dysphoria. She knew she should talk to Mark about it, but it just felt like the ghost in her closet took precedence.

Sarah really liked Felicia and she was terrified of saying or doing the wrong thing. She tried to use humor but then she was afraid her jokes wouldn't land, and she wasn't exactly sure when other people were joking or not, like with what just happened with Felicia.

Felicia returned to the room and stood before her with her hands on her hips. "I can see you overthinking things," she said.

Sarah frowned and nodded. "Really? It's visible? Sorry."

Felicia snickered. "When you start thinking like that, you should just voice it, so I can help you shut it down and set it straight, and then we can move on. If you internalize it, it will just mess with you forever."

Sarah looked at her fearfully, but she swallowed and nodded. “Okay.”

“Do you have class today?”

“Not ’til 10.”

Felicia’s smile was wicked. “Good. Then we have time for a shower first.”

Sarah chewed on her fingernail for a moment and then followed the other woman into the bathroom. She sighed with relief when she saw that Felicia’s shower had a curtain rather than a glass door. There would be no fingers painting cryptic messages on that. She allowed herself to put her last shower experience out of her mind and enjoy her girlfriend for a minute. Is she my girlfriend? They soaped each other and leaned into each other as they rinsed. They kissed under the water and Sarah felt the steam releasing some of her tension. “Do you think we should try to find him? Kevin?”

“The better question is, should we be talking about this right now, in this moment, and the answer is no.”

Sarah did want to talk about it though. She also didn’t want to upset Felicia and mess this up, so she swallowed her retort. She kissed the woman to keep from saying anything she would regret. Felicia responded with passion.

A few minutes later when they were turning the water off and grabbing towels, Felicia said, “Yes. We should find Kevin and talk to him.”

“You said he did some time at Twin Spirits. Do you

know what happened to him after that?"

"No, but I'll do some digging and see what I can come up with."

"Thank you," Sarah said with a genuine smile. She looked Felicia over and marveled at her beauty. It was strange to feel so lucky while you were being haunted. Did life ever just make sense?

"And when we find him," Felicia said as she sat by a magnifying mirror working on her eyebrows, "we'll go see him together. I may not be able to go back to the 80s with you, but I can go with you in the here and now."

"I'd like that," Sarah said as she applied makeup, using the big mirror over the sink.

She feared she would see Regina again, a visual that was etched into her mind for life now, but she also had to be able to live and get ready for her day. She realized then that she held in her hand the same lipstick that the dead girl had used to write on her mirror. She frowned and decided to forgo lipstick today.

30

Sarah went to the vending machine between classes. It felt nice to attend class after a full night's sleep for a change. It was easier for her to focus when she was well-rested. She didn't want to get so bogged down with the madness of the present that she lost sight of her future. It felt like common sense that she would never be an educator without an education.

Sarah ran her card through the reader and pressed the appropriate buttons to send a bag of chips crashing down. She pushed her hand through the lid and grabbed for the bag. Someone or something grabbed her hand from inside the machine. Sarah's eyes went wide. She shook her head and looked around to see if anyone was in earshot. Then she leaned closer to the machine, sweat beading on her brow. She gave her hand a tug and the lid of the hatch banged, but she was held firmly by whatever had her. "Not here too," she whispered. "Please. I need this place to be safe. Let go. Regina…let go."

Whatever had her hand released its grip, and Sarah sighed with relief. She pulled her hand out of the machine without getting the chips, deciding to pay it forward and leave them for the next person. Her stomach wasn't happy with the decision, but it would have to deal. Maybe Felicia would cook something delicious again to soothe its sadness. As she walked away, her phone rang. It sounded extremely loud in the silence of the hallway. Sarah quickened her pace and hurried outside to answer it.

"Sorry to bother you. I hope you're not in class," Mark said.

"It's actually perfect timing. I'm on a break," Sarah replied. "What's up?"

"Well, I had this crazy idea. I thought, what if the killer was never caught because he wasn't from 1987? What if he was able to go through his closet and disappear back into a different time like you do?"

"Jesus," Sarah said, frightened by how much sense it made.

"Right. So, I decided to look into who lived in that

room between 1987 and when you got it. There were only three. After Regina's high-profile and brutal murder, Kevin was committed, and the room stayed vacant until 1993 when I guess enough time had passed for people to either forget or stop caring. Then a man named Kelly had it. He stayed there for a long time, until 2007, and only left because he went to prison on drug charges. When they put it back up a man named Neil moved in. He was there until 2011 and something bad happened. It isn't clear what, but he ended up in Twin Spirits, too, where he still resides. After him, there was no one for a really long time and then there was a man named Fred who moved in, at the beginning of 2020. He stayed until he left in the middle of the night a few months later. He left most of his belongings, didn't pay rent, or tell anyone he was leaving or where he was going. He was just there and then he wasn't."

Sarah pulled out a notebook and wrote down the names and dates he had just told her. "This is good info. Those people all lived in my apartment though, which was Kevin's. You should look into who lived in Regina's apartment on the 11th floor. Apartment 53."

"I did. I couldn't find anything other than an old couple and the people that currently live there. I called Gary, the apartment manager over there. He told me that the apartment was in such bad shape they could never get it fully clean. Thrill seekers kept wanting it for what happened there, and

Gary locked the door and threw away the key, so to speak. No one had officially lived there until that old couple. Something about it felt off to me though. I don't know that he was being honest. Be careful. I don't trust him."

Sarah thought about that for a second. Then she said, "I really appreciate all your help, Mark. It means more than you know. I have to get back to class. I'll see you soon."

"You can test it."

"I'm sorry?"

"My theory. You can test it and know for sure if it's plausible. You just have to see if you can hurt someone in the past. You can make it seem like an accident, knock them over or scratch them or something. If you can then we need to know more. If you can't, then that settles it."

Sarah gave a "Hmm." She remembered Baggins telling her that none of it was real, but what if he was in on it somehow? What if they knew she was coming and they wanted to get in her head, throw her off? That was as crazy—if not more so—than Mark's wild theory. She chose not to voice it, not yet anyway. She would get home and talk to Felicia about all of this. "Sounds dangerous but I'll consider it."

They said their goodbyes and Sarah headed to her next class. She was starting to feel even more lost than she had before she knew anything about the infamous RJ and KT. Could she hurt someone in the past? What would happen if she did? Would it prove anything? How would they react? She wasn't sure she wanted to know. Without even meaning to, Sarah quickened her pace.

31

Sarah stopped by the diner to see Leremy on the way home. She wanted to tell him about Felicia. He would be happy and proud of her, and she felt like she could use some of that. She always wanted his unique perspective on what was going on. Sarah felt a strange sort of comfort and trust with Leremy. She felt like she could tell him anything and it would be okay. That was a rare and difficult thing to find in today's world, and probably in the world of the past too, she thought. Did Regina have a friend she could trust and confide in?

Unfortunately, when she got to the diner, Leremy

wasn't there. The host, David, said he hadn't come in. Sarah told herself she felt more concerned than she should. Leremy was a grown man. She was sure he was fine. Even if he wasn't, it was probably a stomach bug or something, nothing to do with Sunnycrest.

Sarah texted him immediately and stood out in front of the diner waiting for him to reply. Her impatient nerves led her to pace and get odd looks from people going in and out. They probably think I'm on drugs. Screw them. Let them. You try being haunted, assholes. Finally, her phone Ding-ed and Sarah rushed to look at it. It was him and she sighed with relief.

Leremy said she was sweet to visit, and he was sorry for not being there. Then he sent a photo of his face, swollen and bruised with a bad black eye.

Her heart seized. "What happened?" she said, but she didn't wait for him to respond this time. She just hit the call button next to his name.

Sarah paced again as she waited for him to answer, flipping the bird at someone's silent judgment as she did. It was something she would never have done even months ago, but she had no remorse. Who were they? Why did they think they understood her situation or that they were any better than she was? To hell with them.

When Leremy finally did answer on the fifth ring, it was with a weak-sounding groan. Sarah spoke quickly in a panic, demanding to know what had happened to him and why.

"Nothing new," he told her. "My dad sent some goons to pay me back for embarrassing him at the restaurant. Not the first time and won't be the last."

"What?!"

"He will play the good supportive father in public, and then pay me back in private. That's how it goes. That's our dynamic. You know, he has an image to protect."

"For the love of God, Leremy, then why do you go? Why antagonize him if you know he will do this to you? Is it really worth it?" She started walking away from his place of employment out of respect.

"It's just how it is, Sarah. The day I came out he took the belt to me and then called me out of school with the flu. We've been at it ever since. I want to see how much it takes before he snaps publicly and shows his true colors to the world. So I keep pushing. If he kills me one day then everyone will know the monster he is, and I will still win. If I quit fighting, then everyone goes on thinking he's this wonderful saint and that's not just a disservice to me, but to every queer kid like me. I can't do it."

Sarah was angry, but it wasn't with him. She wanted to be mad at him for putting himself in danger, but he did it because he was fighting for something he felt was right. She was doing the same thing with Sunnycrest, wasn't she? Logic said to walk away but her heart wouldn't let her. She sighed into the phone. "It's okay. I get it," she said. "I'm just sorry. The world should be better by now. People should be better. I hate that it's still like this. It's 2021 for God's sake. Damn it."

"Bruises on the outside heal," Leremy told her. "Gimme a day to rest and I'll come visit you, good as new. You'll see."

"Why don't you let me come visit you so you don't have to go there?" Sarah said empathetically. "Your heart has been through enough. The last thing you need is Sunnycrest."

"It's okay. I'm a big boy. I can handle it."

"Alright. Just please be nice to yourself. Go rest, take a bath, and drink some wine."

"Yes ma'am," he said with a chuckle. "'I think I'll do even better. Rain makes this beautiful mango vodka and I happen to have a bottle. I'll put it in a wine glass." He snickered again, and Sarah found herself joining him. This guy was something else. Even in the face of darkness, he found a smile and not just for himself but for her as well. She was starting to think Collin must have been crazy to leave him as well. Or maybe he just couldn't deal with Dad's goons and nursing his injured boyfriend in the aftermath of it. Not everyone has that level of fight in them, or wants it for that matter.

When Sarah hung up and headed back to Sunnycrest, she felt sad and confused. She sought Leremy because he made her feel comfortable and safe, but hearing his truth and seeing what his own father had no qualms about doing to his face left her feeling disgusted. Sarah was living in two worlds, thirty-four years apart, and they were both terrible places full of violence and fear. Her mind went to what the good doctor had told her. Maybe it was in fact time to test his theory. Maybe she could test Felicia's theory at the same time and see if she could bring her. Then if the person she hurt got mad she'd have some backup. Or you'll be selfishly putting someone who is good to you in danger.

Sarah wiped tears from her eyes that she hadn't even realized were there. She was feeling down and needed something good, something positive. When something bad happened, she looked for any win she could find to gain balance. She saw a flower stand and nodded to herself. Then she hurried over and bought a bouquet of roses for Felicia, and as she made the last leg of her trip, she wore a smile. She couldn't wait to see that beautiful, freckled face light up at the sight of them.

Sarah soon felt a terrible headache coming on though, and her smile was short-lived. When she reached the edge of the Sunnycrest property line, she was forced to stop. She closed her eyes against the pain. Behind them, she saw Regina smiling. Her eyes sparkled with stars of love. "No one's ever given me flowers," she said, so happy she was now crying.

Kevin walked over to her, a smile decorating his own face. "Until today." He took her hands in his own. "I'll make sure you keep getting flowers until you're totally sick of them." Regina laughed at him and kissed him as she sniffled and wiped at the tears in her eyes. Then Kevin was gone, and the happy girl's flesh began to peel away from her bone like a banana. Her lips dropped from her face and fell to the ground at her feet with a wet smack, and her eyes popped from their sockets to dangle over her ruined mouth. Her face was a mangled shower of blood. It leaked from every orifice.

Sarah gasped and opened her eyes. She found herself standing next to the big tree and gasped again. Her hand was resting on its cool bark. When she took it away, she saw the carved initials that had been hidden beneath her palm and she shuddered, her eyes immediately going to the window of Apartment 53. A woman inside was staring down at her, maybe the married man's wife. She looked at Sarah with worry and fear though, like Sarah was somehow dangerous. Sarah wanted to call out, to defend herself, but she pulled her eyes from the woman and her gaze returned to the carving in the tree. Maybe she's right.

32

Sarah made her way to the second floor of the building and knocked on the door of Apartment 7. She forced herself to smile as she listened to the many locks disengaging. When the door opened, she extended the flowers in her hand.

Felicia took them with a smile of her own and said, "Believe it or not, no one has ever given me flowers."

The words came out of Sarah's mouth before she could even think of them. Maybe it was because they were fresh in her mind. "I'll make sure you get flowers until you're sick of them."

Felicia laughed and moved to let her in. She put all the locks back in place and then walked past Sarah to retrieve something she could use as a vase for the flowers. Sarah laughed when she saw the other woman use a tall coffee thermos. "I have a vase at my place if you need one."

"Yeah. That might be good, but I'm totally okay with not being fancy as well."

Sarah kissed her gently on the lips. "How was your day?"

"Surprisingly ordinary and uneventful."

Sarah grinned. "Well then, let's change that. I want to test your theory and try to take you with me, through the doorway in Apartment 8."

Felicia seemed to study her for a minute. Then she nodded. "Yeah, okay. I'm down. Let's do it."

Sarah didn't tell her about the other thing she wanted to test. She felt like that would make the trip sound a lot more dangerous and a lot less appealing. She was just tired of all the questions and decided it was time to start getting some answers.

"I'm going to have a drink first," Felicia said. "A little liquid courage. You want one?"

Sarah exhaled. "You know what? I think I do."

Grabbing her bottle and two glasses, Felicia carried them awkwardly until Sarah took one of the glasses from the crook of her arm. Felicia poured the liquor in both glasses and then set the bottle down on the coffee table. Sarah followed her over, sipping at the contents of her glass. Then Felicia turned around with a smile and clinked her glass into Sarah's. "To time travel," she said with a laugh. "To getting some answers to life's great mysteries."

"To hoping you come out of the closet with me," Sarah said with a wink. Then she drank from her glass.

Felicia laughed and drank her own. "Alright. Let's do this," she said.

FIVE

Going Backward

33

Sarah and Felicia held hands as they moved across the hall to door number 8, their hearts racing in tandem. Felicia let go long enough for Sarah to unlock the door. When she was turning the knob to open the door, Felicia had her other hand again. Were they dating? It definitely felt like it to Sarah but they hadn't had a true conversation about it. Things were just happening. Sarah had learned the hard way in the past that that didn't always mean what you thought it did. As soon as things were actually normal, they were going to have to sit down and discuss exactly what they wanted from this, from each other. For now, Sarah thought, just not being alone is enough.

When they were inside, the door closed, they stood still before the closet, their hearts still pounding. "Are we sure about this?" Sarah asked.

"I am if you are," Felicia told her.

"Okay." Sarah nodded, more to herself, and took several deep breaths to steel her nerves. She could feel Felicia's hand tighten on her own and she was thankful for that. Before she could change her mind, she opened the closet door and started taking things out, creating a pile in the living room as she worked to create space. Behind her, Felicia giggled. The sound made Sarah smile even as frightened as she was. It felt like she was a teenager again, at a sleepover playing Bloody Mary in the bathroom mirror. When the closet was all but clear, she said, "After you."

"Oh yeah, sure. Thanks," Felicia said back, widening her eyes just a little. She stepped forward into the closet without letting go, dragging Sarah in tow. Something crunched under her foot and Sarah silently hoped it was hers and she didn't just break something important to Regina or Kevin.

"Alright. Here we go," Sarah said. She sucked in a breath, held it, and pulled the door closed. Felicia's hand gave hers a supportive squeeze just as everything went dark. Seconds ticked by.

"This reminds me of Seven Minutes in Heaven in high

school," Felicia whispered through the dark.

"Honestly, that was almost just as scary for me with everyone being straight and expecting you to want to sit in the dark with a greasy hormonal boy. You ready?"

After a moment of silence, Felicia said, "I forgot that you probably can't see me in the dark. I'm over here nodding. Yes, I'm ready."

Sarah laughed nervously. She touched Felicia and it felt good to not be alone, but it didn't do anything to slow her heart. She reached forward and reopened the door. The giant pile of mess she'd created to make room in the closet was no longer in front of them.

"Holy shit, did it work?" Felicia asked from behind her as Sarah stepped out into the new living room. "It worked, didn't it?"

Sarah turned to her and raised a finger to her lips. "I've come here when they've been home," she whispered.

Felicia nodded. She let go of Sarah's hand and moved toward the kitchen. Then she disappeared. Sarah stood there staring at where she had been. Just like that, she was alone again. She looked at her hand and sighed.

Sarah couldn't leave yet—as much as she wanted to, now that Felicia had gone. She had something else to test. She wasn't even sure how she was going to do it. Maybe go into the hall and find someone, then see if she could hurt them. Sarah had never purposely hurt anyone in her life. It wasn't in her nature to do so. There were boys whose hearts ended up broken but that wasn't something she could help. She couldn't change who she was. She certainly never physically hurt anyone. There was a girl in high school that beat her up once, but Sarah didn't even fight back. She just stood there in shock and took it. It'll just be a scratch, something minor and forgivable. Just try to breathe. Do it and get right back with the answer. You'll be okay. Everything will be okay.

Sarah moved slowly through the apartment. She wanted to make sure Regina and Kevin weren't there before she ventured out. When she got to the bedroom doorway, she gasped. Her whole body started to quiver, and her legs gave out. She fell to her knees in the doorway, still clutching the doorknob.

Today was the day.

Today was the day it happened. Regina must have wanted her to see it.

Regina was lying atop the made bed, or at least what was left of her. It was more brutal than Sarah's imagination had been able to conjure—even at its worst. What she had briefly witnessed in the mirror at Felicia's had been a mere taste of the actual sickening reality.

The entire room had been spattered with blood and gore. It dripped from the lamp and the end table and splayed across the wall and bedspread. Bones were jutting out of torn flesh as if each broken ivory was an arm reaching for help.

They went in every direction. Her guts were spilling from her shredded torso onto the floor like a pile of wet laundry. Her once beautiful flesh was peeled from her skull in ragged violent strips, her muscle, sinew, and bone on full display. The eye that had been missing in the mirror now rested beside her on the bed, staring at Sarah. Whoever the Mangler was, they were no surgeon. There was no grace to this horrible scene, just brutality, sheer and utter enraged violence. It almost felt like it was done with haste, desperation, need. Sarah found herself wondering if she could feel some of the killer's feelings, left behind in the air, the moment swirling with sickness and disgust.

Sarah felt instantly nauseous. She could smell the death, the blood, taste it on her tongue and it turned her stomach sour. Sarah held a hand to her mouth to try to keep it down. She didn't know what it would do to puke here. Would it put her DNA at the scene and send police hunting her in a year she wasn't even born? She remembered Baggins: "None of this is real."

Sarah was shaking her head, tears flowing freely from her poisoned eyes that would never forget these images. All she could hope was that the worst of it had been done post-mortem, that the poor girl was dead before the true rage came out. Maybe she didn't feel it. Maybe she was already gone.

On trembling limbs, Sarah fumbled her way backward, away from the room on all fours. She made it back to the living room and hugged herself tight with shaking arms. She rolled there on the rug and cried. When she stopped, she did so because she felt someone's presence. Sarah knew she was no longer alone.

She looked up and saw Kevin come in. He looked good, normal, nothing like someone that had seen their true love as Sarah had just witnessed her. He must not have known yet. This had to be when he found her. Would he find Sarah here and think she did it? Shit. Shit, shit, shit.

Sarah stayed low to the floor and crawled toward the open closet, trying her best to remain out of his line of sight. From what she could tell, he didn't seem to notice her. Second test long forgotten, Sarah scurried into the closet. She didn't want to close the door with him there. Surely he would hear it, and look. He could see her. She had no idea what kind of consequence that would have. So she sucked in a breath, held it, and hugged her knees to her chest as she waited, her heart wildly pounding. When she heard Kevin's anguished sobs and blood-curdling screams, she reached up with tears spilling from her eyes and pulled the closet door shut.

34

When Sarah opened the closet door, she fell out into her own apartment, shaking and sobbing. Felicia ran to her. She must have been there waiting for Sarah to return after she disappeared. At least she was okay.

"What happened?" she asked. "Are you hurt? I came back here as soon as we broke contact. Did someone do something to you? What happened?"

"Not to me," Sarah choked out as she struggled to regain composure. The images of Regina's broken body, paired with Kevin's tortured sobs, infiltrated her mind where she was sure they would claim permanent residence.

Felicia held her close, pressing Sarah's head into her chest. She hugged her tight and stroked her hair, gently rocking until Sarah's sobs quieted. "I'm here," she said. "You're safe now."

Sarah moved her head and looked at Felicia, but Felicia could see that Sarah wasn't actually viewing her. She was still seeing what she saw through the gateway in her closet. Sarah shook. She looked down and noticed some of the dead girl's blood was on her pants, and her shoes. She turned her hands over and saw it on her palms. Sarah gave a choked sob in time with the sound of Kevin's own that rang through the corridor of her mind. Then she broke down and started crying hysterically, letting it all out.

Felicia picked her up. "Alright. Come on," she said, and dragged Sarah's trembling form to the door. "I need you to help me some." She sighed with relief when Sarah remained upright as she let go.

Sarah swayed back and forth, the images of Regina's horrible death cycling through her mind to the chorus of her lover's pain. When Felicia got the door open, she grabbed Sarah and dragged her across the hall to her own door before letting her go again. Once the new door had been swung wide, Felicia pulled Sarah through it, across her apartment, and to the bathroom where she set her down gently on the floor. Sarah stared blankly at Felicia as she turned the shower on and stuck her hand in the water to check the temperature.

These little moments warmed Sarah, as gone as she was. To see little things like that, the moments that proved how caring this woman was. She didn't want the water to be too cold or too hot after what Sarah had already been through. She wasn't just trying to bring Sarah back but bring her back comfortably.

Then Sarah's attention was drawn back to the blood on her, and she squealed. She started frantically trying to undress, to get it off her and away from her. As she ripped at her clothes and shoes, she kept finding more—a spot on her elbow, a splatter on her hip. She moaned in horror and desperate need to be free of the blood—of the horror that led to it—but she knew in her heart that she would never be free of it. Long after all of this was over, she would still carry this day and the images that were now burned into her mind, with her. They were a part of her now and she heard her mother's voice in her head telling her, "The darkness leaves a stain on you. Stay away from it."

"It's okay. It's gonna be okay," Felicia told her in a soothing tone. She helped Sarah finish undressing and get to her feet. Then she helped her step over the wall of the tub with her quivering legs and get into the spray of water.

Sarah grabbed a bar of soap that rested on a tray protruding from the wall and scrubbed herself vigorously. On the other side of the curtain, Felicia said nothing. She must be waiting for me, Sarah thought. "I saw her—her body—what the Mangler did to her. I can't unsee it. I think I will see it behind my eyes, every waking moment of my life, and then again in my dreams forever and ever."

"I'm so sorry." Felicia's voice was tender through the shower curtain. "I'm sorry you had to see that. I've seen photos from the crime scene. They didn't show everything, but they showed enough that I can imagine how horrible of an experience that was for you. Maybe you can take some solace in knowing that it happened thirty-four years ago, that you're safe. I wish I had something better."

"I want to help her," Sarah said, her voice quiet and almost drowned out by the spraying water. "I want to understand what she is trying to tell me, what she needs, but I don't think I can ever go back there, not after that."

"You know you don't have to go alone anymore. We just have to remain in contact. I have a pair of handcuffs we can use to make sure we don't separate." An embarrassed silence. "Don't ask about why I have them please."

Through her tears, Sarah choked out a laugh. "Can I say I love you yet?"

"Not yet. We haven't even used the handcuffs."

Sarah laughed again. After another minute, she found the steam of the water was making it easier to breathe. "What if we're not safe, Felicia? We don't know the rules. We're finding all of this out as we go. What if they can hurt us? What if they can come through the gateway just like we can? I'm so scared."

Felicia opened the curtain and looked at her. "They can't," she said assuredly. "You're safe. We're okay."

Sarah was shaking less but Felicia still helped her out of the shower and kissed her wet face beside her mouth. "There were people that lived there before me. I wonder if she tried to reach them if they went through this too," she said as Felicia worked to towel her dry. The towel was cloud soft, like the couch cushions, and allowed Sarah to push out the grisly images for a moment to remember the night she and Felicia had made love on that couch.

"Maybe we can find them," Felicia told her. "Ask them. Let's take one day at a time."

Sarah nodded.

Handing her an imposing navy-blue dress, Felicia said, "You're smaller than me, so I can't give you my jeans, but this should work until you get your own clothes. Unless, of course, you want to walk around naked, which I am definitely completely okay with."

Sarah gave a small laugh. "Thank you," she said, accepting the dress. She shrugged it over her still-damp shoulders and aside from being loose in the hips it was okay.

"Come on," Felicia said, taking her hand. "Let's get you a drink and a warm blanket and go put a comedy on."

"That sounds good," Sarah admitted, "but can you not let go of my hand this time?"

"I will hold onto it until I have to work in the morning. I can't really type one-handed," Felicia said with the hint of a smile.

She walked Sarah out to the living room and they both froze in their tracks. Their hands squeezed at each other. There was a man sitting on the couch, facing forward, not looking their way. Sarah watched Felicia's gaze go to the open door, the locks that weren't engaged like they always were. She felt responsible. Felicia didn't lock up because she was taking care of her. The one time she didn't, and someone came in, made themselves comfortable.

The man on the couch had light brown skin and dark black hair and looked to be in his early thirties. Who the hell was he, and why did he help himself to Felicia's couch? What did he want?

Felicia voiced the question Sarah was thinking. "What are you doing? Who are you?"

The man turned slowly to look in their direction for the first time since they'd entered the room. "Let it go," he said. "It won't end well if you don't."

"What the hell does that mean?" Felicia barked angrily, but the man just stood and made his way to the open door. "Hey! I'm talking to you."

The man stopped in the doorway and looked back at them. "It means the past should stay in the past. No good comes from dredging it up. Let it go." He slipped out the door before Felicia could respond. She ran behind him and was still holding Sarah's hand, so she got dragged along, tripping over herself. Sarah watched Felicia poke her head into the hall and then bring it back. She closed the door hard and then after a gentle squeeze, let go of Sarah's hand to engage all the locks. Sarah found herself wishing there were more.

35

Both women sat in the kitchen, their chairs turned to face the front door. Neither wanted to sit on the couch after seeing the stranger sitting on it like he owned it. It felt tainted somehow, even though they thoroughly inspected it after he left. It hadn't seemed like he'd done anything other than sit on it.

"I'm glad I put that dress on and didn't opt for walking around naked," Sarah said with an awkward smile.

"Me too," Felicia said, sipping from a glass of liquor,

"though CreepyMcHomeInvader probably wouldn't agree."

"I've never even seen him before," Sarah said, eyeing the couch. "I don't think he lives here."

"Me neither," Felicia agreed. "Do you think he was from then, that he could have come through? Maybe he just doesn't live here now but he does live here in 1987."

"I don't know." Sarah frowned. "I don't really believe that then is an actual then. I think it's a recreation made by Regina to tell a story, get a point across, and send a message. Can a ghost's created constructs travel on their own? As insane as all of this is, that still feels like a stretch to me."

"Shit," Felicia said with a sigh. Taking another sip from the drink she poured herself, she sat down. "I don't think I know how anything works anymore."

"Do you think this is the type of thing that happened to Roger on floor seven? It doesn't seem like it ended well for him."

Felicia frowned. "That guy was crazy, Sarah. He claimed he never spoke to you after the day you moved in, but I saw him talk to you several times."

Sarah nodded. "I know. That's my point. This stuff, it skews your reality. Time and plans, days and chores, it all gets lost and jumbled. It's happening to me already. I don't want people to talk about me the way they talk about him."

Felicia took her hand across the table and craned her neck to meet Sarah's eyes. "They won't because we're going to solve this thing…together. Let's go back. If she showed you the day she died, it had to be for a reason, right? Maybe there was a clue, something she wanted you to find from that day."

Sarah paled and shook her head subtly and slowly. "I-I can't. I will see it forever, as is. I can't go back. I'm sorry."

"I can't go without you. I can't even let go of you when we're there."

"I can't."

Felicia exhaled, and Sarah pulled at the fabric of the navy-blue dress, thinking she upset her partner. She really hoped the other woman understood. Felicia sipped her drink and said, "Okay. Let's stay productive though. What else do we have?"

Sarah thought for a moment. "There were three people in my apartment between Kevin and me. There's a kind Indian gentleman and his wife in Regina's old apartment now. I don't know about before that. A friend told me there was an old couple but that's it. I feel like there may have been more."

Felicia nodded. "Well, I know who knows the answer for sure. Come on."

As Sarah followed Felicia out of the apartment and down the hall, a new question began to stir in her mind. "You held me, helped me undress, dragged me home, and didn't have a speck of blood on you. How come?"

Felicia thought for a moment. "Hmm. Just lucky, I guess. What are you thinking?"

"I'm not sure yet," Sarah admitted. Without saying it, they both looked around for the strange man that had invaded Felicia's home.

They went down the stairwell to the first floor and knocked on door number 2. After a moment, Felicia knocked again. Finally, the door opened, and Gary peered out, looking annoyed. "What is it with you two now?"

"Let us in. We need to talk," Felicia said.

Even Sarah's brows raised at her level of abrasiveness. Sarah could never be like that. She wasn't sure she would even want to, though she supposed it was useful in situations such as this.

Gary stood in silence for a moment, peering at them from behind the half-open door. He seemed to be contemplating and Sarah couldn't help but wonder if he was considering slamming the door in their faces. Finally, he sighed through his nose and opened the door. Sarah gave her own audible sigh of relief and followed Felicia inside. They took a seat on a plaid couch that looked to be from the early seventies and was used aggressively the whole time. Gary plopped into a brown leather recliner across from them and lit a cigarette. His TV was on, playing a graphic show about zombies. The visuals brought the images of Regina's corpse crashing back into Sarah's head and her stomach lurched. Felicia saw the change in her, snagged the remote off the coffee table, and turned the television off.

Gary took a deep breath and laid his cigarette on a tabletop glass ashtray next to his chair. Sarah noticed that the walls were stained with nicotine, making it look like the apartment suffered from jaundice. "What do you want from me?" Gary asked them.

Felicia got right to the point before Sarah could respond. "We need to know who lived in Apartment 53 before the people who live there now, going all the way back to 1987."

I wanna see if you tell us the same thing you told Mark, Sarah thought after she said it.

Gary tossed his hands up. "I can't just give you that information."

"You're not supposed to, but you can, and it's really important."

Sarah saw the firm no that was coming and stepped in. "Please, Gary. I'm just trying to figure out what is happening in my own apartment."

"What are you talking about?" he asked, dragging on his cigarette.

Felicia fanned the smoke from her face, and said simply, "Regina Johnson."

Gary sat silently, staring at them, the moments passing by, and his cigarette burning down to his yellowed fingertips. When the tower of ash fell to the carpet at his feet, he said, "Terrible what happened to that girl. She was one of the first to not let go of this place, one of the reasons Momma refused to come back, aside from collecting rent and I got this lovely job I so adore."

"Agatha is your mother," Sarah said, more of a statement than a question. "You were so friendly when you showed me the place and got me to sign the lease."

"That's my job, dear."

"But you knew Regina hadn't let go of this place when you scolded Roger for warning me." Again, a statement, not a question. Maybe he did lie to Mark. What are you hiding?

"As I said, that's my job. Besides, Regina wasn't in your apartment. She died on the eleventh floor for God's sake."

"Her boyfriend was in my apartment and there's a gateway between the two."

"Shit," Gary said, getting to his feet. "That explains a lot. Let me get my computer. Hang on." Sarah didn't miss the way he eyed Felicia as he got up and left the room.

Felicia looked at Sarah and nodded. A moment later, Gary returned with a laptop. "This is much easier than the file cabinet days, but I still remember the pain of transferring all that information."

"I bet," Felicia said.

They watched as he typed, his fingers pecking at the keys like a hungry chicken. "Alright. 53. Mom was still here then when Regina was killed. She wouldn't rent 53. It wasn't until I came in '93 that it was put up for rent again. Still, no one took it until '97, almost to the ten-year anniversary of the girl's death."

Maybe that's when the gateway opened, Sarah wondered. She listened as he continued.

"That was a woman named Sheila, the one in '97. I forgot all about her. She didn't last long. Literally ran out of here screaming. It was a disaster. I had to do a lot of damage control. After that, it stayed vacant for another three damn years. In 2000, a guy named Walter lived there for six months, and then another fella named Ralph who lasted almost a year and a half. In 2002 he moved out and it stayed vacant 'til 2003 when an older couple, Paul and Ginger took it. They stayed there, happily from what I could tell, from 2003 until they both passed holding hands in their sleep in 2020. Found 'em myself. Can't quit smoking after that. There was another short-lived guy who disappeared and left me high and dry. Carl. Shortly after he up and vanished, Aarav and Saanvi moved in. How does this help?"

"Wait, someone else died in that apartment?" Sarah said, a sense of dread scurrying up her spine with a chill.

"Two more, but it doesn't seem like they hung around. Again, how does this help?"

"Some guy came into my apartment and told us to stop digging into Regina's death. We figured he knew something. It seemed like a good place to start."

Gary grunted. "Good luck with that. If you don't

mind, I'd like to watch zombies eating brains now." He lit another cigarette and turned his TV back on.

Felicia sighed in frustration, but she got up and took Sarah's hand, leading her out. As they headed up the stairs, Felicia said, "I guess we're gonna spend the night on Google."

When they hit the second floor, Sarah said, "Hang on. Come to my place first." She led Felicia there and opened the door. One look at the closet and she almost threw up, but that wasn't why she was here. Not this time. She forced the images out of her mind and went to her bedroom where she got on her hands and knees and pulled a box out from under her bed.

"What are you doing?" Felicia asked.

Sarah responded by turning toward her and tossing her the snow globe. Felicia reacted quickly and tried to catch it. She did catch it in fact, but her hands couldn't grasp it. It went right through them and fell to the floor where it shattered. "I'm sorry," she said. "I had it. I thought I had it."

"You did," Sarah said, standing up. "But without touching me you can't touch any of it. Proof…" She walked over, carrying one of Kevin's boots. She took one of Felicia's hands with her right hand and held the boot out to her with the other. Felicia grabbed it. Sarah let go of her hand and the boot fell through Felicia's fingers to the floor. She looked at Sarah with wide eyes. Sarah only nodded.

36

"What does it mean?" Felicia asked, deciding the couch was finally safe to sit on again.

"Exactly what you said," Sarah answered as she took the seat next to her. "The haunt is mine. My apartment isn't haunted, I am. You can go there and touch the things from there through me, but not otherwise because you're not the one that's haunted."

In her mind, Sarah thought, What does that mean for Mark? She had dropped that paper on his desk and he'd picked it up, took it home with him, and returned it. Was he somehow involved in Regina's death or life after death? Why didn't he need her touch? She planned to find out. She didn't voice this to Felicia yet. Instead, she said, "Let's try to see what we can find on the people between Regina and Aarav. We should check the people that lived in my place too, just in case."

"Well, Paul and Ginger are dead, so I don't think we need to search for them," Felicia told her. "At least not on the internet. If you want to search the halls, we might find them around here somewhere. Maybe they're still holding hands. That would be so sweet."

"That's okay," Sarah answered quickly. "I'm content to leave them to it, sweet as it is."

Felicia laughed and started typing away on her own computer. After a moment, she said, "Hey. I think this is him." She turned the computer so Sarah could get a better look at the screen.

The man pictured was definitely the man that had been sitting on that very couch, and Sarah shuddered when she saw him again. "Ralph Masterson," Felicia told her. "This is his obit., Sarah. He's dead, hung himself shortly after he left Sunnycrest."

Sarah shook off a chill. Her stomach felt queasy again. She rubbed at her face. "I think I've had enough for today," she said. "Can we call it a night?"

Felicia gave a humorless laugh. "Well, I doubt I'll be able to sleep, but I'll make sure you do. Come on." She took

Sarah's hand and lifted her from the couch. Sarah caught her paying a last glance at the locks on the door, not wanting to make that mistake twice. Would it even make a difference? Ralph was dead. How much did locks even matter in a place like this? When they got to the bed, Sarah said, "Let's just hold each other."

"Okay."

They climbed onto the bed and under the covers and wrapped themselves in each other's warmth, arms and legs tangled. After a minute, Felicia reached over and turned off the bedside lamp.

37

When Sarah awoke, she was alone in the bed again. She felt vulnerable and a little frightened, so she slipped out from under the tangle of sheets and scampered to the bathroom where she used the toilet, her eyes scanning the room for threats and phantoms. Then stumbled sleepily into the kitchen where Felicia was cooking breakfast. Sarah went right to the fresh coffee this time, thinking, I could get used to this. It smelled incredible. She took a deep breath of the wafting aroma as she poured her cup.

"Did you even sleep?" she asked as she sipped at the

steaming contents of her mug.

"Nope. Sure didn't, but I'm glad you did. You needed rest after everything."

"I thought I would have nightmares, but if I did, I don't remember them."

"Well good." Felicia looked over and shot her a smile. "Why don't you skip school today? Call it a mental health day. Give yourself the weekend and start fresh on Monday."

Sarah puffed air. "I feel like I'm already behind. I've been so in my head lately."

Felicia turned and placed two plates of food on the table. She walked over to Sarah, took her hands, and kissed her gently. "That's exactly my point," she said.

Sarah nodded. She took a seat at the table. "What about you?"

"I took the semester off to write and explore some other things."

"Are you a trust fund baby?"

Felicia burst out laughing. "Would I be living at Sunnycrest if I was? No. I just have some dirt on Gary."

Sarah's jaw fell in time with her fork. "You're living here on blackmail?"

Felicia shrugged. "A girl's gotta do what a girl's gotta do in this city. Don't worry. I'm not sleeping with him or anything anymore. I'm all yours."

Sarah looked like she was going to be sick again. Anymore? "You slept with that guy?"

Felicia shrugged and blotted her mouth with her napkin. "Revert back to my previous statement. Girl's gotta do what a girl's gotta do. Speaking of which, what do you think you'll do today? It should be self-care, something to take care of you."

"There's a guy that lived in my apartment before me. He's been in Twin Spirits for the last decade. I think I'm going to pay him a visit."

Felicia stopped eating and gave Sarah a look that said, Come on. Really? "You're not actually aware of what self-care means are you?"

"Honestly, right now it means doing what I can to get my life back, but I'll meet you in the middle. I'm going to call my psychiatrist and see if he'll see me a few days early."

Felicia finished her food and wiped her mouth again. "I guess that's something. I was thinking more like a massage or a pedicure or something, but you do you."

"I'd rather do you," Sarah said, blushing.

Felicia laughed. "You're corny, but yes." She took Sarah's hand and led her to the bedroom. As they moved through the doorway, Sarah felt something lightly brush her neck. It made her skin crawl and she quickly looked back. She saw nothing. She was still looking back as Felicia pulled her to the bed.

38

Sarah stood before the entrance to the Twin Spirits psychiatric ward. It felt strange. It wasn't like Sunnycrest. It wasn't old and creepy, ominous and foreboding. It was nice and welcoming. This warm-feeling place was actually home to hundreds—if not thousands—of broken and mentally ill people, many probably dangerous. The contrast felt somehow wrong to her, like a trap. Still, she walked through the doors.

When Sarah called Mark to reschedule her appointment, she got Neil's last name from him. He also told her that he would come if they wouldn't let her in. He could use his pull if need be. He knew some of the doctors and staff quite well. She didn't ask him the question looming in her mind. How did you hold the paper? She would wait and ask him that in person later.

Sarah walked to the front desk and asked the pleasant-looking woman working there if she could visit with Neil Pryor.

The woman's smile widened. "Well, I'll be," she said. "He told us that he was going to have a visitor today, said the spirits told him so," she laughed. "Sometimes I wonder how many of these people ain't even crazy."

"Maybe the meds just give them superpowers," Sarah said with an awkward smile. The woman gave a forced laugh to ease the weird moment and made her a visitor badge. She then called a young man who smiled warmly and led her to the visiting area. There were brightly-colored couches, chairs and tables. Sarah walked over to one and sat down. She felt nervous and fumbled with the folds of her dress, smoothing the fabric over and over.

Another man, older than the last but looking just as passive, wheeled a man out in a wheelchair, parking him in front of her. He smiled at her and walked away. Sarah looked at the man before her. He was well groomed and judging by his eyes, heavily sedated. "Neil," she started. "My name is Sarah. I live in Apartment 8 over at Sunnycrest."

The man who hadn't made eye contact yet suddenly

seemed to notice her. He snapped to attention like he had broken through the wall of the drugs he was on. "So it's true," he said, his voice quivering. "There was a girl here visiting Roger. You know Roger. Her name was Alice, and she said you were in danger and you were going to come visit me. She asked me to help."

A chill shook Sarah to the core. She wished she knew more about Roger's story. She would have visited him while she was there but she was more concerned with the fact that this total stranger just said she was in danger. "I do know Roger," she said. "How am I in danger, Neil?"

The man shook his head. He looked all around the room like he was in a panic. He looked truly afraid. He shook his head again. "I don't know. I don't know. She didn't tell me. She just said to help. I don't know."

Sarah didn't want him to freak out. They might take him away if he did and she wouldn't get her answers. "Okay. It's okay," she said. "What happened to you when you lived in my apartment, Neil?"

"I was living in two worlds and I couldn't take it. I didn't know what was real anymore. The dead girl wouldn't stop. I begged her to, told her I didn't know what she was trying to tell me and I didn't want to. The gateway she opened brought him with it."

"Who?" Sarah asked, leaning forward to look him in the eyes.

"The Manhattan Mangler. He was gone. That girl was his last victim, but then she opened that door in my closet and he came through it."

"How do you know it was him?" Sarah asked. "Did something happen?"

Neil nodded and started to cry. His shoulders shook with his quiet sobs. "I went to visit my mom, to stay a few days and get away from that damned apartment and the spirits. On the third day, I found her. He massacred her, and tore her to pieces. Mama was a good woman. Sure she wasn't perfect. She cheated on my Daddy but he was a drunk and didn't offer much. Mama went to church and she was kind."

Sarah put a hand to her mouth. She looked around for the people that worked there. They looked back and didn't seem overly concerned. Sarah reached out and touched the man's hand. "I'm really sorry for your loss," she said.

Neil nodded and wiped his nose on the back of his arm, sniffling as he did. "I left. I didn't want anyone to think it was me. I went back to my apartment," he cried. He stared intensely into Sarah's eyes. "I screamed to that ghost that she needed to close the door. I told that damned girl that she got my mother killed. I told her I hated her and she needed to just go on to Heaven or Hell or wherever she damned belonged. I screamed and broke things and nailed that godforsaken closet door shut. Someone called the authorities. They came and got me and brought me here and they never let me leave." He suddenly perked up. He grabbed Sarah's hand tightly enough to alarm her. "Hey. Maybe you can tell them, tell them I'm not crazy. You can tell them it's real and get them to let me out."

"Okay," Sarah said, even though she had no intention of doing so. It was clear to her that he needed to be here. "The closet is open, Neil. I've been living in two worlds too. I don't know what she's telling me either. Do you know anything that can help me?"

He got serious and quiet then, his stare intense. In a moment, Neil took his hand back and broke eye contact. "Yes," he whispered. "Close the door and get out, before he comes through again. He'll be coming, Sarah. Alice was right. You're in terrible danger. Get out." His voice rose as he repeated his warning. It continued to rise until it was a literal scream that made Sarah jump backward away from him. "Get out! Get out! Get out!"

Someone came over and stuck Neil with a needle and another person wheeled him away. Sarah watched in fear and horror, then raced to the exit.

39

As Sarah walked the streets of the city to clear her head, she passed the train hub and thought about how long it had been since she had last gone to see her parents. She would love to do that now, to get away from all of this and remember what normal life was like, but it wasn't an option. After what Neil had said about his mother, she couldn't take the chance. Was she really a danger to the people around her now? What did that mean for Felicia?

That train of thought brought her to Leremy, which in

turn reminded her that he said he was going to come to visit her today. Shit.

Sarah stopped suddenly and got hit in the shoulder by someone going in the other direction. Out of instinct she reached into her purse and felt for her wallet. She sighed as her hand rested on it. City life. Retrieving her phone, Sarah lifted her head and brought her attention back to her surroundings. Regina was on the other end of the crowded street, staring at her. She raised her hand like she was asking for help, reaching, begging. Sarah blinked and no sooner than she had seen the young woman, she was gone. She took a deep breath.

The brief encounter was enough to get Sarah thinking. If she was haunted and not her apartment, if the killer had never been caught, and Neil's story was true, what was to say that Mark's theory wasn't on point? Maybe the Mangler was jumping worlds and she was in very real danger. Just because that version of 1987 wasn't the actual 1987, didn't mean that things couldn't come out of it. She had a box of proof on that tucked under her bed. What if the killer was never alive and he was part of Regina's ghost world using closet doors to enter this world? That would explain how he got into apartments around the city in mid-day to kill those women. How would you catch a killer who didn't even really exist? I'm definitely going to end up back at Twin Spirits—sans the visitor badge.

Sarah sighed. She had more questions than answers, more theories than actual knowledge. She reminded herself that she had been about to check on Leremy when Regina distracted her. If the danger was, in fact, real and he was at her apartment, he could be in trouble. He had enough of his own demons to deal with without Sarah's or Regina's, though she supposed they were now one and the same.

Sarah decided to forgo the usual texting and just call her friend. After several rings, he answered, but he sounded like he was at the end of a wind tunnel. It sounded to her like he said, "It's not finished."

"What?"

"It's not finished. It's never finished."

"Can you hear me?" she asked. "Where are you right now? What time did you plan on coming by?"

The crackle of radio static sounded loud in her ear and Sarah cussed. Finally, she heard a voice clearly, but it wasn't Leremy's. "Help me," Regina said through the white noise. "Make it right. Please."

Before she could respond, the phone rang in her ear and Sarah yelped. How could it be ringing when I'm already on it? What the hell?

Sarah brought the phone away from her ear and looked at the screen. There was an incoming call from Leremy. Sarah shook her head in confusion and answered the phone, returning it to her ear. "Hello?"

"Hey, beautiful. Listen. I'm a total liar. I said I was gonna come visit you today but a cute boy is coming over to help me get over Collin and I so need that right now, so I'm going to have to give you a rain check. Cool?"

Sarah blinked and shook her head. "Yeah. No. That's fine. Busy day for me anyway. I'm not even home right now. What were you trying to tell me when I called you a minute ago?"

She listened to Leremy laugh. "Oh, you're on those good drugs. Maybe I should come by after all." He laughed again.

"What?"

"Honey, you never called me. I called you."

Sarah shook her head again. Her eyes roamed the crowded streets bouncing off the hundreds of people. "Yeah. Sorry. Look, I gotta go. Have fun today. Text me later and tell me all the juicy details. Well, maybe not all of them, like the PG-13 version."

Leremy's laugh sounded again. "Definitely all of them. You're gonna get full-scale erotica from me later. Talk to you then, girl."

Sarah hung up but she didn't put her phone away. She had to check. She had to know. She went to her recent call log and sure enough, there was no outgoing call to Leremy. She swallowed a lump in her throat and returned her phone to her purse. Her eyes moved over the surrounding people once more, searching for Regina but she wasn't there. It was amazing how you could be in a city this big, surrounded by this many people, and still somehow feel completely isolated and alone.

40

Sarah went to a local joint and had a couple of slices of specialty pizza, mainly because she needed to sit down. She also felt like she was in control when she was doing normal things, and taking care of herself. People in crisis forgot to eat and failed to sleep. That wasn't her. Sarah was her father's daughter. She was focused, motivated, goal-oriented, and took care of business. At least, that's what she told herself.

She was early again when she showed up at Mark's office. Another sign she was still in control. Jessica greeted her when she walked in. "Hey there! He's not here just yet but you can wait inside if you'd like or you can hang out here with me. No scones this time though."

"That's ok. I just ate," Sarah said, forcing a smile. "I'll just wait."

"Alrighty. He should be along any minute."

"Sounds good."

Sarah stepped into Mark's office. She considered exploring his desk, searching for a clue as to his connection, but she felt like the moment she began such a thing, he would show up and catch her in the act. Besides, what were the chances he would let people wait there if there was something incriminating to find? This wasn't the movies. Things weren't that easy. If they were, she would search the internet for Regina and a weird website would show up with her entire story and exactly what to do to help her all conveniently mapped out. Sarah laughed at the thought and then realized that Jessica could probably hear her and she blushed, glad no one was there to see it.

Sarah took out her phone to check the time and saw that the good doctor was about to be one minute late.

"Don't worry. I'm never late," a voice said from the doorway. She looked up to see Mark smiling at her. "I'm also never early. How are you?"

Sarah crumpled and smoothed her dress, waiting until he was seated across from her. "How did you touch the paper?" she said when he was.

"I'm sorry?"

"The paper I gave you, from 1987. None of the things that have come through can be held by other people unless they're in direct contact with me, but you picked that paper up and took it home with you."

Mark remained calm and stoic, though his patented smile faltered. "You tested this?"

"I did. Why you? Add that to how I even found out about you and it seems you're connected to all this somehow, doesn't it?"

Mark shook his head. He took his glasses off and placed them on his desk. Then he rubbed at his eyes and the bridge of his nose. "It is peculiar, Sarah, but I don't know any more than you do. I'm not the enemy. I'm trying to help you."

"Are you? I barely know you and my story is pretty mad, but you jumped right in Mark. I want answers. I've had enough of all the endless questions."

Mark nodded. "I can understand your frustration. I would feel the same way in your shoes. I can assure you though, that I don't know anything about Regina other than what I looked up and searched for. I was eleven in 1987, Sarah."

Sarah exhaled. Her fingers tightened on her dress. "Then why did a phantom breeze send me to you, Mark? Why can you hold the things given to me by a ghost? Is this The Sixth Sense? Are you dead?"

Mark chuckled and shook his head. He put his glasses back on. "I assure you, I am very much alive." Then he sighed and his smile fell away. "I'm not connected to Regina, Sarah. It's the building, Sunnycrest. It seems to be calling to me for some reason, but I don't know why. The residents keep coming to me. I feel like I treat that whole building. You're just the most recent addition. I'm not sure they came to hear of me in the same way, but I honestly wouldn't be surprised at this point. The whole thing creeps me out if I'm being honest. I avoid it. That's why when you invited me to come see for myself, I left the restaurant. I don't want to go there because I don't know what it wants from me and I'm afraid."

Sarah sighed. Her fingers released the fabric of her dress and she fell back into her seat. She saw the candor with which he spoke. She knew that he wasn't supposed to talk to her about other patients and probably just broke some cardinal psychiatrist rule. She believed his words were true.

"Did you treat Roger?"

"I can't talk about that, Sarah. Let's focus on you."

"You did. Did he ever talk about a ghost, a child named Alice?"

Mark didn't have to answer the question. She saw him startle, tense. He relaxed then and licked his lips like they were dry. "I can't talk about that with you, Sarah," he said when he regained composure.

Sarah nodded. "You don't have to. I went to visit Neil

at Twin Spirits. He knows Roger, and Alice told him I'm in danger."

Mark's mask fell away. He looked pale and genuinely afraid. Sarah watched as he opened his desk drawer and retrieved his liquor and a small glass. "I know this is unorthodox and unprofessional but do you want some? I have another glass."

Sarah snorted. "I'm good."

Mark nodded. He poured some of the brown liquor into his glass, swished it around, and then downed it. Then he rolled his shoulders and put the bottle and the glass back where he got them from. "Has Regina made any more contact with you?"

Sarah nodded. She started from the beginning and filled him in on everything. He listened intently, or at least gave that impression. When she finished, she expected him to go back to the bottle but he didn't.

"That's a lot," he said. "I'm sorry this is all happening to you. It sounds difficult and scary."

"Both. Yes. More than anything though, I just want to understand. I can't be like you, Mark. I can't just ignore it and avoid it. I don't even think that's an option anymore. It's me. I'm haunted. I can't run from it. I have to figure this damn thing out. I need to help her somehow."

Mark nodded. His thick fingers toyed with his bushy beard. "I hear you and understand your need to solve this problem, to remain in control, but according to you, two other ghosts have warned you away. Why listen to one ghost and not the others?"

Sarah huffed. It was a good question actually. She frowned. "I saw her, Mark. I saw what he did to her. It was overkill. I will never unsee it. Whoever he is, he must have had real hate in his heart. It would take hatred to do what he did to her."

"You also said that the man in the hall—Baggins was it?—said none of it was real. You were seeing what she wanted you to see."

Sarah growled, surprised by her own anger. "She really did die though, Mark. There is news to prove that. Don't victim shame."

Mark put up a defensive hand. "I'm not. I'm not. I'm just playing devil's advocate. You seem to have tunnel vision about this. I'm trying to make sure you see the whole picture, look at all the details."

Sarah sighed. "I understand. I just…she was so happy, in love, and it was ripped from her quite literally. Now she's still suffering, still in need of help. I can't turn my back on that. I can't."

Mark nodded. "I can see that. So let me ask you, what's the next step?"

Sarah's shoulders slumped. She said all too honestly, "I don't know."

SIX

When Worlds Collide

41

Sarah felt frustrated. This day had gone nothing like she'd hoped. First, the meeting with Neil gave her more questions than answers. Then whatever happened with Leremy happened, and finally, what she thought was a lead with the good doctor, Mark was just a dead end. Not to mention her run-in with Regina in the street. It was enough to drive her crazy, but she wouldn't let it. She couldn't. It wouldn't do her or anyone else any good if she did.

It was funny. Such a short time ago she was so lonely and wished she had some people to go through life with. Now she had them and they only made things more complicated, more dangerous. With more people, there was more at stake. The moment she remembered Leremy was going to visit, she felt such fear for him. She thought of him getting to her apartment when she wasn't there, of him finding someone other than her. For a brief instant, she saw him butchered on her bed, opened like a Thanksgiving turkey, the walls and ceiling painted with his life and dripping rhythmically to the floor, and she felt a surge of panic grip her heart. Sarah felt relief when she discovered he had other plans but the realization of the danger she had now put the people she cared about in, lingered.

It pushed Sarah to realize that she had to get to the bottom of all of this. Fast. She couldn't deal with the weight of the stress of knowing someone else could wind up hurt because of something she did or didn't do. Knowing that just made the fact that today was a failure that much more painful. I wish you didn't have to communicate in different ways. I wish you could just tell me what you need, Regina, tell me what I need to do.

Sarah found herself wanting a drink from Felicia's bottle, something to help her relax. The thought bothered her. It was uncharacteristic of her. She was willing to admit to people that she could use to lighten up a little, but desiring alcohol when she felt stressed was not a place she ever wanted to allow herself to get to. She thought of Mark and his hidden bottle.

Still, moments later when Felicia answered her knock with a smile bigger than usual, Sarah sighed and said, "Today sucks and I need a drink."

She expected Felicia to laugh and tell her they would have one together while she talked about why her day was so bad. Instead, Felicia cringed like she tasted something sour, and opened the door. She stepped aside as she did so.

Sarah saw the man standing behind Felicia in the living room and she paled. Her jaw dropped open. "Dad?"

42

Sarah could feel Felicia standing behind her as she faced the washer in the first-floor laundry room. She didn't know where else to go.

"I'm sorry," Felicia's voice said over her shoulder. "I didn't know you'd freak out."

Sarah just stared at the unmoving machines. "This place isn't safe," she said finally.

She could hear Felicia sigh. "I know, but he was already here, standing in the hall, looking for you. It's not like I called him and told him to come over. I just asked him if I could help him. After the other day with the dead dude on my couch, I wanted to know who he was. When he told me, I invited him in. Did I really do the wrong thing?"

Sarah turned around at last and frowned. "No. I don't know. I just don't want my parents anywhere near any of this. Seeing him there just scared the crap out of me."

Felicia nodded and stroked her face gently, brushing a loose strand of black hair from her eyes. "He's still outside. He wouldn't leave even after you yelled at him and told him to. He's waiting for you to calm down and talk to him."

Sarah took a deep breath. "Yeah. Okay."

Felicia rubbed Sarah's shoulders and stepped out of the way. Sarah kissed the side of her mouth and walked to the front door. It opened on its own before she got to the handle and she shivered. When she spied her father standing by the big tree, his fingers on the carving in its bark, she gasped quietly and then hurried his way.

He turned to her as she approached and his eyes were full of concern. "Gwaai Neoi…what has gotten into you? You have never spoken to me in that way."

Sarah glowered. "I know. I'm sorry. I just, I'm staying with my friend because my apartment has Mogwai, like Mother and Maa Maa always spoke of. I don't want you in there. I got scared."

Sarah's father smiled at her. "I didn't think you believed in any of that. I appreciate you caring for me in such an out-of-the-box way. Let's get dinner and talk. You can tell me all about it."

Sarah's eyes moved back to his fingers on the carved letters in the tree. She looked back at him and shook her head. "I'm not hungry. You should go. Please don't come back here. I will come to see you and Mom soon."

Her father studied her for a minute. His fingers left the carving to touch her face and she flinched as if it were contagious. He stared at her for a moment and then said, "Come back with me. Come home for a little."

Sarah cast her eyes downward. "I can't. I'll come soon. I promise. Dad, please."

"I don't like seeing you like this. How is school going?"

"It's good. I will be okay, Dad. Please."

Her father looked sullen again, and he touched her arm. Sarah didn't recoil this time because she knew he was watching for it and he wouldn't leave if he was frightened. Instead, she forced a smile. "You trust me, don't you?"

Her father looked into her eyes. "Do you know why I'm here? Your mother sent me. She's been having bad dreams. She said that Maa Maa came to her and said you were in trouble. You know she won't feel better until she knows you are safe. Do I go home and tell her that you have Mogwai and wouldn't come with me?"

Sarah sighed. Her shoulders slouched. "Don't. Please. I am haunted, Dad. I could bring bad things to the house and

I would never forgive myself. Just tell her I'm okay. Tell her I will come to visit soon."

"You want me to lie."

"Just once. Please. For her own good."

"I have not lied to your mother in forty years. I will not start now."

"You definitely placate her."

"I validate her because I love her. I don't have to share her beliefs to respect them. Now go say goodbye to your girlfriend because you are coming home."

"I can't. I'm sorry."

Sarah knew he would wait around for her all day, that he would sleep in the hall if he had to. She hurried back into the building. She could feel him coming behind her without needing to look back. Her father probably thought she had gone mad, but he didn't understand. How could he? Still, if what Neil said was even partially true, there was no way she could go home.

She went to the stairwell and hurried up, taking the steps two at a time. She could hear him calling her name behind her but she kept going. She knew one place that he couldn't follow her, the one place here that he couldn't go.

She ran to her apartment and opened the door. Then she looked back at her father, who had followed her. She saw the love and fear in his brown eyes. He was about to speak but she didn't give him the chance. Sarah opened the door to the closet and climbed in, closing it quickly before her. She opened it again and stepped out into Regina's bedroom on the eleventh floor, thirty-four years in the past. She was sure that her father ripped the closet open, prepared to demand she get out of there and speak with him. She was also sure that he found it empty.

"Sorry, Felicia," she said, knowing that he was probably headed over there, looking for answers.

43

Sarah rubbed at her face as she looked around the room. Her other hand was tugging at the fabric of her dress. Everything was such a mess. But what was she supposed to do? Her dad was the reason she was stubborn and goal-oriented like she was. He would have kept on if she didn't do something. Coming here was all she could think of. But now what?

Chewing her lip, Sarah ran a hand through her hair. If this wasn't real, then it didn't matter what she touched. There had to be a clue somewhere, right? There had to be something that told her what Regina needed in order to be set free. If she was already here, she might as well put the trip to use and explore.

Sarah went to the dresser and started opening drawer after drawer, rummaging through the contents, throwing things to the floor and nearby bed. "There's nothing here," she growled. "It's just clothes, ticket stubs, jewelry, nothing of use."

"If you're looking for money, she ain't got any," a voice said from behind her. Sarah jumped and failed to suppress the yelp. She turned around slowly and found a handsome young black man standing in the doorway. He looked a few years older than she knew Kevin was at the time.

"I-I'm not looking for money," Sarah stammered. "I'm not stealing anything."

"Then what are you doing in my brother's girlfriend's apartment, trashing the place?" the young man asked as he stepped further into the room.

"That's what I'm trying to figure out. I know this isn't the real past. This is Regina's world, right? But what is she trying to tell me? What does she need? Is she trapped here in Sunnycrest? How do I set her free? If you're here, it's because she wants you to be, right? She wanted me to meet you. Why? Can you help me help her?"

The young man smiled and winked. Then he turned and walked out of the room.

Sarah's eyes widened. She stumbled over the mess

she created to follow him. "What was that?" she asked. "You know something and you're not going to tell me? If you're really Kevin's brother, why wouldn't you want me to know what I could do to help her?"

The young man sat on the couch and put his feet up on the coffee table. He picked up a black box with a joystick and a single red button and he turned his attention to the TV.

Sarah glanced over at it and saw a pixelated cowboy on a pixelated horse attempting to lasso a pixelated cow to a series of boops and beeps. She sighed and went to stand in front of the screen. "Answer me."

The boy sighed and put down his controller. "I'm not really Kevin's brother. I just have to be here because Kevin's brother was here when this day happened. This world may not be real but it's a perfect recreation. Reggie and Kev will be back here with pizza in about an hour if you want to wait around. You play Pong?"

"I don't even know what that is," Sarah admitted. She walked over and sat on the couch beside him. "I could wait for them to return, but Regina is already here in a way, isn't she? I mean, if you're a creation of hers, you're part her, right? You know what she knows?"

The young man sighed and picked up his joystick, focusing his attention on the TV once more. "I just think you're not going to like the answer and maybe it would be better if you actually heard it from her."

Sarah took his hand and leaned in close, looking into his face. "Please. I need to know. Just tell me."

His head rolled over to look at her and he rolled his eyes with a sigh. "Fine. If you want to set her free, you can. In order for her soul to move on, she needs to find a replacement. Is that you?"

Sarah's eyes widened. She backed away from him and then jumped from the couch, shaking her head. She knew she couldn't go back yet because her father would still be there, waiting for her to return. At the same time, she wanted nothing more than to get out of there after hearing those words.

Sarah knew she could leave through Kevin's apartment too. That could work because Kevin and Regina were both on their way here according to Regina's brother. She ran to the door and tugged it open. She looked back at the young man on the couch but he didn't return the gesture. His eyes remained on the TV, and after a moment Sarah left the chorus of beeps and boops to slip out the open door into the hall, gently closing it behind her.

44

Sarah hurried to the elevator and pressed "Down". If she didn't want to replace Regina in this world, was there no other way to break the curse? If I do replace her, does that mean I have to suffer through what happened to her? Would it repeat? Maybe not. Regina seems to have control here. It's a dedicated replica but not chronological because Sarah had already seen her death. That suggested she could do whatever she wanted. Where the hell is this elevator?

"It's not working here. She wants to delay you." Sarah shivered and looked at who was speaking to her. It wasn't until she laid eyes on the girl that she jumped. She shook her head. "Tina? You can't be here. It's 1987."

"Is it?"

Sarah stared at the other girl for a moment. "Well, even if it's not the real past, it's a replica. That would suggest that you were here then, but you can't have been because you're younger than me. Do you have a gateway too? A door in your closet?"

Tina laughed. "No. Nothing like that. Just the me you know and this version of me, eternally younger than you."

Sarah started. "No. That's not possible either. This is just Regina messing with me for some reason. I've seen you working the produce stand with your grandfather. You're very much alive in 2021."

Tina nodded. "Yup. Some folks see me and others think my grandfather is talking to himself and needs to retire. He's almost ninety. Soon he will be with me and that stand he loves so much will just fade into nothing because my parents want no part of it. They've hated it since I died during the robbery all those years ago. Grandpa was going to shut it down too but he saw that I was still showing up for work so he kept it open. Shows up every day even though it's so difficult for him. He does it all for me."

Sarah was stunned. She felt like her brain was going to explode. She was thinking about the times she'd seen Tina Weathers at her grandfather's stand. She talked and laughed, but Sarah couldn't remember her ever actually picking up the produce or helping a customer. Could it be true? Could Tina be a ghost?

"No. It wasn't 1987 when I died, but the dead can walk on each other's roads, Sarah. I was shot in 1999. You better hurry. You're running out of time if you're trying to get away. Oh and Sarah, congratulations on finally getting with Felicia."

Sarah blinked several times as she worked to wrap her brain around everything. "Yeah. Thanks. I'm pretty sure that when my father gets through with her she's not going to want me anymore though."

"When Regina gets through with you, it won't matter. Go."

The elevator sounded a Ding! The doors began to open. Sarah could hear Regina and Kevin talking from the other side of the open doors. "I thought you said it wasn't working," Sarah said as she ran for the stairwell.

"It's her world," Tina said from behind her. Sarah pulled the door open and ran down the stairs as fast as her legs would carry her.

45

Sarah didn't go all the way down to the second floor. She was afraid they would expect her to do just that and take the elevator to beat her there. Was all of this just to earn Sarah's trust, to get her to come here?

Do I have a choice in replacing her, or can she just make it happen if she catches me? I wish someone would tell me the rules. Kevin's brother was right—I didn't like his answer. It was shit, quite honestly. Sarah slipped out on the seventh floor. She paced the hall wondering what to do. It's her world. If she wanted to, couldn't she just appear here in front of me? Maybe she can't. Maybe there are limitations. What is happening with my dad right now? Please don't hate me, Dad.

The bald man she'd encountered here that had creeped her out, was standing at the other end of the hall just staring at her, a smile spread across his thin lips. Something was wrong with him. Was he the Mangler? He adjusted his thick plastic glasses.

"What do you want?" she asked. What was he even doing on this floor? She could hear Tina in her mind, her voice saying, It's her world. But why would Regina send this creep after her? Did Sarah have to die in order to replace her? Please don't let that be the way this works. Would anyone even know what happened to me? Would I just be gone?

The strange man's smile widened, and he started toward her. "You look delicious," he said, his hunger honest. She could hear it in his tone, dripping from his words and it made her sick. Sarah looked at the door to the stairwell. It was between her and him. Could she make it there before he did? She didn't trust the elevator to open for her.

"I remember how good you smell from the last time we met," he said with a moan as he continued toward her. He didn't seem like the Mangler to Sarah. The Mangler had rage and hate that fueled his kills. This guy was something different, another kind of evil. She suddenly remembered something else Tina had said: "The dead can walk each other's roads, Sarah."

The bald man was licking his lips now and doing an old-fashioned two step dance on his way to her. Regina may have nothing to do with this guy. He might have just invited himself to the party. She had to get away from him. Then she could figure out the rest.

Sarah ran for the stairwell door, her heart pounding and limbs shaking as she had to run toward the man to get to it. His hungry eyes watched her, and he moved quicker than she would have imagined he could, darting at an angle to intercept her. Sarah screamed and she reached for the door, her hand grasping the handle. She yanked the door open and slipped through it. The bald man hit the other side of the door with a bang as it fell closed.

Sarah jumped.

She felt like electricity ran through her whole body, her nerves tingling. Then she turned and bounded down the steps. She heard the door bang open behind her and the sound of a man whistling. She pushed herself harder, jumping when she neared the bottom of the landing. She could hear the footsteps behind her and the whistling that went in perfect time with them. Sarah didn't need to know who this guy was or how he got to be here in order to know his intentions.

She reached the second floor and banged her way through the door. She stumbled and almost fell, waving her arms. The whistling sounded behind her. Sarah ran to what in thirty-four years would be her own door. It's my door now, she thought. This isn't really the past and it exists simultaneously within the same walls, two worlds. One of the living and one of the dead.

None of that mattered now. She turned the knob and found the door was locked. Of course, it was. Kevin was out with Regina. This city wasn't safe enough to leave your door unlocked when you weren't home. The whistling got louder. Sarah knew she was running out of time.

She was about to scream when there was a click and the door opened inward without anyone behind it. "I need you," a voice said from behind her and in front of her all at once. It sounded like it was carried on the wind, but there was no wind. "Go!"

Sarah didn't need to be told twice. Her father might have still been waiting for her on the other side of that door, but if he was, it was time for her to face the music. That music would be far better than the whistling that was closing in on her by the moment.

She ran to the closet and ripped the door open. She fell trying to climb in as it was full of stuff. Shoes and folders of papers fell out onto the floor. She slipped on them—the whistling insanely close, and suddenly stopped. Sarah was still. She was trembling and hoped it wasn't noisy. She knew the bald man was in the room with her. His intentions alone, hanging in the air as they were, made her want to shower.

She moved slowly, staying low, and tried to pull herself into the closet. When she looked up, he was there, staring at her and licking his lips. Sarah gasped. She reached up, grabbed the doorknob, and pulled the door shut with a Bang!

46

Sarah told herself that she had to reopen the door and get out before he opened it from his end and got in to join her in the dark of the closet. She could imagine him stepping in, curling up next to her, sniffing her hair, his stale breath on her face, the plastic of his glasses pushing against her face. Even though it was her imagination, she could almost smell his sweat, taste his breath and feel the wetness of his saliva on her cheek as he licked her face in the dark.

Sarah lunged for the knob and stopped with her hand on it. She felt another hand on her shoulder and it made her freeze. She bit back her gasp, slowly turned her head, and saw Regina's beautiful face with a pleading gaze, so close to her own. "I need your help," she said, her words sounding like they were spoken by a hundred overlapping voices.

"I know," Sarah said back quietly. She trembled and her hand squeezed the knob. "But I can't replace you. I'm sorry."

Sarah twisted the knob and pushed the door open, the light of the present day penetrating the darkness of the closet's interior. Behind her, a voice said, "You can. You have to."

Sarah all but fell out of the closet. She was lying there on quivering limbs and she felt the presence of someone else in the room. She expected to find her father there, angry after waiting for her for so long. She lifted her head and looked up to find Leremy bent over, hands on thighs, looking down at her with a smile.

"There you are," he said. "I've been looking all over. I didn't think you were still in the closet. You should have told me that. The closet wouldn't even have me. My father will attest to that. It spit me out when I was seven and discovered my mother's closet. She was a woman that always understood fashion. She has a color-coordinated collection of boas. I mean come on. My little ass used to walk the bathroom rug pretending it was the red carpet and I was Meryl Streep."

The joke didn't even reach Sarah. She was too frightened to see him there and think of the ramifications of that.

"What are you doing here?" she snapped in a panic.

"Wow. Fine, bitch," Leremy said with a laugh. "I thought you'd be happy to see my beautiful face, but whatever."

Sarah sighed. She got to her feet and closed the closet door in a hurry, looking at it nervously. She shook off a chill that ran a race over her bones. "I just meant, I thought you had a date. That's what you said right?"

"I did. A super hot guy that I met after a drag show the other night. His name is Ben. He wanted to meet in public the first time so we did. Then we agreed to his place over mine which turned out to be fucking Sunnycrest, and of course that brought up all kinds of feelings about Collin and I couldn't do anything. I couldn't even get my mini-me to respond, Sarah, so I apologized to sexy Ben and decided to come to find you, except I couldn't find you because you were hiding in your closet for some damn reason. Would you like to explain that now?"

"I'm sorry," Sarah sighed. "I'm sorry your date didn't work out and I'm sorry your friend is a weirdo—that friend being me. Let's talk, but not here, anywhere but here."

"How about across the hall where your dad has Felicia hostage? He is 'old guy hot' by the way."

"What? No."

"Well, of course, you don't think so. He's your dad. That would be weird."

"No. What? No. I mean I don't want to see him."

They opened the door, prepared to step into the hall, and came face-to-face with Sarah's father. "See who?" he asked.

"Too late," Leremy said.

Sarah huffed. "Dad, you have to believe me. I can't go home, not yet."

"I'm going to get better acquainted with your girlfriend," Leremy said. He turned sideways and squeezed past her father. Sarah huffed again.

"Show me," her father said.

Sarah shook her head adamantly. "No. It's too dangerous. Please, Dad, just trust me."

"How can I? Look at how you're behaving. Show me and I will trust you and leave."

Sarah looked back at the closet. Could she really bring her father into Regina's ghost world? If she didn't give him something, he wasn't going to leave though. An idea occurred to her. "Follow me," she said, leading him to her bedroom.

Sarah dug the box of things from Regina out from under her bed. She handed him the newspaper but kept a hand on it. "Look at it."

Her father frowned. "This is from your Mogwai?"

Sarah nodded. She let go of the paper and it fell through his solid hand onto the ground at his feet. "See?"

"You are leaving here and coming home right now."

Sarah shook her head and backed away from him. "It

will follow me, Dad. I can't escape it like that. I will just bring it with me to you and Mom."

"Your mother may know how to help."

Sarah shook her head again. "I can't. I won't."

Her father stood there silently looking into her eyes before he finally released a sigh of his own and turned toward the door. "If anything happens to you, your mother will never forgive me. I will never forgive myself."

Sarah nodded. "I'll be okay. I just need time."

Her father looked at her, his eyes swirling with love and worry. He nodded and walked out. Sarah's shoulders fell, and the weight of worry lifted from them. She stepped into the hall and watched her father get into the elevator. He looked back at her again, fear adding creases to his face. When the elevator doors closed, she turned and wound up face to face with Leremy again. Sarah yelped and jumped.

"Man, she is pissed. You are going to have to deal with that. I'll hang with you another time," he said.

Sarah frowned and looked past him to Felicia's door. "Shit," she said.

"Seriously. You know what they say, redheads are fiery. Like a dragon. Good luck with that."

Sarah felt the weight return to her shoulders. She hugged her friend. He hugged her back. Then she felt him stiffen. Sarah released him and looked at him with concern. He was staring down the hall. She looked that way and saw the same blond man she had spied through her doorway the other night. She looked back at Leremy and he said, "Collin?"

The man turned and ran for the stairwell. "What the hell? Why are you running?" Leremy called after him. Then he left Sarah and took off running as well. Sarah cussed under her breath. She looked at Felicia's closed door, and then over at Leremy running away, then back at Felicia's door.

Sarah growled under her breath, turned, and ran after Leremy. She'll understand. I hope. Please let her understand.

47

Sarah ran into the stairwell. She couldn't see either man but she heard their pounding footsteps racing upward. Sarah took a deep breath and started after them. "Leremy, wait!" she called.

He didn't.

She ran as fast as she could. If the blond man really was Collin, something about him gave her the creeps. Leremy chasing him to the top of the building left her with an uneasy feeling. Where was Collin leading him? Why did he run? Why did he just stare at her the other day? Did anything in this building make a lick of sense? No, Sarah. The answer would be no, she said to herself.

The further she went up the stairs, the further up she heard the pounding feet of those she followed. "Stop!" she yelled to them, but she knew they weren't going to listen. Still, she tried again. "Stop!"

Sarah heard a door slam above her and she pushed herself harder. When she got to the landing, she found she had reached the top. She stood before the door to the thirteenth and final floor of Sunnycrest Apartments. Sarah had never come up here. She had never seen anyone come down from here either, at least not that she was aware of. She knew some people on eleven and twelve, but not thirteen. As far as she knew, this whole floor was vacant and stayed that way.

Sarah had a bad feeling. She tried to take a deep breath but couldn't. There was a lump lodged in her throat. She tried to swallow it but it wouldn't go away. Sarah bit her lip. She looked over her shoulder and peered down the long stairwell behind her. She didn't know what she thought would be on the thirteenth floor that would be more frightening than what she had already run into down on floor two, but she couldn't shake the feeling. You're being ridiculous. Just go. Make sure your friend is okay. Come on, Sarah. Jeez.

Finally managing to swallow the lump in her throat, Sarah took that much-needed deep breath and nodded to herself, agreeing with her inner voice at least enough to urge herself to move. She reached forward and opened the door, albeit slowly. Then she stuck her head through first and said quietly, "Leremy?"

When no answer came, Sarah sucked in a breath and stepped over the threshold, the door easing shut behind her with a dull click. Even as quiet as it was, in the ultimate silence of the moment, the sound of the sealing door made her jump.

Still, she pressed on.

48

Sarah stepped into the hallway of floor thirteen. "Hello?" she said. Then she repeated it a little louder. She cleared her throat and tried again. "Leremy," she whispered loudly.

Sarah still didn't get an answer, but she heard voices from the other end of the hall. She couldn't hear what they were saying but she was sure one of them was Leremy. Sarah walked briskly but quietly toward the sound, stepping carefully like she was afraid of disturbing someone. Who? The building? As she got closer, Sarah heard the words more clearly.

"What are you doing, Collin? Tell me what the hell is

going on? Why did you run all the way up here?"

"Buildings stopped making thirteenth floors out of fear but they were foolish. Thirteens were made as a ward to protect against evil. This is the safest place in the building. Nothing can hurt you up here."

"You've already hurt me plenty. I don't think what floor you're on will make a difference."

Sarah frowned. She suddenly felt like she was intruding on a private moment. She didn't want to interrupt Leremy in finally finding the closure he so desperately needed. She bit her lip, then stopped where she was and leaned against the wall. Sarah didn't want to leave, just in case her gut was right and her friend was in trouble, but she didn't want to go further and intrude either, so she settled on staying where she was, chewing on her knuckle.

"This is important. Please listen," Collin said.

"I'm listening," Leremy answered.

"Your friend in Apartment 8, she's in trouble. The gateway there hides some very bad things, Lerr. You have to get her away from there, away from here, from all of it."

Sarah paled. Her mouth fell open and she pressed harder against the wall. Leremy scoffed and snorted. "You're worried about my friend? You left me and ghosted me. You broke my heart, do you understand that? I've been broken. Why don't you worry about that? Explain yourself."

"I didn't mean to hurt you, Leremy. It's the last thing

I wanted."

"Then why did you?"

"Because someone hurt me."

Leremy blew a raspberry. "Oh please. We've all been hurt. That's a sorry excuse. You could have at least told me."

"That's not what I mean."

"I'm listening."

Collin sighed. Did Sarah just see him flicker? What was going on? Oh no, Collin. Collin belongs to Sunnycrest. Oh, Leremy. Oh no.

"There was a guy that lived in Apartment 8 before your friend. He was weird, fascinating, and yes, attractive. He told me that there was a gateway to the eighties in his place and offered to show it to me. I told myself that it didn't count as cheating on you if I didn't have sex with him. It was all in good fun. Good, harmless fun."

"Finally, the truth comes out," Leremy said bitterly.

"Just listen."

"I am."

Sarah was too. It felt wrong, but she couldn't possibly walk away now.

"It was wrong and I wish I could take it back, Lerr, but I went with him. He was right. He did have a gateway to the eighties, but it wasn't fun that was waiting for us there. It was something terrible, something vicious, and he knew. He took me there, knowing what we were walking into. He fed me to that monster and kept a hand on me as I was butchered so I would remain in that world long enough to die. I don't think he understood how Sunnycrest worked. I don't think he realized that he would see me again. The first time he did, when I asked him why, he just ran out of the building. He left all of his things and ran and never returned." Collin's image twisted and contorted and Sarah couldn't help but think he was remembering the pain of his murder.

Leremy slid to his knees and hung his head. Sarah decided that was the right time to act. She ran up behind him and wrapped her arms around him. "I'm here," she said. "Okay? I'm here honey. I'm here."

"You need to not be," Collin said to her. "Leave this place and take him with you. Please. Keep him safe. And stay away from that closet. It doesn't just let you in. It lets things out."

Leremy shook his head. With Sarah's help, he got to his feet. "You're mad," he said. "You want me to leave? If I live here, I can still see and talk to you. We can still be together."

"It's not safe," Collin told him.

"It is up here. That's what you said. I'll tell them I want one of these apartments. I'll insist upon it. I won't let you go again."

Just then, Sarah watched as Collin faded into nothing. Leremy fell back to his knees in her arms. He was screaming, tears pouring from his eyes. She held him more tightly. She couldn't help but wonder if maybe Collin was right. Maybe there was no answer but to run, to get far enough away from the building to break whatever bond tied her to it. Maybe it was time to go see her parents, after all. Sarah knew the man Collin was talking about. He was the third one in her apartment, Fred. He disappeared and left his belongings. He made it out though, didn't he? If he could escape then she could too, right?

Maybe he was still out there somewhere and she could speak to him. If he was, then he had the answers. He knew who the Mangler was. He fed Collin to that monster. Why? What did he stand to gain from it? Maybe Fred was the Mangler. Could Mark's theory be spot on? Maybe he was living in the now and killing in the past. No. That world wasn't real, right? Sarah didn't know what was real anymore. People were lying and hiding things and she couldn't tell who or what. Maybe her dad was right and her Mom would be able to help.

"Come on," she said, trying to pull Leremy up to his feet. He slapped her arm away and dropped back to the ground. Sarah frowned. She sat down next to him. They would go together when he was ready. Then she would face the music with Felicia. Then, with any amount of luck, all three of them would get the hell out of Sunnycrest. She just hoped that whatever was happening here was willing to let them go.

"It's not," a voice whispered into her ear from nowhere. Sarah shivered. It felt even more evasive as she hadn't spoken out loud. Her eyes moved around the seemingly empty hallway to see who was there. She saw no one. Even Collin was gone. From what she could see, she and Leremy were the only people on the thirteenth floor, but Sarah knew better. This was Sunnycrest, after all. In her mind, she heard Regina from the closet: "I need you."

Sarah frowned, then pulled Leremy to her and held him tightly. He sobbed into her bosom. "I wished it upon him." He shook through his tears. "When we were talking the other day, I wished it upon him."

"You didn't mean it," Sarah said, petting his head. "He knows you didn't mean it."

Sarah could feel a thankful hand grasp her shoulder, but when she looked, nothing was there. She reached over and patted the unseen hand anyway, a wordless, You're welcome.

SEVEN

One is the Loneliest Number

49

Leremy hadn't been exaggerating. Felicia was really mad. "You left me here with your angry, confused father, while you hid in another dimension that none of us could fucking go to, and now you want me to just bail on everything and leave with you?"

Sarah huffed. "Dad wouldn't have gone to you if you didn't introduce yourself and let him in your apartment. I didn't do that."

"Shit."

Sarah wasn't clear on what that shit meant. Was it

Shit, this is ridiculous, or Shit, she's right? "I'm sorry. I was just so scared for him and I knew he wouldn't give up. It's not in him to give up."

"He still didn't!" Felicia bellowed.

"I know. I'm sorry, but I think you could be in danger because of me and I don't want anything to happen to you. Please. Hate me on the road."

"No. Maybe we can meet up later, but for now, I need some time."

Sarah huffed and stepped back so Felicia could close the door. She turned then and surveyed the hall. It was weirdly quiet. Leremy was still up on the thirteenth floor. He refused to come down. She didn't know if he ever would. Now Felicia was furious and wanted time away from her. In a single day, the two people she had finally acquired were both gone. Had she burned the bridge with Mark too? Maybe she should call him.

Sarah sighed loudly. She hated the idea but if she was going to leave she needed to go into her own apartment long enough to pack. She realized then that her toothbrush was still at Felicia's. She looked at the closed door and frowned. I'll buy a new one.

Going into her place, she opened her bedroom closet and grabbed a small suitcase, stuffing it with clothes. She paused, her hand hovering over a particular hanger. There was a dress hanging there, one that didn't belong to her. She recognized it and it almost stopped her heart. It was the one Regina was wearing when she died. Sarah touched the fabric of it, lifting it to inspect it further. It was still ripped and torn, cut and frayed, in so many different places.

"You didn't give it to me from before you died? You gave it to me afterwards. Why?"

Of course, there was no answer, at least not in words. She just heard the click and squeak of the living room closet door popping open. An invitation.

Sarah fought against the chill that raced over her bones. "No," she said. "I'm leaving. I'm sorry. I hope you find peace."

She stuffed more clothes in her bag and grabbed what she needed for her classes, packing it, as well. The closet door slammed shut and she jumped, crying out. Sarah held a hand over her heart as she worked to catch her breath.

Click. Squeeeeeeee....

The closet door came open again.

Sarah shook her head. She left the bedroom and headed for the apartment door. She couldn't resist the urge though, and looked back at the closet. It seemed to feel her looking, and it opened wider.

Come, it said to her.

"No." Sarah didn't even close the door when she left. She just rushed out. Then she reached the stairwell door and thought about Collin. She closed her eyes and cussed. What if someone else went in while she was gone and got hurt? They couldn't, could they? Fred had to hold onto Collin like she had to hold Felicia. Still, her heart wouldn't let her take the chance. Sarah hurried back and closed the apartment door, locking it and checking to make sure it was secure.

Then she turned back toward the stairs and jumped when an old woman stood rigidly before her. "Regina is very troubled," the old lady said to her. "But running and hiding isn't the answer. She knows that better than anyone."

Sarah opened her mouth to respond only to find herself alone in the hallway. "Of course," she growled. Then she stormed into the stairwell, pounded her way down the steps, and burst out onto the first floor. Tina was at the mailboxes.

"Hey neighbor," she said with a wave and a smile.

Sarah just rolled her eyes and grunted. Then she stomped her way out of the building. When she got outside, she had barely reached the big tree when she had the feeling of being watched. Sarah turned and looked at Sunnycrest looming over her. In a window, high up on the eleventh floor, Regina was staring out at her, palms on the glass. Sarah broke away, turned, and hurried toward the street as fast as her legs would allow.

50

Sarah felt guilty running away, knowing that Leremy and Felicia were still in that building. She felt like she was running away from them. Due to her RSD, she always felt like she was ruining relationships, always feeling like everyone secretly hated her, even when they were nice. It was a way of rationalizing running away from people, but the problem was, it left her hating herself for doing it. She couldn't run from that.

Sarah reached the train station before she even made a full decision on where she was going. She stopped and looked at the mob of people, all packed in tight, lying and sitting on the floor as they waited for their train, others rushing in every direction. There was a strange comfort in the chaos of the city. It was consistent. You could count on it.

Today, it made her uneasy. She was expecting to see Regina among the crowd, blocking her path and working to coax her into going back home, opening the door to a closet that wasn't attached to anything.

Sarah looked at the list of trains and their times and destinations as well as which ones were on which lines, and she felt overwhelmed. She had done this plenty of times before but not when feeling panicked and afraid. All of the lines may have well said blah blah blah. She felt a headache coming on and put her hand to it. Someone asked if she was alright and Sarah smiled and waved.

When they left, Sarah sighed and took out her phone. She placed a call to Mark and waited, hoping he would answer and not Jessica. Instead, no one answered. Sarah huffed and waited for the beep to leave a message. "Mark, hi. This is Sarah. If you get a chance, I need you to see if you can find out about someone for me. You seem to have a knack for that kind of thing, better than me at least. The third guy in Apartment 8 was a dude named Fred. It's really important I speak to him, but he might be dangerous so be careful if you find him. Jessica, if you're the one hearing this then please just—"

The ending beep sounded and cut her off. Sarah groaned. She just hoped the message went through. Now what? she asked herself.

Sarah called her father. She knew her mother would be too frantic. He answered, "You've come to your senses. You're coming home."

"Maybe. Sort of," she said, chewing on her lip, her eyes still roaming the passing crowd in search of someone who shouldn't be there. For a moment she thought she saw the bald man from 1987 staring back at her, but he was part of the past, wasn't he? Could he be from the present, someone who could travel back like she could?

"Sarah?"

She shook her head. "Yeah. Sorry. Would you help me get a hotel so I can get away from Sunnycrest, but not come home to your house? Call it a compromise."

"Sure. Yes. Of course. Just come home," her father said, his voice laced with worry.

"Thanks, Dad."

"There's a train heading this way in an hour. I'll pick you up when it gets here."

"Thanks for that too," Sarah said. "For everything, always. I love you."

"I love you too. See you soon."

When Sarah's dad hung up, she followed suit and pocketed her phone. When she looked up, the bald man was standing a few yards away, wearing the same sinister smile she had gotten to know. Sarah gasped and his smile widened. He adjusted his glasses, his grin never faltering.

Sarah moved through the crowd. She was trying to find the train her father had mentioned. She could buy a ticket on board for extra money that she didn't care to spend at this point. Sarah kept looking over her shoulder but she didn't have to. She could feel the man's stare. She knew he was still with her, still following. She felt something touch her arm and she jumped, looking all around. It must have been a bug or something because she was alone.

No. Not alone. She looked back and the bald man gave another wave and matching smile. Sarah took her phone out and dialed Felicia. Please pick up. Please pick up.

"What?"

"Oh Thank God. Listen. I know you're mad, but there was a bald guy in Regina's world, in 1987. He was in Apartment 55."

"I'm not doing this anymore."

"Please. Just listen. He's in the here and now, following me at the train station. Please talk to Gary, find out who he was, or is, or I don't know. Call me back. Please."

Sarah listened as Felicia sighed. "So now you're okay with me manipulating Gary when it's for something you need?"

"I didn't say to sleep with him."

"Maybe I will."

Sarah didn't say anything. She knew Felicia was just

looking for an argument because her feelings were hurt. That much was, in fact, Sarah's fault. She just said, "Call me back," and hung up. When she looked over her shoulder, the man was right behind her. Her heart jumped. Adrenaline ran through her and made her skin tingle.

"Where are you going?" he asked. "Let's talk, and get to know each other better."

Sarah turned and ran before he could say another word.

51

Sarah found her train and ran down the steps as fast as she could. She hurried to the closed doors of the nearest train car and tapped her foot, staring over her shoulder for the man that was following her until the doors finally slid open. Then she rushed inside and found a seat. She sat there in silence, her heart pounding. Only when the doors slid shut and the train started moving did she find the ability to breathe again. That is, until the bald man walked up the aisle and sat across from her, staring at her with that unnerving smile of his. She almost screamed but she caught it, not wanting him to have the satisfaction, the power that her fear would bring him.

Sarah was about to ask him what he wanted and why he was following her when her phone rang in her pocket. She reached down and dug it out of her pants without taking her eyes off the eerily smiling man seated across from her. Ever so slowly, she lifted the phone to her ear. "Hello?"

"It's me," Felicia said into her ear. "Gary wasn't home so I let myself in."

"You let yourself in," Sarah said, staring at the man staring at her.

"Yeah. I have a key. One of the perks of our deal. That guy is involved in some shady stuff, Sarah. He doesn't want anyone to know and I made sure to know. Anyway, he had his computer with him so I'm having to do this the old-fashioned way and go through the old files. You owe me."

"I do." Sarah wasn't sure if the man across from her was listening but she tried to keep her responses to a minimum just in case.

"1987, found it. Okay, fifty-five…fifty-five. Here it is…" Sarah stared at the bald man's grinning face as she listened to what Felicia had to say. "Okay, yeah, this has got to be him. He does look skeezy. His name is Milton Waters. Forty-five. Lived by himself. Oh wow, according to this file, apparently old Agatha evicted our guy Milton after he tried to force himself on Regina. That's all I've got."

"Okay. Thank you and I'm sorry again."

"What are you doing?" That was Gary's voice. Sarah listened with worry as he and Felicia started to argue. Then Felicia hung up and there was just silence. Shit.

Sarah looked at the man across from her. It made sense to her why Regina would include Milton in her recreation of that world, but what she didn't understand is what he was doing here. He wasn't the him from today because he would have to be almost eighty and he certainly wasn't. Forty-five was a much closer fit. Also, the current day him wouldn't know Sarah. So the real question was, "What are you doing out of Sunnycrest? Out of the world Regina made for you?"

Milton showed some teeth. He leaned forward across the aisle, pushing his face closer to hers. "You think you know Regina. You know nothing. Regina didn't make my world. She made her own. I just walk in it."

He reached a hand over and traced lazy circles on her knee with the tip of his index finger. Sarah trembled. She felt instantly nauseous and she wanted to scream but she bit it back. "So, you're dead too."

"As a doornail," he said, that hand moving around her knee to the inside of her thigh.

Sarah's eyes fell, to stare at his hand for a moment. She clamped her legs shut tight before it could climb any further.

He laughed at that, a delighted chuckle. "I picked the wrong girl one day. Bitch stabbed me right in the neck, but I guess the point is, there was no Mr. Scrooge lesson, deary. I am in death what I was in life."

Milton tried to force his hand up further, to push her legs open, and Sarah resisted him. Then he shimmered, faded away, and came back. His smile faltered but he found it again. "Why can't we be friends?" he asked her. Sarah watched nervously, unable to find her voice, as he shimmered again, blinked out for longer, and then returned. "Come find me when you come home. I promise to make you scream."

A chill ran through Sarah and she looked down at his hand, the fingers trying to worm their way up to her most private space. Then the hand shimmered and blinked out. This time it didn't return.

Raising her gaze from her lap and staring at the empty seat across from her, she waited for Milton to return once more. It stayed empty, but she couldn't shake the unease that he'd left her with, or the dampness of his wormy fingers on her skin. Her own hands wiped at her knee and legs. She wanted to shower. Apparently, Sunnycrest had many demons, and there was a limit to how far those demons could go from the building. They could venture out, fairly far even, but there was a limit, thank God.

This was what Collin was trying to tell her. She would be safe if she got far enough away. Those were the words he used, Far enough. Then she remembered the voice that whispered into her ear that Sunnycrest wouldn't let her go. Was that the truth or another lie, another manipulation? Sarah didn't know. All she knew was that she wanted to go home. She wiped at her leg again.

52

Even though Milton was long gone, Sarah couldn't get off the train fast enough when it reached her stop. She saw her father. He was there waiting, watching the cars and looking to see which one she was going to step out of. Sarah spotted him before he saw her and she ran in his direction. He caught her in his arms and she hugged him tight. He wrapped her up like a blanket and took a deep breath.

"It's going to be okay," he told her.

Sarah didn't believe that, but she was still glad to hear it, especially from him. "I think you were right. It'll be okay if

I come home," she said. Home is far enough.

Her father looked at her knowingly and said, "Your mother has made dinner for you. The table is already set."

Sarah couldn't help but laugh. When they pulled up at the house it was like a sigh of relief. She didn't want to come here but after everything, it felt so good to be home. To be safe.

"I want to shower first," she said, looking at the dinner table. The food smelled wonderful. Unlike Felicia, Sarah was not a cook. Her mother simply nodded, and Sarah bounded up the steps to the bathroom. Sarah turned the water on and in moments the room filled with steam. She couldn't wait to wash away Milton's icy touch, to cleanse herself of everything that had happened in the past few days. It wasn't until she was in the tub, the hot water beating down on her naked form, that her mood changed. She missed Felicia and worried for her after the way that phone call ended. Sarah hoped she didn't put the other woman in any more danger than she already had. I didn't tell her to break into someone's apartment though. I had no idea she was going to do that.

Sarah worried for Leremy too. She felt like a terrible friend for abandoning him. He was so broken. Maybe now that they were alone Collin would help him through it, but something in her gut made her think he was going to hate her. She told herself it was in her head. It was her RSD. Even if it was, it didn't make her feel any better.

A pang of guilt struck her for how she ran from Regina, as well. At the end of the day, Regina was a victim who just wanted to go home. She was another girl—a girl like Sarah—who was scared and alone, and desperate. Sarah couldn't imagine what it would be like to be in Regina's position. *Well, I can, but I don't want to.* She heard Kevin's little brother again: "She needs someone to replace her. Is that you?"

Sarah stood in the hot water, scrubbing her skin red and thinking about the dead girl. Regina needed help but could Sarah really give it to her? Not if that meant replacing her, living in some limbo world within the brick-and-mortar of Sunnycrest. She couldn't willingly do that. She couldn't be stuck there, trapped, bound to that place forever. She was ready to move and never look at it again.

Regina had needed help for so long—so many lonely, isolated years and no one had come through for her. What she was asking was too great of a price and now Sarah was destined to be the next in a long line of people to let her down. That fact felt like a weight on Sarah's chest, pushing the air from her lungs. She breathed in the steam rising from the water that pelted her to remind herself how to breathe. There had to be another way to set Regina free, something Sarah could actually do, but she had no idea what it was.

When she cut the water off, Sarah just felt like crying. She was ready to just collapse there on the bathroom floor and sob until she couldn't anymore, but her parents were downstairs waiting for her. She knew them enough to know that they were likely growing more concerned for her with each passing moment. Sarah hurried to scrub herself dry and throw on a fresh clean dress from her bag. Then she hurried downstairs wearing her best smile.

When Sarah took her seat at the table—the same seat she'd sat in since she was old enough to sit in a seat—she closed her eyes and breathed in the aromas of the steaming food. Her mother would make the trip to Chinatown in the city once a week in order to get ingredients for her cooking.

Even though Sarah had been born and raised here, her mother and father grew up in Malaysia. Her mother's cooking remained authentic. Sarah remembered how much her friends loved coming over for dinner when she was growing up. Her best friend, Michele, used to say it was like going to a gourmet restaurant. She wasn't wrong.

Sarah wondered how Michele was doing. She went to college in Texas and Sarah did a poor job at staying in touch. Sarah wanted to call her all the time but she felt like she had already let too much time pass and Michele probably hated her now. The longer it went, the more she missed her friend and the more she felt like she could never call her. It was a shame. They had been friends since first grade. Sarah knew it could just be in her head, her RSD at work again, but she didn't know how to fight that. If she took the chance and called, and Michele was mean or hateful, that would hurt so much worse than just losing her to drifting apart and going separate ways. It was better to just stay away and protect her heart. At least that's what she told herself.

Look how well you did with Leremy and Felicia. People are better off without your friendship. Michele is probably doing great because you're not in her life.

Sarah's mother reached across the table and put a supportive hand over hers. "Your father told me," she said plainly.

Sarah shot a look at her father.

"Don't do that," her mother said with a serious look to punctuate it. "Your father never hides things from me and I don't hide things from him. You would do well to understand that before you get married. Trust and honesty are necessary to make a marriage work."

Sarah looked at her mother, amused. "Yes, Mom."

After they ate and Sarah's father talked business for a bit, he took the dishes into the kitchen and Sarah's mother stayed with her. "I made you something," she said, reaching into a pocket. Sarah blinked when she saw the beautiful hand-carved amulet on a necklace. "It's Peach wood. It protects against spirits."

"It's gorgeous. Thank you." Sarah immediately put the necklace on.

"I got you some incense and firecrackers too. Set them off if you need to expel evil."

"I think the incense will go over a lot better with my

neighbors," Sarah laughed.

Her mother gave a mischievous smile. "According to your father, your neighbor is your girlfriend and she is not very happy with you at the moment."

Sarah looked down at the table, bit her lower lip. "That's true."

"And it's okay," her mother said. "Humans make mistakes and they need to be able to overlook the mistakes of others. If they can't, they aren't worth your time. There are many fish in the sea, Sarah."

Sarah met her mother's eyes and smiled. "Thanks, Mom."

Her mom patted her hand and walked away. "Get some good sleep. I put a crying Buddha by your bed. It will help."

"I love you," Sarah said.

Her father came back in with a grin. "I told you your mother would know how to help."

"You were right," Sarah said, feeling calm for the first time since this all began. "And Mom was right too. I need some rest. Goodnight. Love you."

Her father leaned over and kissed her cheek. Then she turned and went back upstairs. When Sarah got back to her room, there was already a stick of incense burning. She smiled and sat on her bed, taking her phone out to call Felicia. She had to do it now while she was calm and feeling good, or she would convince herself not to call at all.

It rang a few times—too many—and Sarah's confidence started to waver. Then finally, Felicia answered. "Hey. I was worried about you," she said. "What happened with Milton?"

"You were worried about me?" Sarah asked. "I was worried about you with skeezy Gary. I thought you were mad at me."

Felicia laughed. "Gary is easy to handle and I was mad at you. People get mad, Sarah. I'm probably going to get mad at you again at some point. You'll get mad at me sometimes too. That's life."

Sarah took a deep breath. The scent of the incense felt calming to her. "I know. You're right. I have a tendency to overreact to things like that."

"Duly noted. So tell me about Milton."

"He...vanished. I think I got far enough away that he couldn't stay with me any longer."

"Shit. He was a ghost. That's extra creepy."

"I guess. I was kinda relieved to be honest. So what did happen with Gary?"

"Nothing. He just bitched like he always does. It's fine. He'll get over it."

Sarah hesitated a moment but then said, "Okay. I trust you. You haven't seen Leremy, have you?"

"Yeah. I got him. He's sleeping on the couch. He's a

little drunk, but he's alright."

"Oh my god, thank you."

"Of course. Your people are my people, Sarah. That's how relationships work."

"We're in a relationship?"

"Duh. So, you coming home tomorrow?"

Sarah sighed. "I don't think so. I'm not ready. I need to figure out how to end this before I can go back there."

Felicia laughed. "You make it sound so easy."

"There has to be a way. There just has to be."

"Board up the fucking closet and move into my place. Problem solved."

Sarah mumbled, "Not for Regina."

"You still want to help her." It wasn't a question.

"Look at what she went through. Now she's been trapped for thirty-four years. I can't leave her like that. I couldn't live with myself."

She could hear Felicia sigh, even though it was quiet. "What if that's just how it is, Sarah? Maybe some stuff shouldn't be messed with."

"Have you found anything about where Kevin is? Maybe he can help."

"I haven't. I'm still trying, but nothing yet. I don't think he wants to be found."

"Yeah," Sarah said. They said their goodbyes and blew kisses and Sarah hung up. She was glad that Felicia and Leremy were together and that Felicia didn't seem to be mad anymore. Having less to worry about made things feel easier, and more manageable.

Sarah got up and went to get ready for bed. She brushed her teeth with a newly bought electric toothbrush and flossed for good measure. Then she went to her closet. She hesitated even though she knew this closet had nothing to do with Regina. This house wasn't Sunnycrest. There was nothing to connect it all. I've got closet-phobia now. You gave me closet trauma, Regina. Jeez.

Licking at her lips as she opened the door, Sarah jumped away, taking a defensive stance. It was just a closet as it had always been. It looked like her mother had even kept it clean for her. She grabbed a hanger with a long nightshirt emblazoned with a Tweety bird graphic. Sarah smiled at it and slipped it off the hanger. Then she shrugged out of her clothes and slipped the nightshirt on. It was another small comfort of home. Maybe Felicia is right, she wondered.

Maybe she should just move on and allow herself to have the good life that Regina never got. Would that be cruel? Selfish? It felt like it would.

Sarah closed the closet and went back to bed. She climbed under the covers. Then she saw the crying Buddha on the nightstand below her lamp, and smiled. It was the same statue that helped her when she was plagued by night terrors in her youth.

"Goodnight," she said to him as she had when she was a child, before reaching over to pat his head.

Then she reached up and turned off the bedside lamp. The room fell into darkness. Sarah yawned and closed her eyes as soon as her head hit the pillow. Then there was a click and a creak as the closet door came open and her eyes reopened. No.

53

Sarah stiffened, eyes open, peering into the darkness. She wouldn't allow herself to get up and check the closet. She told herself that Regina couldn't reach her here. Milton was proof of that. It was a coincidence or her imagination. She told herself to ignore it, to sleep, but she couldn't. She just stared through the darkness at her childhood ceiling.

Sleep was impossible now, Sarah knew. Maybe I just didn't close it all the way. I would know if I got up and checked, but that could also be what Regina wants me to do. I can't allow her to exist here in my parent's home, in my safe place. I just can't.

Lying there in the dark, Sarah tried to think of other things and failed at it. She told herself that checking and believing in it could bring it to life, and give it power. The only way to overcome this intrusion into her childhood home was to ignore it. These were the same things she lay awake telling herself as a child when the night terrors came. She didn't sleep then and she wasn't going to sleep now.

Sarah clutched the amulet her mother had given her. She told herself it would protect her and keep her safe. Everything was going to be okay. No, it's not. Come on, yes it is, don't do that.

This routine continued for hours, Sarah tossing and turning just like the thoughts in her mind until exhaustion finally won out. The next thing she knew, daylight was shining upon her through the open curtains of her window. She groaned and pulled her pillow over her head, holding it in place with both hands, knowing she had far too little sleep to be functional.

After a minute or two of lying like that, she realized just as well, that she wasn't going to be able to fall back to sleep. With another groan, she got up and stumbled her way to the bathroom. As she passed by the closet she took note that the door was closed as it should be.

It was my imagination, she thought. I knew it. It didn't even really open. It's just PTSD or something.

After using the toilet and brushing her teeth again, Sarah splashed cold water on her face, then shuffled back to the bedroom.

She went to the closet to grab a dress for the day and realized she hadn't hung her clothes up yet. She couldn't live in childhood outfits. Sleeping was one thing, but facing the world was another. Sarah sighed and went to her bag. She unzipped it and popped the top open, grabbing a dress from right on top. Everything she packed were things she liked and wore all the time so she didn't need to think on it much.

Sarah got out of the nightshirt and hung it back in the closet. Then she dressed in the outfit she selected and yawned, still sleepy. She thought about how nice it was waking up at Felicia's with hot coffee and breakfast ready for her. Still, she wanted to hang up her clothes while she was up here before she went down to the kitchen for caffeine. Her father always used to have a pot of coffee despite her mother constantly declaring that it was terrible for him and he should drink tea. Sarah hadn't seen it in the kitchen at dinner though. Maybe Mom finally won and he got rid of it. Maybe it burned out or broke and he just decided it would be easier to not replace it.

One by one, Sarah grabbed the things from her bag and put them on hangers, lining them up in her closet. Suddenly she stopped and stared at the garment in her hands. It was the tattered dress that Regina had died in, stained with her long-dried blood. Sarah just stared at it, rolling it over in her hands. Had Regina somehow snuck it into her bag before she left Sunnycrest? Sarah thought about the sound of the closet door opening in the dark last night. Could Regina have come through then and left it for her?

No. She shook her head. She was safe here. She was far enough away. She had to be.

Sarah put the torn, bloody dress in the pocket of her suitcase by itself. Then she made the decision to leave the rest for later and went downstairs.

Her mother met her at the bottom of the stairs. She was in a coat and holding her pocketbook. "Your father is already at work. I have to go. Make yourself some breakfast."

"Coffee?"

"Coffee is bad for you. Have some tea."

Sarah watched her mother leave and she groaned. "Coffee is good for me," she said once she was alone, and started the teapot boiling. "It is very good for me." She went back up to her room.

Checking her phone, she saw there was nothing new. No notifications. Sarah rubbed her eyes and went back to hanging up her clothes as she listened for the whistle of the kettle to inform her that she could finally get caffeinated.

When she went to hang up a favorite shirt of hers, she stopped. "Shit."

The tattered, blood-stained dress was now there hanging in her closet with everything else. Sarah left it there and closed the closet door. She heard a girl's high-pitched screams carried up to her from downstairs. Her breath caught in her chest. It took her a moment to realize it was just the kettle. Sarah shook her head, annoyed at herself, and bound down the stairs.

She poured the boiling water over the tea bags and sat at the table, letting it steep for a minute. Her head hurt. Sarah tried to think of what Regina was trying to say with the dress. It was hard to think without caffeine. Maybe the dress was just Regina's way of making sure she wasn't forgotten, a reminder to Sarah to come back. After all these years, all the failed attempts, her desperation had to be growing. Sarah hated to think what it would be like to be in her position, which was why she could never agree to set her free, not that way. There has to be another way.

The first sip of hot tea burned her tongue and made her cuss. Reluctantly, Sarah let it sit longer, her head craving caffeine enough to hurt. Sarah thought about Fred, about Collin's story. Regina's recreation still contained the man who killed her. Fred gave Collin to him. He brought Collin there on purpose, enticing him with the time period. Why? Was he just another psychopath, someone evil like Milton or was he trying to accomplish something? What would that be? What could he gain by helping the Mangler to murder? Was the Mangler dead, a ghost walking the halls of Regina's recreated Sunnycrest, or was he real? Collin had said things could come out of that world too. Did he mean the Mangler? There were too many questions and no answers.

Sarah closed her eyes and pressed her thumbs against her temples as her headache worsened. She decided tea wasn't going to do it and made her way out of the house for coffee. She walked to the bagel store down the road and she thought about how she and Michele would get up at 4 a.m. just to walk over there and get the first bagels of the day when they were hot. I really should call her. But you won't. Still, I should.

Sarah walked inside, and ordered a large black coffee and an egg and onion bagel with melted butter. When it was ready, she thanked the green-haired boy behind the counter with a smile and went to a table against the wall where she gleefully inhaled the steam rising from the tall paper cup.

With only one sip of coffee taken, and before even touching her bagel, her phone rang. She expected it to be either her parents checking in on her or Felicia giving her an update on Leremy. When she retrieved the phone from her purse, she discovered it was neither. She answered the call.

"Hi, Sarah. This is Jessica from Dr. Stephenson's office. I got your message and I wanted to give you a call back."

Sarah sipped her coffee. "Oh, hi. I'm sorry. Mark had seemed interested in my situation and in helping me figure it out so I was reaching out. I'm sorry."

"Honey, don't be sorry," Jessica said with a laugh. "First of all, he's not the one good at finding things out about people, at least not outside of that office of his. He does the 'finding people inside themselves' and I do the 'finding people in the world'. I'm really an invaluable resource. His entire practice would crumble if he got rid of me and he knows it."

"Oh wow. Umm…okay. I—"

Jessica laughed again. "I'm teasing honey. Listen, the guy you wanted to know about, Fred, is out in Patchogue." She gave Sarah the address, which she wrote on her napkin. "I hope you find what you're looking for. Just give me a call if you need anything else. Mark told me it was alright to help you with anything you need. I don't know anything about your personal situation, honey, but it seems you struck a chord with our friendly neighborhood doctor."

"Thanks. Thank you. For everything. Really. Thank Mark too. Please."

Sarah looked at the address. Jessica didn't know Sarah had gone home, but the home in Patchogue where Fred lived was actually not far from her parents' house, where she currently was. It was just a few stops on the train. Her parents would lock her in her bedroom if they knew she intended to go talk to someone who got away with murder, but she had to tell someone. She sent Felicia a text message. She didn't plan on talking if Felicia called or texted back, but it was important for someone to know where she was if things went bad.

Finishing her coffee and bagel, Sarah then headed out. It was time to finally get some answers.

54

As she rode the train, Sarah's fingers toyed with the packs of firecrackers in her jacket pocket. Would they really help against the dead? She had to admit it felt better to be armed, even if it wound up useless. Her fingers left her pocket and went up to the amulet.

Fred wasn't dead though.

Part of her wished she brought something more than firecrackers with her. He's not the one who killed Collin, she reminded herself. He assisted, yeah. The guy isn't innocent, but from what I know, he isn't a killer himself. Then again, if he was willing to drag Collin to his death, what else would he be willing to do? It'll be fine. He's not gonna hurt me. He's going to help me. This is a real lead. Everything is going to be better soon. The thought didn't do that much to ease her nerves, and her fingers toyed with the fabric of her dress, scrunching it and smoothing it in repetition.

Sarah felt like the other passengers were staring at her and when she looked up, found that a young man seated diagonally from her actually was. She forced a smile, smoothed her dress and held her hands together in her lap.

When she stepped off the train, Sarah took a deep breath and looked around at the streets. It was a far cry from the city that was hustling and bustling a couple of hours away. In fact, there was only one other person on the road before her—a man walking his dog, and he eyed her suspiciously like she was about to rob him. Sarah scoffed at this. She bit her lip and tried to figure out how to get to where she needed to go. Sighing, she took out her phone to use the GPS. She had several missed calls from Felicia and Leremy. Sarah checked her texts and saw her friends were yelling at her there too. Shit.

"Are you insane?"

"Don't go there at all, but especially don't go there alone."

"Why aren't you answering your phone?!"

The messages went on and on, twenty-three in all. What could she even say at this point? Ack. I'm sorry. I'm already here. I can't turn back. I have to do this.

Sarah opened her GPS, putting in Fred's address. What did her friends want her to do, bring them? If it was as dangerous as they seemed to think it was, the last thing she was going to do was put them in danger. She'd done enough of that since bringing them into her world. Still, it nagged at her that she had damaged their friendships even more than she had already and they were going to hate her after this. She adored them and didn't want to lose them. Just the thought left an ache in her chest.

I'm doing what I need to do.

Fred was the only one who had been to Regina's world and also knew who the Mangler was. If she could find the Mangler and make him pay for his crimes, maybe that would be enough to set Regina free. It could be a way to save her without replacing her. Sarah knew she couldn't call the police and have them go out to Fred's house. They would think she was trying to prank them or that she was mentally unstable. They might even be right. The last few days she was beginning to wonder about herself. Following the map on her phone, Sarah walked the suburban streets.

She passed by many small houses with decent yards, and a seafood restaurant, but nothing remotely supernatural from what she could tell. Sarah was confident that the ghosts of Sunnycrest couldn't reach her out here on the island. Of course, if Fred was dangerous maybe they wouldn't need to.

Don't kill me, Fred. I'll haunt you if you do. I live at Sunnycrest.

She walked for a while until she was tired and sore and questioning her own judgment. Then the map was done. If the volume had been on, it would have said, "Your destination is on your left," so Sarah said it herself.

The yard was huge and the house was far back behind a wall of trees and large bushes. Sarah bit her lip and her fingers toyed with the fabric of her dress. Maybe her friends were right and this was a terrible idea. She sighed. Those friends were also back at Sunnycrest with the dead that could be a threat to them if Sarah didn't do something to stop it. She wanted to see her friends, to go home, but in order to do that, she had to do this first. She didn't see it as a choice.

With a deep breath, she started the walk. The day was eerily quiet. It had Sarah looking around and also chiding herself for being paranoid. Then with a huge flutter of wings, a murder of crows fled from a nearby tree and Sarah shivered. She smoothed her dress and kept going. Let's just get this over with.

55

Sarah went past the trees and bushes, up the walkway, and the following steps to the porch. She looked back and couldn't see the road. Sarah bit her lip and started to sweat, despite the chill in the air. If anything did happen to her there, no one would ever know. There weren't passersby to see or houses close enough to hear. Her fingers rubbed against her palms.

That's why I texted Leremy and Felicia. They may be mad but they'll send the police if I don't come back.

Sarah took a deep breath and knocked on the door before she lost her nerve and changed her mind. The sound was louder than she was prepared for and it made her jump.

A moment later the door opened. It definitely wasn't Fred standing before her. The person at the door was a woman, young and pretty with a big smile. “Can I help you?”

Sarah wondered if she might have been at the wrong house. She used the GPS but maybe she typed the address wrong or wrote it down wrong on the napkin when Jessica first told it to her. “Hi. Sorry. Uh, I'm looking for Fred Pearson.”

“Uncle Fred isn't here right now. He won't be back until later. Who did you say you were?”

Sarah smiled despite her roiling nerves. “I'm Sarah. I'm a friend of a friend. I just wanted to ask him about something, about a mutual friend that I haven't been able to find.”

The woman at the door seemed to eye her suspiciously. Sarah tried another smile. “Does he have your number?” Fred's niece asked. “I'll tell him you stopped by and have him call you.”

“He doesn't actually. I wish he did. I got a new phone and lost a lot of people's numbers. That's kinda why I came all the way out here. It's okay. I can just try back later.”

“Or just give me your new number now and I'll give it to him,” the woman at the door said, looking at her like she was an idiot.

“Right. Yeah. Of course. Sure. Do you want to write it down or do you have a phone I should put it in or…”

The young woman rolled her eyes. She reached into the pocket of her skinny jeans and pulled her phone free, handing it to Sarah. “Great. Thanks,” Sarah said with yet another smile. She didn't know if she should put in her real number or not. Chewing her lip, she added herself to the girl's contacts. Then with a nod, she handed the phone back.

Fred's niece didn't seem to have gained any trust, judging by the look on her face. "Okay. Well, I'll pass that along and tell him to give you a call, Sarah."

"Sounds good," Sarah answered. She gave a wave and then headed away. She stopped when she got to the first big bush. Then she stood behind the bush and looked back at the house through the branches. The young woman she had just spoken to didn't go back inside and shut the door. Instead, she came outside. She walked out of sight to the side of the house.

Gritting her teeth, Sarah wished she could see what was happening. She rounded the bush and tried for a better look, her heart pounding. *Please don't let me get caught.*

Fred's niece seemed to have gone to some kind of shed or storage building beside the house. She was standing by the door, waiting. Then the door opened and a man appeared. Sarah didn't know if it was Fred or not, but if it was, Collin was right—he was handsome, all olive skin and jet-black hair. Sarah strained to listen to what was being said. She couldn't hear. Then she saw the woman hand the man her phone. That had to be Fred. His niece must have been telling him about their encounter. He had been home the whole time and the young woman just didn't trust Sarah, not that she could blame her. *I probably seemed shady as hell. You would too if you* were in my shoes. I bet you don't know what your dear uncle did to poor Collin, do you?

Sarah's phone vibrated in her hand, and she silently sighed with relief that she had turned the ringer off. She hurried back behind the giant bush and watched again through the branches, waiting for Fred's niece to go back into the house. She knew it was Fred calling, but didn't dare answer the phone—not while they could possibly hear her. She could always call back and apologize for missing it for some reason.

Fred's niece walked by, looked over her shoulder, and went up into the house, shutting the door. Why did she look back? Did she know Sarah was still there? Sarah chewed her lip as she contemplated what to do next. She looked over her own shoulder, eyeing the street behind her. There was no one walking by but there could be at any moment. She couldn't stay there forever, lurking around in someone's yard like a burglar. She could head to the road and then call him back or just go to that building and talk to him in person. It wasn't the safer option, but he also couldn't hang up on her face to face.

Sarah took a deep breath and decided to just go for it. She rounded the bush and went to do what she came there for. Alright Fred, time to face the music. Let's hear what you have to say. I just hope to God it's useful.

56

When Sarah got to the door of the building, she stopped short. She didn't know how to do this. Should she knock? She cringed and gritted her teeth. With a sigh, she tried to open the door. If it was locked she would seem even creepier than she already did, and it could get her in trouble.

It wasn't.

The door came open and Sarah found herself standing face to face with Fred, who was glaring at her through hard gray eyes. She gasped and went rigid. The man before her smiled at this. "You must be Sarah," he said. "I don't know you, so why don't you tell me what the hell is going on."

Sarah swallowed. She stepped into what looked to be a workshop. It seemed Uncle Fred was in the middle of building a dresser of some kind. She reached behind herself and closed the door. "I know about what you did…with Collin," she said.

Sarah watched Fred's face shift, his eyes going hard. His hand slid over a wrench on the table he stood by. Sarah held up a defensive hand. "I haven't told anyone and even if I did, no one would believe me."

Fred sighed and pulled his hand back. "So what do you want?"

"I want to know why. I want to know who the Mangler is. I want to know how to set Regina free so I can live in peace."

Fred studied her for a minute. "You're in Apartment 8 at Sunnycrest."

Sarah nodded.

"It's still happening."

She nodded again. "So help me end it. Help me understand and I'll leave you alone. Why did you help the Mangler kill Collin?"

Fred scoffed at her and snorted. "You think you know things but you don't know shit. You want to know what to do? Stay out of that building. Find somewhere else to live, and don't go questioning people at their homes when they know you haven't told anyone their secret and can take it to the grave."

Sarah's eyes widened. She moved around a large workbench and grabbed a screwdriver. "I told you that so you wouldn't kill me."

"Then you're not very smart."

"But I am because I lied. I can show you the texts. Several people know where I am, and why. Now can we please talk?"

Fred studied her some more, his eyes painfully scrutinizing.

"Are you going to kill me with your niece right over at the house?"

Sarah watched Fred's jaw clench, the muscles in his cheeks throbbing as he worked to contain his temper. This guy definitely had anger issues. "Collin liked me. He was… that way. I saw it as an out, a chance for freedom, so I took it. I live with it every day. Happy?"

Sarah shook her head. She still held the screwdriver in front of her and kept the table between them. "No. How would killing Collin help? Who is the Mangler? People in 1987 told me point blank that it wasn't the actual past, that the world wasn't even real. It was a recreation made by Regina. So how could the Mangler still kill there? I've seen other ghosts, people who have died more recently that walked those halls. It's part of Sunnycrest's weird rules. I don't know. Is that it? Is the Mangler a ghost too?"

Fred laughed. He actually laughed at her. It wasn't this humorless cynical laugh. It was genuine laughter. "You come here like you know things but the fact is, you don't understand anything. You're going to die or you're going to kill and none of it will change anything. Now get the hell off my property."

Sarah shook her head. "I'm not leaving, Fred. I have no other options. For you to say I don't understand anything means that you do, so tell me. Help me understand, Fred. Why did you see Collin as a way out? What did you expect to gain from that?"

Fred's mouth wore a smile but his eyes were full of hate. He grabbed a circular saw and pressed the button so the blade spun in its chamber. Sarah knew he was doing it to frighten her so she worked hard not to show any reaction—though below the table the fingers of her hand not holding the screwdriver tugged at the fabric of her dress. She watched Fred walk over and stand in front of the only door, and she couldn't help but swallow the lump that rose in her throat. Her screwdriver was starting to feel inadequate.

Inhaling deep, Fred blew it out slowly, and rolled his shoulders. "The Mangler hides there, in that world. I brought Collin there so I could learn. I wanted to see how it was done, to recreate it in the here and now. If I was anywhere other than Sunnycrest I could have done it, but at Sunnycrest your victims come back, talk to you, and want to know why. Even when you tell them outright that there was no reason 'why them', that they were in the wrong place at the wrong time and it was that simple, they still don't accept it.

"They keep going on and on until they make you crazy. Of course, it's a catch 22, isn't it? I wouldn't be able to kill someone in a world where no one would ever find them or know what I did if I didn't do it at Sunnycrest. It's like the Garden of Eden, the most delicious enticing apple that happens to be poisoned and cursed."

Sarah looked him over. He was trying to threaten her, to frighten her, but something was off. "Have you killed since? Have you used the Mangler's methods outside of Sunnycrest?"

Fred seemed lost in thought for a minute, then he sighed. "No, no I haven't. Not before today."

Sarah realized the conversation was over then. Fred started the saw and moved toward her. She moved around the table, keeping her distance from him. Her hand left the folds of her dress to reach into her jacket pocket. Her other hand clutched the screwdriver.

"You shouldn't have come here," Fred told her. "You should have just left the whole thing alone. Didn't Ralph visit you? Didn't he tell you that like he told me? Why are we as humans so self-destructive that we can't listen to a simple warning?"

The saw was spinning and grinding. Sarah kept her eyes on the man holding it as she worked to unwrap a pack of firecrackers with one hand under the table. Fred swung the spinning saw at her face. It failed to reach; the length of the cord causing it to pull up a foot or so short, but it was enough to make Sarah cry out, which in turn brought a chuckle out of her host.

Sarah threw the screwdriver at him and he easily swatted it away, but it was enough for her to take the lighter with that hand and touch it to the fuse of the firecrackers. Sarah circled the table and lunged for the door. She threw the firecrackers in Fred's face just as they started to go off. He raised the spinning saw over his head and then the firecracker assault began. Pop! Pop! Pop! Pop!

Fred cussed and dropped the saw from his hand. Sarah grabbed for the door but Collin's killer recovered quickly and grabbed for her. She screamed as he caught her arm before she could open the door.

It opened anyway and a gun came through, followed by a deep voice that said, "Let her go. Now."

Fred snarled at the newcomer and grabbed a machete off the nearby wall with his free hand.

"Don't," the man holding the gun told him. "I will shoot you. I don't want to, but I will. Let her go."

Sarah tried to see who had come to her rescue but the door was blocking her view. She saw the gun though and that was enough to satisfy her. Then another voice joined the chaos. "Uncle Fred? Uncle Fred, what's happening?"

Fred huffed and let go of Sarah's arm. "Nothing, Aimee. These people were just leaving."

Sarah ran through the open door. She turned her head at the man holding it open. He was an older black man with white hair and Coke-bottle glasses. "I'm parked on the road," he said. "Go."

Sarah looked at Fred's niece and saw the worry and fear on her face. Sarah grimaced, but didn't try to say anything. What could she say that would explain any of this or make it better? She just turned and ran for the road.

As she ran, she looked over her shoulder. The man who came to her rescue was hurrying behind her and behind him, Fred was hugging his niece and looking Sarah's way. His eyes were hard and burning with hatred.

EIGHT

Kevin

57

Sarah sat turned around in her chair, watching out the rear windshield until Fred's property could no longer be seen. Would he really have killed her? It sure seemed like it, but something in her gut still said no. Maybe it was the niece, Aimee, but Sarah tried not to forget what he did to Collin. No matter what it seemed, she knew what he was capable of. Silently, she apologized to her mother for wasting the fireworks on the living. Her hand unconsciously moved to the amulet around her neck.

When she finally turned around in her seat, her eyes

fell on the man that had saved her. She realized that she had no idea who he was or what he was capable of either. What she did know was that he had a gun and she was in his moving vehicle. She had been too quick to trust him in her hurry to get away from Fred. "Who are you?"

The driver looked over at her for a moment and then quickly put his eyes back on the road. "You know exactly who I am."

Sarah stared at him. It took a moment but then she saw it. She saw him with darker hair, without the thin wrinkles that lined his face. "Kevin. You look older than you should be." She cringed as soon as she spoke.

That was the type of thing that came out of her mouth without thinking, the type of thing that would repeat in her head for days and months to come, attached to guilt and shame and remorse. She still lost sleep over things she said when she was a child. Hearing him scoff when she said it didn't help in the least.

Sarah was still beating herself up when he said, "Grief ages you."

Sarah nodded. She cringed again. "Right. Of course. Yeah. I'm sorry. I didn't… I don't know what I—"

"It's okay," he told her.

Sarah was looking at him when he pulled the car to a stop. She looked around nervously then and realized he had taken her to the train station. She shook her head and turned back to face him. "No, no, wait…I can't. I've been looking for you."

"I know."

"I don't even know how you found me."

"I know."

"So you know I can't leave. Kevin…I have to talk to you. I have to."

Kevin turned to face her, the car still idling. "You couldn't find me because I didn't want to talk about Regina. I found you because you were trying so hard to find me and it set off all my alarms. The only thing you need to do, Sarah, is go home to your family. Leave me alone. Leave Regina alone. Leave all of this alone and go live your life."

Sarah shook her head. "I can't. I'm sorry. I can't."

Kevin hit the button on his own door to open the lock on hers. "Get out."

Sarah shook her head again. "No."

"Get on the train and go home. Live while you can."

Sarah felt like she was going to cry. If Kevin left, she knew that was it. There was nothing left to do after that. She was facing the end and she couldn't grasp what that meant in this moment. She looked at him with pleading eyes full of fresh tears. "She is trapped, Kevin. She needs help. Please. You love her. I need to save her."

"You can't!" he screamed. His voice boomed within the confines of the car. With a growl, he threw the car back into drive and sped off with a screech.

Sarah fell back into her seat, wide-eyed. She didn't say anything else. She just reached over and tugged on her seat belt, locking it into place. She didn't know where Kevin was going, but she had been going along for the ride since Regina first came into her life. There was no getting off now. She pulled her phone from her pocket and texted Leremy and Felicia in a group message. "You were right. Fred was dangerous and it was dumb to go there, but I'm okay. I found Kevin. I'll see you soon, hopefully with the answer on how to solve this thing."

58

Sarah sat in the passenger seat for a long time, riding in silence. She stared out the window at the passing scenery, wondering where Kevin was taking her. She didn't ask. He was obviously on edge—by the way he gripped the steering wheel tight, like he was choking it—and Sarah didn't want to do anything else to make him call it quits and send her packing.

She had wanted to say more to her friends, explain that Kevin actually found her and what little she'd learned so far, but she didn't want to sit there texting for a long time. She was afraid it would make him paranoid and set him off. She just said what she needed to and tucked her phone back in her purse. Now, watching the trees and houses fly by the window, Sarah considered taking her phone back out, holding it so she could call for help quickly if she needed to. Her gut told her that Kevin wouldn't hurt her, but she didn't know how reliable her instincts were. With nothing else to do, she went back to watching the passing scenery. The quiet felt heavy and stressful. Kevin wasn't saying anything. Occasionally he would glance over at her, but he didn't utter a word. Sarah felt like she could reach out and touch the tension sucking the air out of the car like it was tangible. She pressed the button to roll down her window, suddenly desperate for a breath of fresh air, her lungs constricting.

Kevin must have gotten tired of the silence too. He still didn't say anything to her, but he tapped a button on his steering wheel and clicked the radio on. It blared bubblegum pop music, not anything that Sarah would have listened to on her own, but she welcomed the sound of it now. At least it's something.

After a while, Sarah could no longer take it and finally said, "Where are we going?"

Kevin shot her a quick glance. "Home. Out of reach."

Sarah blinked but offered no verbal response. She had thought they were already out of reach. Maybe the reach was different per the spirit and they had varying levels of power. She knew Regina's presence was strong. She thought about the ripped, brutalized dress that was probably still hanging in her childhood closet. I should have gotten that thing out of Mom and Dad's house. I should have burned it.

After that, they rode in silence—apart from the crooning love songs on the radio, and the whistling wind that howled through her open window. They rode for hours. Sarah actually fell asleep for a time and woke with a start, earning her a glance from Kevin. A glance out the window told her they had crossed State lines. Where the hell are you taking me? Maybe he meant out of reach from the authorities.

Sarah watched as Kevin pulled the car off the main road and onto what didn't seem like a road at all. He drove through the trees, the car jumping and bouncing over rocks and gravel. Sarah felt a pang of fear, knowing she was going into the middle of nowhere with a stranger. He tried to get you to go. You're the one that insisted upon coming along. If he kills you, it's your own damn fault. I wish I wasn't out of firecrackers.

Sarah saw a cabin coming into view. Has he been living out here this whole time? Hiding out here? Regina's touch stretched far, very far. Why would he want to escape her though? He loved her. Something didn't sit right with Sarah but she couldn't put her finger on it.

"I lived many places before this," Kevin said, as they went up the hill toward the log cabin. "I kept moving, kept trying, for so many years before I made it here." He pulled the car to a crunching halt outside the cabin and cut the engine. Then he turned to look at Sarah. "We go in, have your talk, and then you go. Once you leave, I never want to see or hear from you again, and that includes being pinged because you're searching for my name and calling around looking for me."

Sarah nodded shyly. "I understand. I promise."

"Good," he said. "I'll see you inside." Kevin got out of the car quickly, slamming the door and hurrying toward the cabin. Sarah grasped the amulet her mother gave her as she watched through the windshield, spying Kevin going in and shutting the door behind him. She took a deep breath and then another, and at last pushed the door open.

Sarah was finally going to get the answers she had sought for the last several exhausting days. This was all she wanted, but for some reason, the idea of actually getting it felt terrifying to her. She supposed she never really believed she would. Sarah had poured herself into this but she never really thought it was actually going to end. It was what she wanted but she didn't have faith in it. Now the end was looming before her and the weight of it felt heavy.

Maybe there was hope of a normal life after all, a life with Felicia. She was going to have a lot to make up in school, but she knew she could do it. Hell, if she could solve this and free Regina from the trap of this world, she believed she could do anything. Kevin had said that Regina couldn't be saved but Sarah didn't believe that. If she did, she wouldn't have come here, gone this far. She had never been the type to give up and she wasn't about to start now.

Even though she was far enough out that Regina couldn't hear her, Sarah said into the night, "It'll be over soon. Don't worry. I found Kevin and soon we will both be free. I'm so sorry you've suffered for so long. Just hang tight."

With that, Sarah took a deep breath and ran up the walkway. Fireflies blinked and fluttered, lighting the way like tiny lanterns of hope. Sarah climbed the steps to the cabin door. Something howled behind her, but she didn't look over her shoulder. She wasn't looking back this time, only forward. She reached before her, grabbed the handle, and pulled the door open.

59

Sarah stepped into the cabin and found the interior a lot more modern than she expected. It was nicely furnished and well decorated with impressive art, and Kevin was sitting in a swivel chair beside a large computer desk fitted with several monitors. "Anytime someone searches for my name it flags it and tells me. On this one over here, I can track the IP addresses and find out who wants me. Then over here I can follow your cell phone and locate you as I did, just in time, it seems."

"So you were trying to find me just to tell me to stop

trying to find you?" Sarah asked, sitting on an enormous couch nearby.

"Well I saw your other searches recently and I realized you had to be at Sunnycrest with Regina, so I was really trying to find you to tell you to leave it all alone—me, Regina, that damned building, all of it."

"Has that changed?"

Kevin stood from his chair. "No. That's still my stance, but you're your own person. What you do is up to you."

"Okay, good. Well, I plan to free Regina and live happily ever after with my girlfriend at a newly 1987-free Sunnycrest."

"It's not going to happen, but good luck," Kevin said as he stepped into the kitchen and fixed himself a glass of red wine. "Pinot Noir?"

"Sure," Sarah said with a shrug. "I understand why you don't want to talk about it. I know you were in Twin Spirits after Regina's murder. It must have been really hard for you to deal with. I can't even imagine being in your shoes."

"You have no idea." Kevin walked back into the room and handed Sarah a glass of wine. Then he sat in a chair positioned at an angle by the couch. "We were young when we met. Regina had it hard, but you wouldn't have known it. She was so alive, so joyful and appreciative."

Sarah was listening to him and sipping her wine. She glanced quickly at her phone and saw that she hadn't received any response from Felicia or Leremy. Her parents had finally checked in. She made quick work of texting them back to tell them she was fine and to thank them for everything.

"Regina's mother was an addict so she ended up in foster care. She would have been better off with the addict. Her foster mother was a white lady with a penchant for violence. Betty Markowski. Doesn't sound like a sociopath's name, does it? She definitely got off on what she did to those kids though and she got paid to do it. The system is a mess but that's a different story, right?" Sarah nodded. She didn't want to interrupt.

"She ran away at sixteen, got a job and her own place, and never lost her smile. She was able to get her GED while living at Sunnycrest and she planned on going to college, but she never got to fulfill that dream. This was a girl that didn't have a chance from the start of life and made one. She rose above so much, just to lose it all."

"She sounds really great," Sarah said when she finally spoke.

"What she was was broken, broken, and really good at hiding it from the world, from her boyfriend even. I used to be jealous of her, of her way to smile through it all and find the good in life. I didn't realize until she was gone that I didn't really know her at all, not who she really was. She was masking for everyone. It was part of her survival instinct. It was the way she learned to cope, to get on. I believed it."

"You speak like someone who really loved her."

"Oh, I did. I really loved her, but I didn't love the real her. There was a quiet anger in her, a hatred even, just lurking below the surface. No one saw it but it was there like the proverbial monster, hiding in the darkness under the bed."

Sarah was confused. "I'm sorry. I don't understand. You're talking about her like she was evil or something. That's not generally how I talk about people I love."

"Yeah. I know. I think I'm going to need something harder than wine." He got up and headed back to the kitchen with his empty glass. Sarah didn't follow him. She knew he didn't want this conversation so she figured she needed to let him do it at his own speed. She took the opportunity to check her phone again. Still nothing.

She sent a text to both Felicia and Leremy. "Everything okay? No ghost trouble I hope."

Maybe they really do hate me now after what I did earlier. Maybe they're just tired of my drama and they're over it. Did I finally burn my very few important bridges?

Sarah added a text saying, "Sorry about worrying you earlier. Hope you're not too mad at me. Love you."

When she got done and looked up from her phone, Kevin was sitting beside her again. He passed a glass of brown liquor across the coffee table to her. She didn't want to turn it down so she accepted it and said thank you.

"It's like she was two different people," he said after a

sip from his glass. "She was who she was with me, this sweet, beautiful soul, someone so strong and vibrant with limitless potential. She loved children and was always doing things to help them anytime she could. She taught an art class to underprivileged children. She had some of their pieces hanging in her apartment."

Sarah thought about it and was sure she hadn't seen anything like that. They must not have made it into her recreation.

"I thought we would have kids of our own someday. I really planned on marrying her. The only darkness I saw in her came out toward other women. I thought she was just jealous, and a little bit insecure. She wouldn't be alone in that."

"Definitely not," Sarah said and sipped the liquor.

"But it was more than that, Sarah." Kevin downed his glass and reached by his feet for where the bottle rested. He poured another glass and gestured toward Sarah, but she put up a hand.

"I'm good. Thanks," she said. "I don't drink much so my tolerance is not very high. I'd like to be able to hear and comprehend all that you're saying." She laughed but it sounded forced and awkward. "Go on."

"You sure you really want to hear this?"

"I have to. It's no longer about what I want or don't want."

Kevin nodded. "When Regina's foster mother was going to beat her, Regina would hide. She would curl up in the closet and sometimes the woman would lock it from the outside and leave her in there for hours. Other times she would open it and drag Regina out to do what she intended, be it belt buckles, ladles, the broom, or hangers from that very closet."

"My god…"

"I was not present for Regina's childhood. I only know what she told me and what I saw with my own eyes. The closet became a place to escape evil for her, Sarah. There was one night I remember, one of the first nights I realized something was very wrong inside her." He paused and licked his lips. It was obviously painful to remember, and Sarah didn't want to push him so she just waited.

She averted her eyes. It felt awkward to just sit there and stare at him until he was ready to speak. If it were her that would only make it more difficult to do so.

Then she heard his voice and looked back his way, meeting his eyes as he said, "Regina had gotten furious at this woman for cheating on her boyfriend. We didn't even know them. It was none of our business but she was trembling with rage and she hid in the closet. I talked to her through the door trying to coax her out but just had to wait until she was ready, until it was safe to come out. She wasn't hiding from the adulterous woman or her humiliated boyfriend. She was hiding from her own dark side, from her own anger and her own terrible thoughts, of which it seemed there were many."

"That poor girl. The trauma must have really set in deep and messed her up. That's awful. I can't even imagine what it must have been like for her."

Kevin nodded. He wiped bourbon off his mouth with the back of his hand and then took another swig. "Deeper than any of us knew, that's for sure. I still don't know if it was that Betty made her feel like a bad girl and abused her for it, so she hated bad girls and thought they deserved to be punished. Or if it was her hatred for the evil that was Betty, that made her hate bad women and think they should be punished. I don't know." He took another drink. "Either way, the end result was the same."

"Wait. I'm not following you. Deserved to be punished? What end result? Did Regina do something?"

"Sarah, Regina was the Manhattan Mangler."

Sarah's mouth dropped open like a trap door.

60

Sarah was stunned. What was he saying? How could it be? It didn't make any sense. She decided she needed that drink after all. She downed what was left in her glass and grabbed his bottle without asking, pouring more with surprisingly shaky hands. Sarah topped off his while she was at it, still without asking, but he nodded thanks. "I'm sorry. I just…I don't understand how that's possible. The Mangler tore Regina to pieces. I saw it myself. I saw her body. If I close my eyes I can still see it. I'll never be able to unsee it, Kevin. There's no way she could have been the Mangler and the Mangler's victim."

"You saw what she wanted you to see."

Sarah shook her head. "No, no, no. There are news articles about her murder. She was the Mangler's final victim. That is real. I won't let you gaslight me and make me think I'm crazy. It's been in the paper. Other people know about it."

Kevin gave a humorless laugh. "I'm not gaslighting you. She was the Mangler's last victim. That part is true, and because once she died the Mangler couldn't kill anymore unless there was a copycat."

Sarah heard the words in her head. She needs someone to replace her.

"No," she said, shaking her head. "This isn't right. No."

Kevin took a deep breath. He let it out slowly and started talking, despite Sarah's protests. "I started putting the pieces together. I figured her out. I was heartbroken and didn't want to accept it, but I couldn't run from it so I called her out on it. I didn't call the police. Maybe I should have. I just confronted her. Like you said, I loved her, monster or not. We had a fight and I walked out. I was trembling with adrenaline. I walked the city for hours trying to deal with all my conflicting emotions. When I got back she was dead. She left me a note, an apology, and a promise to always love me. Can you believe that? Even after everything. You know, I believed it, still do actually, so I took the note, hid it, and reported her murder.

"I decided to let her be a victim since that's what she was when you get down to it. It was easy to pass off, even if it shattered me to do so. I mean, the tools were the same, the cuts the same, the M.O. the same. It was so easy for the cops to add her to the Mangler's list. Of course, after she died, the Mangler's reign of terror stopped. People thought he just quit and got away with it, went into hiding somewhere. His murder tools were left at the crime scene this time which had never happened before. They took it as a sign that his mission was complete, that he was done and closing shop. I guess in truth they weren't far off."

Sarah took another shot. She was about to go for one more but the vision of Regina's mutilated body infiltrated her mind and her stomach started to swim like a wild sea of churning waves during a storm. She put the glass and the bottle down on the ground. Her head spun when she bent over and she knew she made the right decision. "You're telling me she tortured and murdered herself in such a slow and brutal way? How could she do that? How could anyone do that?"

"Regina killed bad women. She saw what she did as justice. She was the executioner, ridding the world of the guilty. When I discovered her truth and she was forced to look at herself in the mirror, she realized that she was a bad woman, no better than those that met her blades. In her mind, in that moment, she deserved to suffer. That's the part that still gets me. Regina was good. She was a beautiful soul, just stained and broken by evil. She was corrupted, and tainted, but the good was still there. It was. I saw it every day. That bitch Betty who got to live a full life and die of old age made her believe that she deserved to suffer, that the women she hurt deserved to suffer. Betty was the only one who deserved to suffer and she was the only one who didn't. How is that fair at all?"

Sarah's eyes widened. Her eyes found the liquor, but she thought better of it. "You still loved her, even after you knew."

"I loved the good side of her. Like I said, she was two different people. I was in love with one of them and terrified and sad for the other."

"The Mangler's victims were killed in their homes in broad daylight. Do you think she wanted to get caught, to suffer for the things she was doing?"

Kevin sighed. He stared into the contents of his glass as he moved it in circles, the liquid swirling within. "I don't know. I know it made sense to me why no one suspected a pretty, happy, bubbly young woman of being the perpetrator of such heinous brutality. She probably walked right past everyone, smiling and waving, and when people were asked who could have done this, they never even thought of her as a possibility."

"Jeez. No one saw that side of her but her victims. She must not have even seen it herself until you brought it up to her."

"Yeah," Kevin said with a sigh. "In that sense, I'm responsible for her death." He leaned back and turned his glass up until it was empty.

Sarah wanted to say something comforting to him but what could she say, after all these years that he had gone on living with such a thing? She leaned back and put her hands to her head. This was a lot to take in. "So there's no way to set her free, to get her to move on? We can't save her from herself right?"

Kevin just nodded. He poured another drink and leaned back in his chair.

"No one knows but you?"

"And now you."

Sarah sighed. She leaned forward and buried her face in her hands. "I'm still not sure what to make of it. I'm sorry. It's just hard to wrap my head around. It doesn't make sense. I guess I can't see how anyone can do that to themselves. It must have taken her the whole time you were gone. How could she stand to keep going once she started? She had to be in so much pain. I just don't see how that could be real."

Kevin huffed. He got up from his seat and stumbled, but caught himself. "Well thank you for pointing out that if I had gotten home sooner, I might have been able to save her. I've thought about that every day for thirty-four years."

He walked to a china cabinet against the wall and tugged open the top drawer. He moved some things, pulled something out, and returned. He dropped a piece of paper in Sarah's lap and then fell back into his seat. He immediately returned to his glass.

Sarah unfolded the paper and looked at it and she gasped. She was crying before she even realized it. Kevin was telling the truth. The aged, yellowed paper was the note that Regina left him before she killed herself.

I'm so sorry, Kevin.

I'm sorry I wasn't better for you. You deserved me to be. You deserve someone better. I never meant to be bad—my whole life, I never meant to be bad, but I always was and I wanted so desperately to make it right. I tried to fix the broken, to correct the bad, but I couldn't make it right by punishing other bad women. So now it is time to finally do what is needed to fix the bad that is me, to save the world from another terrible woman.

It's time for me to punish myself, to destroy something wicked, and leave the rest to God. Hopefully, he can take bad women like me

away from the world and spare
people the suffering and hurt that
we cause.

I love you, Kevin. I've loved you
since I first looked into your
beautiful eyes and I will love you
eternally.

I hope one day you can forgive me
as I cannot forgive myself.

Love forever, Regina

Then, just like on the tree, she drew a heart and wrote RJ and KT in its center.

"I'm so sorry," Sarah said, looking at him with tear-filled eyes. "Oh my god, that's terrible. I'm just so sorry."

"Me too," he said before he downed the contents of his glass one more time.

Sarah was racked by sobs. "I just can't imagine seeing the world through such a lens. Did she think men were innocent? How skewed! Men are statistically far worse, no offense."

"None taken."

"I just… Damn it. Some girls can be so brainwashed by adults to believe that our gender is awful, to believe everything is our fault. The idea that it was another woman that put those thoughts and feelings in her is sickening. What happened to Betty to make her hate women so much? Did she have a misogynist father who told her how terrible she was, who beat her for not being the son he wanted? How far back is the first link to this chain of pain and terror? It probably sounds fucked up to you, but part of me even feels bad for Betty."

Then Sarah remembered Baggins in the hallway. Most Bettys aren't named Betty, so I guess I shouldn't pass judgment like that.

"Shit," she said, earning her a quizzical look from Kevin. "What was a Betty in 80s slang? Did you ever hear that term when you were young?"

Kevin still looked confused, but he said, "It had a few meanings. I think it started as like a surfer or skater thing, a Betty being a girl on a board, but a lot of people just used it to mean a bitch."

"Or a bad woman," Sarah said, sighing. The dead communicate in strange ways. "Regina was trying to tell me from the very beginning, trying to help me to understand. I think maybe she was even testing me, seeing if I was good enough to live...or if I was a Betty."

She heard Baggins again. See you around, not-Betty.

"My God, would I have been killed if I had handled that encounter differently?" she mumbled, more to herself than said to Kevin. "The name Betty was significant to her because it was Betty who made her believe she was bad and so many other women were bad too. It also happened to be a slang term from the era that she could use to explain the situation to me without outright saying it. It was her truth encoded. It was there right in front of me the whole time and I missed it. This probably sounds bad but I think I need to call my psychiatrist."

Kevin gave a humorless laugh. "No. That sounds really appropriate actually. I might call mine too."

61

Kevin finally laid down his empty glass without filling it. "So you understand now? She hasn't killed you yet, so she must not see you as bad, but there's no margin for error with her. You being a woman, if you do anything she deems immoral or wrong, you're dead. You know you can't go back there. It's not safe. Call your psychiatrist. Then you can stay here until you find somewhere else to go."

Sarah tried to literally shake off the drunkenness that now plagued her. "What about the other women there? What about my girlfriend? They're in danger too. I can't just leave them to die."

"Tell them to leave or they will eventually die. That's just all there is to it. Death couldn't stop her. What can?"

"There's got to be another way."

"There isn't."

"What about you? She loves you. You could be the answer. You can appeal to the good in her."

Kevin chuckled and rolled his eyes. "You don't think I thought about that in thirty-four years? I thought maybe if I killed myself and bound my soul to that building so I could be with her she would stay as the good side of herself, except that in life when we were actually together, she was still the dark side of herself as well, right? I didn't know it, but the whole time we were together, she was brutally murdering women, Sarah. Me being with her didn't stop her in life and it won't stop her in death. I'll just be trapped there forever with a murderer. I can't handle that."

"But you finding out was enough to make her end it, end herself."

"Which ended nothing. Did it?"

Sarah sighed. She leaned forward but the room started spinning, so she leaned back again. "She said I had to replace her. Would that work? Would that save Felicia and the others, if I took her place? Maybe she could finally move on then. I'll live in her world and she could go to heaven and find the peace she's deserved since childhood."

Kevin laughed out loud, and it boomed in the quiet of the cabin living room. Sarah stared at him uncomfortably, wondering in her drunken haze what could have been so funny about what she had just said to him. He stared at her then, his eyes hard. "You are truly naive as I was when I gave my heart to her. She doesn't want you to replace her in purgatory, you fool. That's her world. She's not bound to that world. She's bound to the building. Regina created that world."

"But other people can only go to it if they're touching me and when Fred took Collin there he had to keep a hand on Collin while the Mangler killed him so he wouldn't disappear and go back to our reality."

"While Regina killed him, you mean, and that's because it's her world and you can only enter it if you're invited. She could have invited this man, Collin, if she wanted to kill him, but that wasn't what she wanted. She kills women. What she wanted was to manipulate the other man, Fred. She wanted him to learn her ways, to be a part of it, to see how he reacted to that. She wanted the same thing from him that she wants from you, Sarah. She wants someone to take over her work. She wants someone to replace her as the Mangler. In Fred's instance, a man was a better choice because he wouldn't become a bad woman for doing the things she needed him to do. He wouldn't find himself stuck in the puzzle she found herself in when she was doing the work."

Sarah realized the truth in what he was saying and she

felt so entirely defeated. Her shoulders fell under the invisible weight, and her back arched. "Damn it. How could she be so lost? I wish I could just talk to her, break through, and get her to understand that women who aren't perfect aren't automatically evil. Maybe she could see how much evil men have brought to the world, to see that evil comes in all shapes and sizes and genders, but so does good. She deserves that realization. She's been hating herself for far too long."

"And she's far too gone. You will never convince her of anything other than that you are bad. She will see your plea as a ploy to get her to allow evil to exist and dub you a liar and a bad woman for it. Then she'll kill you…slowly. You really want to free her so badly? Take over her work. Then she'll be free and you'll be a monster and none of it will matter."

"I could never do anything close to that to anyone. I feel guilty when I kill bugs, even after they bite me."

"Well, that's how you set her free. You take over her work and then she can move on, but she can't leave all those terrible women out there in the world going unpunished. It's what binds her to this world, to Sunnycrest. She feels like there's too much to do still, too much unfinished work. She can't walk away from it. You think you're going to convince her after all this time that she's wrong? Not a chance in hell. Literally. You really want to set her free? That's what it will take. Become the Mangler. Or…do like I said to begin with and let this all go. Walk away, Sarah."

Sarah sighed. She worked to get to her feet, but was so off balance that she had to catch herself on a nearby bookcase, and almost took the piece of furniture down with her. As it was, several books toppled off the shelves onto the floor and she frowned at the mess, but knew she couldn't look down at it in this moment, or try to bend and pick it up. The room spun and her stomach lurched. Throwing up on Kevin's books would probably upset him even more. She could hear him asking if she were alright but it sounded like he was speaking through a tunnel. "I'm not much of a drinker," she stammered. "Which way to the bathroom? I'm so sorry but I think I'm going to be sick."

Her elbow was grabbed then. She could feel Kevin leading her. He reached before her and opened the door, and the light made her squint. Her stomach lurched again and she fell to her knees before the toilet. Kevin held her hair back while she puked viciously into the bowl. When the assault finally ended, Sarah fell back against the wall. She groaned and squinted up at him. "I'm so sorry."

"It's alright," he told her. "You can crash here tonight. There's a guest bedroom. In the morning I'll take you wherever you want to go."

Sarah grabbed the edge of the sink and pulled herself to her feet. She turned the water on. First, she splashed some on her face. Then she filled her cupped hands and gargled with cold water. She did it several more times and then started drinking it. She could feel Kevin still standing behind her, bracing her in case she lost balance again. When she finally stopped, Sarah wiped her hands with a nearby hand towel. Then she took a deep breath and turned to face Kevin, who was looking at her sympathetically.

"You alright?" he asked.

"Yes," she said. "No… I don't know."

"Sleep it off."

"I can't. I have to go. What you said earlier, about Regina. My girlfriend, Felicia. She lives right across the hall from Regina's little world. Felicia is a good woman. She's really good to me, but she's been blackmailing the building manager, living there for free, and using him. Wouldn't that put her on Regina's bad list? How much does she know about what goes on at Sunnycrest?"

"Understand that I, myself, am not judging her, but yes. Regina would see her as a bad woman. It doesn't take much. She wants women to fail. She looks for flaws, for an excuse. You should call your girlfriend, explain the situation, and tell her to get out of there. That is if she'll listen."

Sarah frowned. "I've been texting her for hours. She's not responding. What if it's already too late? I gotta go." She took out her phone and made the call. It rang and rang and rang. She put the phone on speaker and held it out. "Kevin, I have to get back."

"How exactly? I'm in no shape to drive and neither

are you if even you had a car. We're in a different State, hours away and off the beaten path. I had to pay a lot of money to get them to put wi-fi out here for me. Whatever happens, it's going to have to wait until morning. There's no other way. I'm sorry."

A message came on about Felicia's voicemail being full. Sarah hung up the phone. "If I wait 'til morning, someone I love could die."

"If you don't, you and I could die and I'm not okay with that. Get some sleep." With that, he began to walk away. He pointed down the hall. "The guest bedroom is down there. There're more blankets and pillows in the closet if you want them."

Sarah shook her head. "No. No closets. I'd sleep on a bed of nails before I'd open another closet. Maybe she'll be okay because I'm not there and Regina needs me to bring Felicia to her, which of course I will never ever do."

"Regina will invite her if she wants her. She doesn't need you for that. She just needs you to start killing so she can finally stop. If she believes someone will continue her work, she can finally walk away, but you're not going to do that, right? So pray for Felicia and get some sleep."

Sarah kept a hand on the wall and tried to stumble her way to the guest bedroom, but she stopped midway. She looked back at Kevin and asked, "Did you know?"

"Know what?"

"Did you know the drink would keep me here? Did you sabotage me going back there? Is that why you wanted to come all the way out here to talk? Why you wouldn't talk in the car? Did you know she was gonna kill Felicia?"

Kevin stopped walking and huffed. "I didn't know anything about your girlfriend until you said it, other than the fact that she's been looking for me too, and so has a local psychiatrist for some reason—the one you wanted to call, I'm guessing? I did know you were hellbent on being a good Samaritan and you would run into the fires of Hell if you thought it was right. Otherwise, you would have let this go and left it alone a long time ago. I also knew you couldn't save Regina. Maybe you can't save Felicia either, but you can still save yourself. You can save Sarah."

"So you made a decision on my behalf. I'm not okay with that."

"Then be angry," he said. "It's too late to change it." Sarah watched him walk away, declaring the conversation over. With a sigh of frustration, she turned back around and made her way to the guest bedroom.

She fell onto the bed when she got there. Even as drunk as she was, though, sleep wouldn't claim her. She was too anxious, too afraid, too worried. She just lay there in the dark, staring at the finished wood ceiling, finding images in the patterns of the wood grain. There were faces staring at her, judging her for her failures. It made her wonder if maybe

Regina had ADHD. It could have been undiagnosed, but the accompanying RSD would leave her in a state of self-loathing that Sarah understood all too well. It also led you to believe that no one cared and everyone was terrible. Maybe if she had just gotten medication and treatment all of this could have been avoided. The world failed Regina. Now she was too far gone.

Sarah could hear an owl outside the window and the endless rustle of the cicadas. Every once in a while, when she couldn't take it anymore, she would take her phone out and try Felicia again. There was never any answer, and it made her want to scream, but Kevin was right. She was literally trapped here. Short of stealing his car, there was nothing she could do. If she did make the choice to steal his car, would Regina know? Would that be enough to put Sarah on the bad list?

A few times throughout the night, Sarah tried Leremy but she couldn't reach him either. Was he just so broken up over Collin? Was he with him, talking to him and catching up? Felicia had said he was drunk but okay. He had been with her, on her couch. Could Regina have hurt him too? She only killed women in life but since her death, she did kill Collin. Maybe the rules were changing. She was willing to kill outside her M.O. if it fit her greater purpose, it seemed. She must have been so lost. Even now, with her friends in danger, Sarah couldn't help but feel for the girl. Like Kevin, her anger was with Betty Markowski, or even more so whoever broke Betty and made her the female-hating abuser she ended up as.

Sarah couldn't believe that a woman would just be born that way and become that on her own. In her mind, there had to be a man at the end of the chain, a man like Leremy's father, that set all this in motion.

"I hope Hell is real and you're burning in it," she said into the dark.

62

Sarah didn't know when she fell asleep, but she woke with a start. Panic filled her; the frantic beats of her racing heart was like it was trying to run back home without her. Sun shone through the cabin window and birds chirped outside. She jumped to her feet and found she was still a little dizzy, still a little drunk. She groaned.

What time was it? She tried to look at her phone but it had died during the night and she didn't have a charger on her. She had been kind of flying by the seat of her pants, not really planning ahead. That's what they were mad at me for and they were right. They might wind up dead and it'll be my fault. I screwed everything up.

Sarah focused on putting one foot in front of the other until she made it back to the cabin's living room, where Kevin sat in the same chair he had been in the night before. This time he had a mug of steaming coffee instead of a glass of liquor. "Have some coffee. I made it strong. It'll help," he said when she entered.

"I don't want coffee. I want to go. My phone is dead. I can't even call her anymore. I just need to get there."

"Have some coffee."

Sarah growled but she stormed to the kitchen, her anger finding her legs for her. She poured a cup of coffee into the mug he set out, splashing some on the counter in the process. Then she carried it back and stood before him. "Okay. Now get your keys. Let's go."

"No matter how fast we run out of here, we're still hours away. That's not going to change if you have some coffee."

"All the more reason to go!" she screamed. "Every second could matter! What if you knew before she died, that you could save Regina? Wouldn't you have rushed back to do it?"

Kevin sighed but got to his feet. He grabbed his keys off a hook by the door and went out the front door. Sarah rushed to follow him, the door swinging shut with a Bang behind her. When she reached the car, she closed the door just as hard. Kevin looked annoyed but he didn't say anything. He just started the engine, backed up, and turned around. Then he followed the almost-indecipherable dirt road back to the highway. Only when he was back on the paved road, passing signs that spoke of civilization did he open his mouth. "And what exactly do you plan to do if I take you back to Sunnycrest? Please tell me your genius plan."

Sarah glared at him. "What the hell do you mean? I'm going to get Felicia and Leremy, if either one of them is even still alive, and I'm going to drag them out of there with me. Then when they're somewhere safe, I'm going to speak to Gary and tell him that number 8 needs to be closed forever and never rented to anyone again. I'll tell him to move Aarav and Saanvi out of 53 too, to get them into a different apartment and lock that one up forever as well. Regina can't hurt anyone she can't reach. We'll lock her up and board her away and then maybe she'll finally give up and just move on."

Kevin snorted. He focused on the road ahead of him. "Yeah," he said. "Let me know how that pans out."

"What do you want me to do then?"

"Walk away," he told her. "Just walk away."

"I can't. I couldn't live with that."

Kevin glanced at her and then put his eyes back on the road. "I tried everything. When I was in Twin Spirits, Regina was there with me. She haunted me. She was always in my closet, crying and reaching for me but then pulling away and hiding her face. I finally got them to seal up my closet, even though one doctor thought it was enabling and unhelpful, but once they did, my treatment went better, the meds kicked in, and the therapy finally worked. It led to my release.

"When I got out, she followed me home. She would come out of my closet while I slept, ask me if I still loved her, ask me to understand why she had to do what she did, to see that she was just doing the Lord's work, destroying evil. I tried both telling her I couldn't, then telling her I did. Neither worked. She followed me to the next place, where she killed my neighbor, a woman who was deemed bad for some reason unbeknownst to me. No one connected it to the thirty-four-year-old crimes as the Mangler was long forgotten outside serial killer enthusiasts.

"When I moved again, even further away, she came with me once more. She apologized for what she had done to the lady next door and begged for my forgiveness. She said she didn't want to hurt me and that it had to be done. I screamed at her. I screamed that these women weren't bad and that she was not the person to judge them, that only God could judge them, and she said to me that God was who she worked for. She really believes it, Sarah. I told her that it had to end, that she had to stop. I told her that I didn't want to see her anymore, ever again, and that she belonged in hell with the devil, not with God. She screamed and sobbed for days on end, keeping me awake, and driving me mad." Kevin didn't blink as he spoke, eyes fixed to the road.

"I moved again. Again, she came with me. Again, she killed. Again, I couldn't tell the police anything because they don't really take kindly to stories about how my dead ex-girlfriend did it, especially as a Black man. They did add me to the list of suspects though, as I was living nearby both victims and I was browner than they were. I thought it was going to be pinned on me, and my life was over. I cried and I prayed. You have no idea what I felt like. By the grace of God, I managed to escape persecution and then I left the State. I wanted to get as far away from those cops and people as I could. I wanted to get far away from Regina too. I went far. I changed my name and set up my computer system and went off the grid. Now, with you getting caught up in her web, Regina found her way back to me. I knew I couldn't escape forever, that it was too good to be true. Her fingers are dug in deep. She will never truly let me go. Never."

Sarah took a deep breath, staring out the window. "Regina didn't find you. You came to me. You put yourself back into the story, Kevin. You could have stayed hidden away and out of it if you chose to."

"Yes of course, and another person would have died at Regina's hand, someone I could have saved. How many times could I let that happen?"

"But you don't care about the other people that you could have saved. You had no problem getting drunk while she may have been killing them?"

"I didn't know about them until I was half in the bottle and you don't know about me so stop rushing to judgment. And my name is Donald now. Kevin died. Regina killed him. Call me Donald if you call me by name."

Sarah exhaled. She didn't argue further. She realized that she was just directing her anger where she could, even if it was undeserved. She realized that Kevin—Donald—was just like her. He was stuck and trying to find a way to do the right thing. He was plagued by the guilt and the consequences of it all. He was lost. She was lost. Regina was lost. The whole thing was a giant mess and it seemed like there was no way out. Still, just like Donald, knowing that wasn't going to stop her from trying. As the scenery passed by the windows, Sarah stared down at the black screen of her dead phone. She wished with everything she had that her friends were okay.

63

Donald pulled up in front of Sunnycrest and left the car idling. Sarah went to get out in a hurry, but he stopped her, grabbing her arm. She looked back at him, and he stared into her eyes. "You can still walk away. You don't know what you're walking into. I don't know what's waiting for you in there, but I do know I'm not going in there. So if you walk through those doors, I can't save you, but if you stay in the car we can drive away…together. I'll help you find a new place to live, somewhere safe. You can start over."

Sarah answered him by pulling her arm free and getting out of the car. She could hear him sigh. He didn't try any harder. He didn't call her back or get out of the car himself to try to coax her back in. That speech was his last-ditch effort, as far as he was willing to go. The moment she reached the front door of that cursed building, she seized the handle and looked back at him as she opened it wide. Then she watched him drive away with a screech of tires. He wanted to put distance between himself and this building, and Sarah understood it. She knew it was most likely the last time she was ever going to see him, no matter how this thing panned out. He would probably move again, maybe even change his name once more, doing his best to escape Regina's reach. Sarah wondered if he ever would. Would any of them?

It doesn't matter how much he runs or changes, Sarah thought as she entered the building, dim lights swinging overhead like pendulums. He still wasn't free. In his mind, his heart, maybe even his soul, Regina still had him. She would always have him. Ghosts haunt people, not places.

Sarah felt a strange sense of terror walking up the stairs to the second floor. It was the first time since this all began that she felt truly afraid. She now knew there was a monster in her midst. If Felicia and Leremy were still alive, would she even have the ability to save them? She honestly didn't know, but she grasped the amulet hanging around her neck as she ascended those cold stone steps. Please be okay.

When she came out onto the second floor her breath

caught in her chest. The hallway was empty and quiet. Sarah didn't know why, but for some reason that built upon her fear, and a chill danced over her spine. She took slow careful steps toward Felicia's apartment. Sarah kept her hand on the amulet and tried to clear her throat and remind her body how to breathe.

She reached the door to Apartment 7 and her hand trembled as she knocked. Felicia never did give her a key. Sarah stood in the hall waiting impatiently. The silence was so thick it was unnerving. She knocked again. This time she called out, "Felicia, it's me. Are you in there? Felicia!" Dammit. What do I do?

Nothing but deafening silence.

Sarah was about to knock again but she stopped mid-motion. Her hand moved down to the knob and she decided to give it a try. She turned it slowly and the door popped open with a whine that cut through the silence of the hall. Sarah swallowed and stepped into the apartment. "Felicia, are you here?"

The place was a mess. It looked as if it had been robbed but Sarah knew better. She knew what happened. They were taken. If Donald was right and they were invited, it seemed their invitation was an aggressive one. Did Regina have help? Was there someone other than her that could bring them into the closet-worlds of Sunnycrest?

You better not have hurt them! Sarah sighed at herself.

Or what? I'm full of empty threats. What can I do outside of failing again?

Sarah had to know though, to make sure, so she made her way to the bedroom. In her mind she saw Felicia atop the bed, her midsection open and her eyes removed, but when she got there all she saw was an empty, still-made bed. It didn't mean Felicia was still alive, but it was a small victory for the moment and she would take it.

Sarah heard a sound coming from the kitchen, something like a crunch of a potato chip under the sole of a shoe. She whirled around and hurried that way, but not without at least glancing into the bathroom to make sure it was clear. When she got to the kitchen, she discovered she wasn't alone, but the person there wasn't either of the two she was hoping to find.

Gary stood before her.

The kitchen was as trashed as the living room, the refrigerator opened, and the contents spilled out onto the floor. Some cabinets were open too.

"Hell of a mess," Gary said. "I'm gonna have to have Tom work overtime to clean this up and this two-faced bitch didn't even pay me rent. I just took it up the ass on this one."

Sarah's mouth fell open. Her head slowly moved side to side in disbelief. "What happened? What are you doing here?" she asked once she found her voice.

"You're wasting time looking around here," he said,

not answering her questions. "You know where they are."

Sarah gasped. She looked back through the living room, through the open door, and across the hall at her own door, the door to Apartment 8.

"Bingo," Gary said. "You know, if you would just replace her, the killings can happen outside of this building and maybe we can get the ratio of living to dead tenants to a better rate, huh? This is a business after all."

Sarah's eyes widened. "You knew. You knew this whole time and you rented it to me anyway. You made me think that poor Roger was mad when he tried to warn me and you knew what I was moving into. You keep renting those two apartments to help her find a replacement because it would be better for your business. If the killings happen in reality they can happen anywhere, but if she isn't replaced they can only happen here. You're sick. Are you hiding the evidence? Cleaning up after her to protect your business and investment?"

Gary scoffed at her. "You think you know everything. It's the only way to get her to stop. Are you honestly going to tell me if you were in my shoes you would do something different? You wouldn't try to find someone to replace her so this shit would finally be over? You wouldn't want to make that kind of evil go away? I mean, sure there would be a new evil, but it wouldn't be here. My home, my business, my tenants—they would all be alive and well. You make your choices, you know?"

Sarah didn't answer because she couldn't. She couldn't answer because she didn't honestly know the answer. She knew what she hoped she would do, but she couldn't say that what she would actually do was the same. It didn't stop her from hating him though, from finding him disgusting and thinking he was probably the type of man that set all this in motion in the first place. She just glared at him. Then she found the air in her lungs and she took a deep breath. "I'm going to try to get my friends back," she said, "and I'm not going to replace her so forget it. If you want a replacement for her, why don't you just replace her your-damned-self?"

Gary blew out a frustrated puff of air through his nose. "I'm not going to kill people and wind up in prison, you nut. Someone else can do that. I just want to protect Sunnycrest. If you're not going to replace her, then I'm just going to have to rent it out after you and try again—and hope the next one is the one. I might as well hang the sign now. I'll go take out an ad."

He crunched through the kitchen, walked past her out of the apartment and down the hall to the elevator.

Sarah walked into the hall. She called his name and he turned to look at her as the elevator doors came open. "You're an asshole," she said. "You know that?"

"Yep." Gary just stepped into the elevator and the doors rattled closed behind him. Felicia had said the guy was into some shady shit and that she wasn't the bad guy, but Sarah never expected this. She didn't have time to dwell on it. She took a deep breath and opened the door to Apartment 8.

It was quiet and still and not as messy as Felicia's. It almost looked exactly as she had left it. She didn't need anyone to tell her this apartment was empty. She knew she was the only one there, at least in this dimension, in this time period, this version of reality. The others were waiting for her in a mocked-up 1987 horror land. Sarah licked at her lips and walked to the closet. She opened the door, climbed in, and pulled it shut without hesitation. Then she just as quickly reopened it and stepped out. There was no more room for hesitation.

Sarah was in the living room of Apartment 53, Regina's apartment. This time the children's art was, in fact, hanging on the walls—bright, colorful images of children with loving parents that Regina never got to experience, animals and houses, all beaming with happiness. *Why did she put them there now? Is she trying to tell me something?*

She moved across the room to the bedroom. She slowed down when she neared the entranceway, terrified of what she was going to find when she crossed the threshold. Everything was still so quiet, so still. She had expected screaming and fighting, but there was nothing, just that terrible awful quiet.

Trying to take a deep breath, she couldn't get one. The air felt stuck in her chest. She turned the corner and stepped through the open doorway into the bedroom, her whole body tingling with nerves.

Sarah froze as soon as she entered. She was right to be afraid. Felicia was lying atop the bed, splayed out like she was tied to the bedposts, though nothing visible held her in place. Regina stood at the side of the bed looking as beautiful as ever, a long, serrated blade in her right hand, glinting in the light of the nearby lamp. Leremy was standing against the wall, shivering in fear. Sarah could see he was trying to move, trying to speak. He couldn't do either.

Regina must have noticed Sarah looking his way because she said, "He's meant to bear witness, to see the exchange take place."

"Are you so broken that you expect me to kill my own girlfriend?" Sarah asked her, her voice trembling as badly as her limbs.

"You must. She is going to die either way. If you don't kill her and learn the way, then you must watch me kill her and learn the way from that. Regardless, you will learn the way."

Sarah shook her head. Tears fell from her eyes to wet her cheeks. "I am not going to replace you!" she snarled. "I am not like you. You have got to stop this!"

"There is only one way for me to stop," Regina said. She rounded the bed and extended her arm in an attempt to hand Sarah the awful, terrifying blade in her hand. Sarah stared at the teeth along its edge. She felt like she was going to throw up just thinking about what it could do, what it had done, what this poor girl had done to herself with it, the images of it all flashing through her mind in grisly detail. "Take it."

Sarah sent a shaking hand out and grabbed the blade from her. The moment it was in her palm, she said, "I'm sorry," and swung it as hard as she could. The blade cleaved into Regina's throat, the teeth mangling the meat of her neck. Shredded chunks hung free as a fountain of blood flowed out, cascading to the floor like a crimson waterfall.

Then everything was dark. Sarah understood at once that she was in the closet again. She reached up, twisted the doorknob, and stepped back into the living room of Apartment 53. She looked at the children's art on the wall and shook her head. NO. No, no, no. I'm still here. Is she still here, as well? Is Felicia? Leremy?

Sarah walked toward the bedroom again, her steps slow and nervous. When she turned the corner and stepped through the open doorway, the scene was exactly as it was the first time—Regina's milky throat intact and whole, the blade in her hand instead of Sarah's.

Sarah's mouth fell open. She clamped it shut and grit her teeth and she quivered, her tears flowing freely. She looked down at her empty hand. "You can't die," she said, voicing the truth that she desperately didn't want to accept.

"I'm already dead. There is only one way for this to

go."

"No."

Regina circled the bed, just as she had the first time, and extended the blade out toward her. "Take it. Set me free. Please. Do what you must. It's the only way."

Sarah wiped tears from her eyes. She shook her head aggressively. She looked at Felicia, who was looking back at her through the most frightened eyes Sarah had ever seen. She strained against her invisible bonds, pulling and tugging to no avail. Tears escaped from the sides of her wide eyes that seemed to be restrained as well, unable to blink.

"Take it," Regina said. When Sarah only shook her head again, Regina grabbed for her arm and her hand passed right through it. She looked at her palm in confusion.

Sarah's mouth dropped open. "You can't hurt me either." It must be because of the amulet, she thought. Oh, thank you, Mom. I love you so much. "So we can't hurt each other. It's a stalemate. Please, Regina, just let it end."

"There's only one way to end it." She extended her arm with the blade again. "You cannot leave this place unless I let you. If you don't do what you must to take my place then this moment will repeat on a loop forever until you do. This is my world. I am in control. I will never let you go unless you let me go first."

Sarah saw movement out of the corner of her eye but she didn't dare look in that direction because it didn't seem like Regina noticed it. She kept her eyes on the beautiful monster before her. "Or you can just stop, you can be the person Kevin loved and stop the killing. You can realize that Betty wasn't right, that she was probably victimized like you were, that you've all been hurt, and betrayed. You're a victim. Don't create more victims. That's all you're doing, all she did. Let it go, Regina. Break the cycle."

Sarah spied the movement again. She didn't turn but she could have sworn she saw Collin. She remembered what Tina had told her. The dead can walk each other's roads.

Maybe Regina could trap the living here, but the dead could walk freely. Collin must have come for Leremy. Save him!

"Please Regina," Sarah pleaded. "Please just stop this. Felicia isn't Betty. None of these women were. Betty was probably a victim once too, before she did those terrible things to you. Think about it—victims creating victims, on and on forever. Isn't that exhausting? You have to be so tired, Regina. You can't keep going. You have to stop."

"Take it," Regina said, gesturing toward the blade in her hand.

Growling in frustration, Sarah jumped when Regina pulled her attention from her and whipped her head toward the doorway. Sarah followed her gaze. Collin was pulling Leremy from the room. "Bring him back!" Regina shouted.

Sarah stepped in front of her. "You can't hurt me and

I won't let you hurt him."

Regina trembled for a moment and then bent over, a scream of primal rage bursting from her. Her face stretched itself, losing its natural beauty. The lower jaw dropped all the way to the floor, skin pulling like putty. For the first time, she looked the part of the monster she'd been playing for so long. Then she reeled it back in. Her jaw sucked back up and she was once again exquisite and the innocent, broken girl she had also been, like Donald said—two conflicting sides living in tandem. "It doesn't matter. We don't need him. We'll do it without him. Take it!" she boomed, extending the blade out once more.

"No." Sarah looked to the bed, to her frightened, resisting, girlfriend thrashing against invisible ropes or chains. "It's over," she told Regina. "You have to let it be over. Forgive her. Forgive yourself."

Everything went dark. Sarah cussed when she realized she was in the closet again. She knew when she opened it that it wasn't going to take her home. She opened it anyway and stepped back out into Apartment 53. This time she walked briskly to the bedroom. It was the same as before but Leremy wasn't there. That made Sarah smile. Now she just had to figure out how to get Felicia home and she would win.

She could win this. She felt energized.

Regina had lost her cool and hadn't regained it. She was still trembling with fury and unspent adrenaline. "How many times must we do this, because we can do it an infinite amount," she said as she stormed around the bed and extended the blade. "Take it. I ache to be free, to be able to live and love again. Help me."

"I wish I could," Sarah said honestly. Then it hit her. She saw the answer clearly and she cried quietly. Kevin had been right. There was no saving Regina. There was no stopping her. But Sarah had also been right, the gateways needed to be locked and inaccessible. There was only one way to make it happen. "Okay. Give it to me," she said.

Regina studied her for a moment. She must have felt that Sarah was up to something. Then after a minute she made her decision and handed Sarah the blade. "You know better than to swing it at me," she said. "It won't work."

"I do," Sarah said, tears streaming down her cheeks. "You can't hurt me, but I can, and the dead can walk in this world, walk between them."

Regina's eyes went wide. "What? No," she snapped, but she had no time to move, and no way to stop it if she wanted to while Sarah was wearing the Peach wood amulet.

With a firm, up shaking hand, Sarah dragged the serrated blade across her own throat. The pain was intense, and she immediately started choking. The sight of her own blood was surreal. She plunged the knife into her gut as she fell to her knees. She thought about how she told Donald that she could never do anything like this.

I guess I was wrong, she thought as she ripped herself open and spilled herself out onto the bedroom floor.

She wasn't doing it because she believed she was bad though. She knew she wasn't bad. There was nothing toxic about her womanhood or femininity. She was doing it because she was good, because she did know how to love, and also—like Donald had said—she couldn't let someone die that she had the ability to save. She heard Felicia scream, but her own pain passed quickly. The pain left with her life. It didn't take long.

Then Sarah was standing outside herself looking down on her own mangled body. The pain returned to her in a sudden crashing wave. She had a terrible headache. Her body burned like her organs were on fire, but she had no body, did she? Still, it was agonizing. Was this what Regina lived with all these years? It was no wonder she was desperate to be replaced. If only she could have just let it go. She could have set herself free. Even now, Regina was screaming. She was running for the knife still grasped in Sarah's dead hand, fury pouring from her black-colored lips.

Sarah didn't try to stop her. Instead, she raced over her dead physical form and hurried to the bed. She grabbed Felicia and the invisible bonds snapped free. Felicia screamed as Sarah tore her from the bed, dragging her to the doorway.

Regina had gotten the blade, and she snarled and swung it. Sarah swung Felicia around her in the same instance. The blade cleaved through Sarah's incorporeal form, spilling her undead insides on the carpet once more, and they kept moving, the wounds healing as they did. In a moment it was as if it never even happened.

Pushing Felicia in front of her as she went, Sarah rushed through the living room toward the closet. Regina screamed in an inhuman way—a ghostly shriek, high pitched and piercing, more like a wailing siren than anything alive could utter—and she chased after them. She slashed and slashed with her blade and it continued to pass through Sarah's ghostly arms and back and legs, splitting her open, tearing her, and spilling her only for the wounds to heal immediately. Sarah gritted her teeth against the pain that remained after the wounds closed. The pain stacked upon itself, adding to each hurt—a torturous mountain she couldn't get rid of. When she made this decision, she didn't know it would hurt so much.

One swipe went far enough to cleave into Felicia's arm, jagged steel teeth ripping through her flesh as it pulled away. Felicia cried in pain. Sarah just pushed her ahead. She didn't need to tell Felicia to open the closet. Together they barreled inside and yanked the door shut with a bang!

Regina's blade burst through the wood, metal teeth getting stuck. She screamed from the other side as she struggled to pull it free so she could strike again. The metal sawed against the wood loudly. Shh-Shh-Shh-Shhk.

Sarah reached up and opened the closet.

Regina wasn't on the other side. They were back in present-day Apartment 8, but they didn't stop there. They ran into the hall and then to the staircase. Felicia went to run down, to get out of the building and Sarah yelled, "Wait!" stopping her in her tracks. Then she led Felicia up the stairs to floor thirteen. "Collin said it's safe up here," she explained. "Spirits can't hurt you up here."

Felicia looked at her then and started bawling her eyes out. "Sarah," she cried. "Why? There had to be another way."

"There was only one other way and I wasn't going to do that to you."

"So you did it to yourself?" Felicia fell to her knees in the hall of floor thirteen, so similar to the way Leremy had that day with Collin.

"Yes, because you have the power to stop this, to stop her, forever."

Felicia wiped her eyes and sniffled. She looked up at her dead girlfriend. "What do you mean? How?"

"Use your leverage. Gary is in on it. He is going to keep bringing in people like me and the couple in 53 to try to find her replacement. You have to tell him it's over. Tell him to move them out of 53 and lock those two apartments for good. He needs to board up the closets and then lock the doors and throw away the keys. They need to be off limits to people forever, Felicia. I could never make him do that, but you can. This is how we win."

"I don't feel like I'm winning," Felicia cried. She tried to hug Sarah's legs and found she could no longer touch her. She passed right through, like Sarah was just an image, a hologram projection of her likeness. Felicia was racked by sobs again.

"I need you to do this," Sarah said to her. "Don't let my death be in vain."

After more sobs, Felicia finally got control and said quietly, "I won't. I promise you. He'll do exactly as I say or I'll nail that son of a bitch's balls to the wall."

Sarah smiled. "Thank you," she said.

Then she was gone.

64

Mark Stephenson stepped into his office and stopped before Jessica's desk. "Hey, have you heard anything from Sarah? I haven't been able to get a hold of her and after what happened with Roger…"

Jessica smiled at him. "I just saw her actually. She stopped in to tell me to thank you. She said her situation is resolved and she really appreciates all your help. She added that your situation is, however, not resolved and said you should go to Sunnycrest. On that part, I completely disagree. That place gives me the creeps and I would recommend avoiding it forever."

"Hmm..." Mark said. "Thanks for letting me know. That's a huge weight off. I'll consider what both of you suggested. My three o'clock still on schedule?"

Jessica nodded and shot him a beaming smile. "Ready and waiting."

"Fantastic. I don't know what I would do without you."

"I don't either," she said with a laugh.

Mark echoed her laugh and then walked past her and pushed his way into his office. He walked past the man fiddling with a Rubik's cube, rounded his desk, and took his seat. "Hey, Rasmus. It's good to see you," he said with a genuine smile. "How are things going? Did you try what I said with your boss at your job?"

"Not yet," the freckled blond man said. "I've been distracted the past few days."

"Well, you're in the right place," Mark said with a warm laugh. "Let's talk about it."

Rasmus sighed. He leaned forward and put the puzzle cube back on Mark's desk where he got it from. "It's hard to figure out where to even begin with stuff like this. You know where I live, right? What do you know about the Sunnycrest Apartments?"

The warmth left Mark's face. His smile fell away, and he just stared across his desk at his patient. Shit, he thought.

He almost said it out loud, but he bit it back. "Enough," he said when he found his voice. "Quite a bit actually. It seems all the residents find their way to me at some point. Let me guess. Ghosts?"

Rasmus's eyes widened. "Wow, you really are a good psychiatrist. Yes, ghosts. I was afraid I wouldn't be able to talk about it here, that you would think I needed to be committed or something, but now I feel so much better."

That makes one of us, Mark thought, and forced his smile to return. "This is a safe space, Rasmus. You can talk to me about anything. In fact, at this point, I think I've heard it all, so let's see if you can enlighten me with something new."

"I can definitely try," Rasmus said with a nervous laugh.

"So let's have it. Start from the beginning. I've helped you before. I'll do everything I can to help you now."

Rasmus nodded. "Thank you," he said. "I really do appreciate you, Mark."

Mark nodded, as well. He smiled again but behind his eyes, he saw a brown-haired boy in a red shirt. Is it you? He couldn't help but wonder. Are you the reason Sunnycrest won't let me go? Are you waiting there for me? I was eleven years old for God's sake.

Mark's fingers toyed with the knob of the drawer that hid his alcohol. He felt like he was going to need its help with courage. Before long he was going to have to face the music—

the music that was a waltz played by a children's band class. He could hear the choir singing eerily in his mind, and it gave him chills he hoped Rasmus didn't notice.

As it turned out, Sarah had been right. He couldn't avoid Sunnycrest forever, and he knew it. He sure wanted to try though. Mark forced the thoughts out of his mind and changed his focus, doing his best to listen and pay attention to the man who needed him right now at this moment. It wasn't Mark's time yet. This was the time for Rasmus's story, though Mark was sure he was going to end up playing his part in it. He always did.

He said a silent prayer as he asked, "Who's haunting you, Rasmus?"

Acknowledgments

First off, I need to thank David-Jack Fletcher and Lee Cross James for believing in my book, showing me that publishing can be a kind, gentle process, and becoming the friends I needed. I need to thank Carlos E. Rivera for welcoming me with kindness.

I would also like to thank Shelly Jarvis for always being in my corner, formatting, and just being my best friend, Peter Blakey-Novis and the good people at Red Cape Publishing, Mark Towse for being my perfect writing partner and a good, genuine friend, Thomas Rickman and the folks at Pinhead's Graveyard for helping me and letting me be part of their horror family (I really do appreciate you all more than I can say), and my family (Mom, Dad, Chris and family, Catherine, Robin, Juju, Elliot, Boe, and Travis and family).

I want to thank the cons that have supported me like Asheville Comicon, Frankencon, Creepycon, the West Virginia book fair, and all the pop-up shops and craft fairs I found a place in. Thanks to all the stellar reviewers that have been huge in helping get me to readers: First and foremost, Corrina and No Remorse Reviews, Donna Latham, Mike Rankin, Diana Richie, Danielle Yeager, Karla Kay, RoseDevoursBooks, Bethany, Amina Ali, Casey S, Cristy Villemaire, Quinnbook, Robin Knabel, that horror bish, Haunted Reader, Christina Pfeiffer, and Patrick McNulty, Luca Rizzo, and Robb Carter. Reviews mean a lot in the indie world. Every reader who leaves a review is also appreciated endlessly.

Thank you to the other misfit toys: Erica Summers and Mick Collins, to my forever friend: Mark Young, the talented Ruth Anna Evans, Garry (shares everything) Struthers, Tina Marie, my good friend J. Scott Coatsworth (I don't know where I'd be without your guidance and friendship), Tiffany Tiffany, Eli Pope, the Fear From the Heartland Crew, Natalie, Stew and family, Craig, Erica Wetzel-Fields, Ashley Jade, Amanda Ohnmeiss, JJ and their horror book club, Holly Horreur, Brandi Hudson-Hicks, Ben Klaiber, Ray and Jen Grooms, Jon Suttle, Soda (and family) Gloria, TT and Ximena, and all my cousins and extended family as well.

I would also like to give some love to the amazing authors who I've gotten to work with or have just become friends with recently because they deserve recognition and gratitude. Candace Nola, Angel Van Atta, Otis Bateman, Judith Sonnett, Matt Gleason, Lucas Mangum, RJRoles, and Jason Myers, Dee Caples, Christy Aldridge, Ayralea Lander, DE McCluskey, Cat Voleur, Brian Berry, Duncan Ralston, Lance Dale, Richard Kodai, David Green, Tim Mendees, Kelvin VA Allison, Shaun Hupp, Chris Bonner, and Kristen Vincent.

Last but of course, never the least, thank YOU. Every reader who cares and follows, purchases, and reviews, talks about and appreciates, befriends and supports myself and my books. None of this would exist without you. I am living my dream and it's because of you.

About the Author

Chisto is the author of the Sunnycrest Apartment series which consists of "Accidental Murderer in Apartment 34" and the "Gateway in Apartment 8" with more on the way. He cowrote the novella The Bucket List with Mark Towse, wrote the popular novella The World Beneath, and the extreme horror Two of a Kind that has a prequel and sequel on the way.

He's published nearly 300 stories for anthologies and podcasts. He lives in North Carolina with his family and awesome pets. You can find him at www.chistohealy.com and on all social media @chistohealy. Feel free to reach out and connect.